To Nicky

DARK TIDINGS

A genuine first
edition ...

K. Magger

I

Dark Tidings

Published by: Ragged Cover Publishing

Written by: Ken Magee

*

ISBN 978-1-908090-2-25

Dedication

To Carol, for putting up with the long hours... and years!

Also, big thanks to everyone who helped me get this story into print. In particular, Paddy for being the first to read it, Jenny for her enthusiasm about my efforts, Chris for keeping my technology ticking, and Daniel, Lewis, Allegra, Athena and Alexander for constantly reminding me that magic is real.

Finally, gratitude to Keith and Marian at Ragged Cover Publishing for their patience with the newcomer.

1

No rest for the wicked

Way back in the medieval mists of time, long before most people counted which century was which, Tung shivered violently on an ice-cold, stone floor.

Dark, dank and putrid were the words an ancient estate agent might have used to glamorise this miserable dungeon. There were no words horrible or nauseating enough to describe what it was really like. To be fair though, it was not all bad, at least the green slime, which oozed like pus from small cracks in the walls, added some colour to the drab greyness.

Tung huddled in the darkest corner of the freezing, granite cell wishing he was dead. He would not have to wait long for his wish to come true because he was due to be tortured to death the very next day. Now he just prayed for sleep, because it would give him merciful nothingness before the excruciating morning.

Roll on death, he thought, it could not come a moment too soon. He was soaking wet, bruised, starving and parched with thirst. Yes, roll on death.

By some miracle his brain dragged his racked body into an uneasy slumber. Thank all the gods for sleep, at least he had not been denied that last sanctuary. His nightmares replayed his pathetic life as his subconscious tried to figure out how he had ended up in this tragic predicament. The work of the devil, no doubt... with a little help from his fiends.

The tortured dreams relived sixteen years of poverty, every day a battle to find enough food to survive. He had been born to a mother who, all through his childhood, had struggled relentlessly on his behalf, trying to stop his father drinking and gambling away whatever meagre wage he had earned. It was a futile struggle, trying to turn beer money into food money. So, most of the time, the family went hungry and, to add real injury to insult, there was usually a beating for anyone daft enough to complain.

Tung had loved his mother dearly, but before he turned twelve, she had lost the will to fight and had either died or run away; he never discovered which. Things got a lot worse after that and then only stealing could put food in both his and his younger sister's mouths. Without his mother, there was no one to protect him from his father's drunken wrath, so the beatings increased in regularity and harshness. His childhood descended into a nightmarish hell of torment and deprivation. His deepest distress was that he was helpless to protect his sister from these paternal abuses.

As he slept, his memory began to reconstruct the day of his first theft. That day was destined to determine how the rest of his life would play out.

✧ ✧ ✧

He was a tiny child and his victim was a giant of a man whose purse bulged with gold and silver coins. He had watched the man for weeks and deeply resented how he seemed to have an endless supply of money to waste on fripperies. This was to become an enduring theme in his life... resentment. Resentment sprinkled with an unhealthy dusting of jealousy, spite and bitterness.

He had first spotted the man buying a gaudy hat at an up-market market stall. He had followed him for the rest of that day, and on many occasions since. He crept in the shadows, always ten or so steps behind. He tracked him from the market, where he had first spied the man's money, to the big house where all the ladies lived. It seemed odd to him that so many pretty ladies should all live together, but they seemed to enjoy a lot of men visitors so they were certainly not short of male role models. That was something Tung desperately lacked; the only male in his life was his father and he was not even a good example for the devil to follow.

On the day of his first big heist, he followed the man from the lady-house to the local ale house. He watched through grimy windows as the man ate mountains of meat and drank tankards of bubbly, brown liquid. He always noticed how the man became increasingly careless the more tankards he sank, and on this particular evening there had been a lot of tankards. Tung watched and waited.

Eventually the man emerged and made his way unsteadily towards the castle area of the town. He did what he always did and took a shortcut through the dark entry that ran past one side of the tavern. Half way down the entry Tung sprung. Starting from a few feet behind, he raced past at full speed and, without so much as a break in step, grabbed the purse. Unfortunately, it was so well attached to the man's trousers that Tung's body stopped abruptly, but his feet kept going, ending up flailing in the air. A ridiculous and hilarious sight for the uninvolved bystander, of which, that night in that secluded alley, there were of course none.

Tung's momentum and aerial acrobatics broke the leather tether and the purse fell to the cobbles spilling its contents everywhere. There followed that eternal split second when neither of them knew quite what to do. The man stared at Tung in total bewilderment. Tung seized the moment and the purse, and ran for it. He ran and ran until he was as far away as his legs could carry him, and then he ran some more. He eventually found a secluded hiding place among some rotting sheep's carcasses which had been dumped in the market square. He lovingly examined the brown leather purse that he held reverently in his hand. It was not bulging anymore, having selfishly emptied itself at the crime scene.

He inspected his booty closely and found, right at the bottom of the pouch, a lepton. It was the lowest denomination of all coins, but it had some value, albeit tiny.

"Result!" shouted Tung as he started to plan his celebration. "I have found my calling."

He did not know that this one event would change his life forever. He could not have known the dire consequences of this relatively innocuous act.

✿ ✿ ✿

Without warning the cell door was flung open. His dream ended abruptly, the night's silence vanished as the rusty hinges squealed and screeched. A grey-bearded, old man was catapulted into the room. He did an involuntary double somersault across the stone floor and landed upside down on top of Tung.

Suddenly everyone was screaming. The old man screamed as he bounced off Tung and smashed heavily onto the floor. Tung screamed as he crashed back into consciousness. The guards screamed as they slammed the heavy, wooden door.

"You'll fester in hell for this, you snivelling toadies!" the old man bellowed at the now-bolted door. The door did not reply.

He shouted a few more obscenities at the door before he noticed Tung. Immediately he began an undignified struggle to regain his composure. He adjusted his position to a semi-upright slouch and brushed the worst of the dirt off his robe. He cleared his throat.

"I am Madrick."

He straightened his back as he spoke. He waited for a reaction, but his opening line had been met by a silence stony enough to make any mountain justly proud. Tung just stared blankly at the stranger; surely this could not be happening.

The old man placed a bony hand on Tung's shoulder and shook him. To his horror Tung realised that this was a real nightmare and not a dream.

"I am Madrick," he repeated. "I am the Royal Wizard, by appointment to the King."

Tung was so exhausted, he was barely able to form a response, but somehow he managed. He punched Madrick square on the forehead, turned his back, closed his eyes and prayed once again for sleep.

Madrick rubbed his bruised brow, it hurt, but he did not take the hint. He shook Tung roughly.

"I may be able to help you get out of this dreadful place, but only if you listen very carefully to what I have to say."

Madrick straightened a little more, his eyes brightened and his face began to take on a new life. Here comes a story, thought Tung, and he was right.

2

A not so humble opinion

Michael thought of himself as a self-taught, computer whizz-kid. Others thought of him as a geek and a hacker - one of those guys who was just a bit too smart for his own good and someone who had no idea what the word 'responsibility' meant.

He did not care what other people thought about him. Over the last eighteen months he had devised a plan which would take down one of the planet's most immoral organisations. 'Other people' might think much more highly of him when that happened. Then he might be interested in what they thought.

Today was the day he would kick his plan into action, today he would start the ball rolling - the demolition ball.

Michael knew that, as far as his plan was concerned, this was definitely the most important day so far. He was starting a new job in the computer department of a major international bank based right in the heart of the city. Big bank, big city, big salary. In reality he was not interested in the salary, he was interested in the fact that he would be working in a bank. In particular, he was interested in this bank.

The International Investment Bank of Europe (IIBE) was far and away the richest bank there had ever been. It had more money than the combined assets of the United States Federal Reserve and the National Bank of China; and, as if that was not enough, it owned one or two of the principal banks in most of the world's developed countries as well. He liked to describe it as having more banks than the Mississippi river. That was possibly being unfair to the Mississippi, because IIBE was much murkier and its banks were much slipperier.

IIBE also had a web of commercial links to virtually all the financial organisations on the planet and, in Michael's not so humble opinion, it cheated and exploited every single one of them.

He looked in the mirror and tried to decide if the image he saw, reflected how he wanted others to see him. He liked it; the neat hair, grey suit, crisp white shirt and dark purple tie definitely worked for him. He still disliked the beard and moustache, but they were an important part of the plan and they made him look older than his years. He knew that looking a few years older would help him to become accepted because nobody liked a know-it-all who was too young.

Overall he was very happy; the reflection screamed confidence, capability and knowledge. He knew he looked good, he knew he looked the business.

He was ready for anything the world could throw at him. He had always known that most people's best laid plans were destroyed by contact with reality, but he was not most people and he was convinced that his plan was indestructible.

3

A tale to tell

Tung felt a massive frustration welling up inside him. What evil had contrived to make him spend his last few hours listening to the ravings of a demented old man? Unfortunately he had no choice, so he had to listen. He was, literally, a captive audience.

"You will find this hard to believe," began Madrick, "but I was not always known as a fantastic wizard."

Tung had no difficulty whatsoever believing it because he had no idea who this idiot was. He had heard of the Royal Wizard, but it seemed pretty unlikely that this old fool was a royal anything. He said nothing in the hope that the story would be a short one.

"I was not the worst apprentice in the Sorebun Sorcery Academy," continued Madrick, "but it would be fair to say, I was never the pointiest stick in the quiver. Then things changed. Then, something special happened.

"I was exploring a forgotten corner of the school library, right at the back, where it was quieter than a tomb and darker than a wolf's mouth. I sensed that my epic search would soon be over. I felt it in my waters that this was the day I would find the Holy Grail - the librarian's secret wine store.

"I climbed on a few stacked tomes so I could search the highest shelves. I pushed some large volumes aside and peered through the gap and that is when I discovered it. Right at the back of that dusty, top shelf there was a large, decaying map scroll. I stretched into the darkness and gingerly lifted it down. I brushed the cobwebs off and started to undo the red strip of leather which bound the ancient map. As I unrolled the parchment a smaller, less significant looking scroll slid out and fell at my feet.

"I bent down and picked it up. It was a spell scroll. I

had never held one in my hand before, but I recognised it immediately. I checked that there was no one around and then slipped it inside my robe before I rushed full pelt back to my room. Can you imagine how excited I was?"

"I can imagine," remarked Tung who actually could not imagine it at all, his idea of excitement always involved wine, women and boisterous song. This story did not even have a tune. He was finding this even less exciting than watching witches burn - at least smouldering witches smelt good.

"Once back in the privacy of my own room I examined my little treasure. All sorts of thoughts flashed through my mind. What could the spell be? The Gold Spell? The Kill Spell? The Spell of Inducement? I held the yellowed parchment closer to my candle.

"The Thunderbolt Spell? The All-seeing-eye Spell? In the flickering candlelight I read the words on the ancient parchment."

Tung, somewhat trance-like, watched the old man and tried to work out where this was going. He had a sneaking suspicion that, wherever it was going, it was going to take a long time to get there. He was becoming more and more agitated because the old man seemed to be, unnecessarily, prolonging the agony.

"What was the wretched spell? Tell me right now or you can finish telling your story to the rats."

"Be patient my young friend, I am coming to that."

He was savouring the tension that was building and he had no intention of hurrying himself to reach the climax.

"As I read the magical manuscript I became more and more excited. This spell was one of the most powerful of all spells. This spell was one of the great wizard legends. This spell was only rumoured to exist... but there it was. And I had it right there in my hand. It was indeed..." Madrick paused for effect, straightened his back and boomed, "THE SPELL SPELL!"

"The spell spell?" repeated Tung flatly unimpressed. "That's the world's most powerful spell?"

An intelligent man might have thought it sounded more like a lexicographer's fantasy party than a great wizard legend. But Tung was not an intelligent man, so his uneducated brain thought 'magic stutter' and that made him laugh.

Madrick immediately realised that Tung was not in the least overawed, he was not even slightly impressed. He considered explaining to Tung the nature of wizards, spells and magic scrolls. He considered telling him how a wizard loses the memory of a spell once he has spoken it, hence the importance of the written spell parchment. He considered explaining that even the most skilful wizards had to return to the spell scrolls to relearn spoken spells. He considered it, but decided it was not worth the effort.

"Scrolls are bleeding important you know. The more powerful the spell the more bloodily important the scroll is," Madrick said angrily.

He was becoming apoplectic because Tung was still laughing. He had no idea how he could make this imbecile understand, but he knew he would have to, if he was going to have any chance of escaping from this dreadful place. Suddenly the laughter stopped.

"I know scrolls are important," said Tung. "I know about these things."

"Only wizards, magicians and male witches know about these things," insisted Madrick indignantly. Silently he added 'and maybe female witches', however the female of the species was a complete mystery to him.

"And only wizards really, truly know."

"Wizards and me," Tung persisted. He was not sure whether he should tell Madrick about the time he broke into the Sorebun Academy. It was almost certainly a very bad idea... so naturally he told him the story.

"I broke into the Sorebun School once. No one in their

right mind would do it twice. I searched long and hard, far and wide, high and low, for something worth stealing, eventually I found the scroll library - the Great White Library.

"Of course I got caught, but not before I discovered what you wizards actually spend your lives doing. You search the world for scrolls; the more you collect the more powerful you become. And the more you collect, the less there are left for the Black Wizards. It is a good versus evil arms race.

"Anyway, I was duly interrogated by the Great Grand Wizard himself. At first he suspected that I belonged to the Order of Black Wizards. He thought I was there to steal the scrolls for that evil brotherhood. Mind you it did not take him long to discover that I was a rather sad, common cutpurse. On that note, I was unceremoniously ejected from the building, but not before he had blessed me with a few curses I would prefer to forget… including one which did actually make me forget a lot of things! So you see, I do understand."

Tung was clearly pleased with himself and Madrick was somewhat taken aback, but he was thrilled that his cellmate had at least some grasp of these mysteries. With renewed vigour he continued his story.

"The Spell Spell, what more could a wizard wish for? I had a decision to make. I could hand my find in to the Academy and become a hero. I would go down in the annals of history as the wizard who found the most powerful spell ever created. Or I could keep it for myself.

"Being a hero in history does not put bread on the table and anyway, I was the one who found it so I decided I would keep it for myself. I hid the scroll in my room and pondered the possibilities. I knew I could not use it immediately without drawing attention to myself. I would have to bide my time, otherwise the powers that be would just steal it from me. They are sneaky men who are not to be trusted.

"I vowed to keep my head down and graduate from the

Academy. Then, when I was established in the world, I would unleash my secret weapon... judiciously."

Madrick was becoming more animated by the second as he relived the saga in his mind.

"Hold on a tick, Rick. If you have the most powerful spell in the universe, why not use the damned thing to get yourself out of here?"

"Well," conceded the old man losing a little bit of his earlier enthusiasm, "there is just one small catch."

"Isn't there always?" whispered Tung who could sense the rapid approach of the tidal wave of disappointment - life is a beach and the tide is coming in fast.

"Explain it to me magic man, what's the problem?"

Madrick ignored him and continued.

"The Spell Spell can create any spell in the universe. Imagine the power, to create a spell from absolutely nothing. It is a bit like 'and for my third wish, I will have three more wishes.' It is the spell that just keeps giving - until it plays the cruellest trick of all. As I told you there is one catch. You see, each spell that is created must be used before the next can be created."

Tung had worked it out now, so he stopped the old man in mid-flow.

"And the scroll's previous owner had not used the last spell so it's not worth the parchment it is scribbled on - or rather scribed on."

"Good guess, but I am the one who has not used the last spell. It is me that has caused the problem."

As he spoke he slipped his hand inside his robe and, after some scrabbling around, which would remind you a lot of flea-scratching, he withdrew a scroll. He passed the small, rather insignificant, yellowed scroll to Tung who unrolled it and began to study the ancient manuscript. It made absolutely no sense to him, partly because it was written in a strange, mystical script, but mainly because Tung could not read. He was totally illiterate. Tung thought hard.

"I know what the real catch is. When you say 'it will magic up any spell' you mean *any* spell. You do the hocus-pocus, but you have absolutely no control over what spell is created. And you have hocus-pocused up a spell that you can't use."

"Exactly right, you are a surprisingly astute young man."

Madrick stood up. He began to circle Tung, occasionally stroking his long, grey beard as he continued his tale.

4

Michael

Michael was twenty-one and he had been messing around with computers since he was about six. His love of the early games had helped him understand the basics about how PC software worked. Later he discovered the internet and all the things it had to offer a teenage boy. His parents tried to restrict his access using parental controls and passwords, but to Michael, that was a challenge rather than a hindrance. He quickly learnt workarounds and this sparked off his interest in security systems, encryption and the like. He became a prolific reader and actually enjoyed ploughing through thick, technical manuals. They were the electronic equivalent of a Mac triple cheeseburger and he loved them. He happily trawled complicated internet forums and spent all his pocket-money on computing magazines; his appetite for knowledge was insatiable.

He had few friends because all he ever wanted to do was work with computers. It was a lonely childhood, but oddly, a very happy one. His parents were loving and supportive, his material needs were all well catered for and his passion for technology was fulfilled. What more could anyone ask for?

Soon he was a genuine expert and a legend among the internet techno-geeks. Apart from being truly knowledgeable, he learnt very early on that, whatever happens, you must always behave exactly as though you meant it to happen. This makes you look very clever indeed.

The acclaim that he attracted gave him a self-confidence beyond his years and this eventually matured into a social confidence which was unusual for a computer buff who had kept himself to himself. He had well thought out opinions on most topics and a relevant anecdote or joke for nearly any situation. He was funny, articulate and very good with people. He was an all round likeable guy.

At only nineteen, he joined Noviru, an emerging high-tech company which produced intelligent, anti-virus software. Their software was revolutionary; it learnt from its experience in the real world and it evolved by itself to counter the ever changing threat from internet crackers and hackers. Revolutionary and evolutionary.

He worked in the Malware Creation Department, MC for short, that amused him because MC was the texting abbreviation for Merry Christmas, but they made presents that no one wanted! Malware Creation was not the department's official name of course. In fact, the department did not exist; officially.

His job was to create Viruses, Worms, Trojans, and Spyware; all targeting the big banks and other financial institutions. He sometimes felt that the term 'malware' was a bit harsh because his creations did nothing particularly malicious, so maybe 'peskyware' was nearer the mark. Whatever you called them, they were annoying enough to be the ultimate selling tool for the Noviru sales team. How else could a small company grab the undivided attention of these multinational giants?

Generally, his software just alerted the target that its system had been breached. For example, it would force a message into their IT infrastructure such as 'This message demonstrates your vulnerability. Contact Noviru if you want total protection.'

As time went on, he injected his own personality into the mix and tried humour to grab their attention. Messages like 'Planet Earth is shutting down in twenty minutes. Please save all your files and log off' were so irritating that they often did the trick.

There were times when his software was a bit sneakier, for instance, he loved messing with the target's automated telephone answering systems. He would add 'Press seven if you would like a list of how technology has improved our lives.' Or he would rig it so callers were trapped in the holding music and every so often, they would get a message which indicated their position in the queue; one place further back than their last message. Nearly everyone has encountered one of these telephonic frustrations because they have called companies which chose not to call Noviru.

As soon as the targets realised they could not shift the intruding messages using their conventional methods, most of them reluctantly called for help. Inevitably the first meeting was extremely hostile; lots of shouting, plenty of accusations and threats of legal action... and worse. However, when it all calmed down, there was usually a sale at the end of it.

That was just the tip of his digital iceberg, he had his own plans for some of these titanic target companies. He had created some software intruders which were infinitely more devious than anything that Noviru had.

5

A spell of trouble

Madrick did have a story to tell regardless of whether anyone wanted to listen. He started his tale.

"I graduated from the Academy and was presented with a few minor scrolls. This is how a wizard makes his way in the world initially. I used these scrolls well, but every so often I slipped in a 'special' with the Spell Spell and secretly created a new enchantment, and that made me stick out from the crowd. Anyway, I became so famous that I was invited, or rather commanded, to attend the court of King Mifal. He liked what he saw and made me his Royal Wizard in attendance. That meant I was given access to his personal store of scrolls so I became even more powerful. He had a reasonable collection of minor scrolls, some of which were interesting, but he had nothing of major import because that was the way it was with 'private' collections. The Wizards tolerated kings, great lords, emperors and the like to build small collections of insignificant scrolls because there really was no point in starting unnecessary wars about inconsequential artefacts. Anyway, I digress.

"To begin with it all went very well and I pleased Mifal with my stunning magic. I amazed him with my versatility. He thought I was exceptionally clever to use his scrolls so 'imaginatively' - his previous wizard had never achieved such impressive feats. But of course, it was really the Spell Spell that was doing the truly splendiferous stuff.

"Most of my created spells were wonderful and I used them to great effect. I am actually very good at this, even though I say so myself. As my reputation grew, I had to keep my wits about me because my wizard teachers from Sorebun were a little suspicious to say the least. Every so often they would send wizardly spies to spy on me and try to discover how I had changed from one of their pretty ordinary students into such a famous and respected wizard. As I said, I was very careful so they never did work it out.

"I revelled in my position as the King's personal wizard. I loved the prestige it brought me. My talents had finally been recognised and I was genuinely content. At last, I had found my place in the world. That all changed when Mifal stripped me of my exalted position about an hour ago."

Madrick continued pacing the cell. It was one of the castle's biggest communal dungeons, designed to hold up to eighty prisoners at a time, so he had plenty of room to pace. He had settled into a sort of circular orbit with Tung as the central point. It was beginning to make Tung dizzy so, when the planet Madrick next passed close enough, he grabbed the sleeve and applied just enough downward tug to make Madrick sit. The old man hardly noticed and continued his story as if nothing had happened.

"Ungratefulness, that is what landed me here in this dreadful dungeon. Yes, ungratefulness. I did miracles for Mifal and made him the greatest, and happiest, king in the history of this land.

"I am sure you wondered how Katrina, the most beautiful woman in the entire world, fell in love with the ugly, old oaf. Well, you are looking at the man who made it happen. One of my spells, thank you very much."

Madrick began to rise, but Tung spotted the movement in time to lay a restraining hand on the old man's knee. He did not want the old buzzard circling him again. Madrick shifted his weight slightly, but luckily, he did not stand up.

"So Mifal had the queen he wanted and he was feeling at one with the entire universe, with one slight exception. He wanted more from me. He had seen results from all his personal scrolls and he was bored.

"I needed something spectacular and so returned to my own wondrous scroll. I created my next spell. That was when total disaster struck. I had created the one spell that I could not use. Now the scroll you have in your hand is as worthless as a harlot's love."

Madrick paused and thought about the considerable experience he had of that particular worthless commodity. The pause lasted so long that Tung started to worry that the old man had passed out or died or something. He prodded Madrick with his finger to try and get him talking again. It worked.

"I had created the one spell that I could not use. How could I be so unfortunate? O me miserum."

Madrick stared listlessly at the cell ceiling. Tung thought he was going to lapse into silence again, but thankfully he did not. In the resonant, whispering voice he reserved for the mystical bits, he continued.

"I will tell you of this spell, listen carefully. This is the really important part of the whole story. If you are going to concentrate on anything I say, concentrate on the next bit.

"This spell was born in the dim and murky past when the ancient wizards battled for supremacy. They were the true magical ones; they were the special people who actually created the spells which exist today. This particular spell was created by Kargill, the most powerful of all the ancient wizards. Its purpose was to save the lives of those ancients who had been defeated in a magic duel. This spell began a sort of 'honour among ancients'... just like thieves have.

"Basically the spell completely took away a wizard's power. The vanquished wizard spoke the spell and thus lost the ability to ever, repeat ever, use magic again. Of course, without magic he was no longer a threat to the victor so his life could be spared.

"That is the spell I have inside me now, the Wizard's Finale Spell. If I speak the spell I will become powerless, if I don't then I am powerless. This is the ultimate dilemma for me. O me miserum... again.

"That is why I'm in this stinking dungeon. King Mifal had given me until midnight to perform another spectacular miracle for him. To use his exact words 'No miracle, no Madrick.'.... a man of few words our king."

"He has certainly said very few to me," remarked Tung under his breath.

Madrick had once again lapsed into silence. He sat dejectedly with his hands covering his face. He was making sad, little whiney noises. Tung studied him and thought about the spell, the Scroll and the possibility of escape. Could there be something in this for him, he wondered, could he really be staring at a way out?

Eventually Madrick spoke again. He had abandoned the mystical lilt in his voice, now his intonation seemed much more urgent. Now he was speaking rapidly as if his life depended on it - which, of course, it did.

"If you do exactly what I tell you we have a chance to escape from this place, but only if we work together. I propose entering a solemn pact with you, a life or death, eternal and soul-binding pact."

"You mean do a deal?" asked Tung after he had sifted and simplified the words.

"Don't mess me around. You must know that you have nothing to lose. Right now, you have the life expectancy of a mayfly in June."

"You mean do a deal?" repeated Tung.

"Fair enough, do a deal, whatever. The 'deal' I offer you requires me to say the damned Finale Spell and then I will help you use the Scroll to get both of us out of here. But heed this warning and heed it well, the Scroll makes a very dangerous friend unless you have had the sort of training that I have had."

The last bit was true, but Madrick had only added it to make Tung feel that he would still need him once he had the power of the Scroll.

"Do we have a... deal?"

Tung did not need a degree in logic to know that this was his last chance; his only chance. He spat enthusiastically on his palm and offered it to Madrick. The old man declined the outstretched, dripping hand and patted Tung on the shoulder. Then he began the rather boring explanation of how the spell scroll worked.

For the next half hour Madrick described the intricacies of the Spell Spell. Tung concentrated harder than he ever had before; he recognised a do-or-die moment when he saw one - he had let plenty of them drift past him before now. Madrick had nearly finished and he thought Tung had understood everything so far. He could not be sure, but they would find out soon enough.

"So, when you trigger the spell you will see words in your mind, and a picture. These, together, identify the spell you have created. Because I have been trained I will know what the spell does. I, and only I, will know the best way to use it. I, and only I, will know how to use it without you killing yourself. Together, and only together, we will harness the power."

He decided he had maybe overdone the 'you need me' part of his speech. Now it was time to focus on the big opportunity that the spell offered them.

"In your hands, the spell will not be working for the likes of Mifal, it will be working for us. Together we will fulfil our wildest dreams, each and every one of them. And wild dream number one... is to escape."

With the explanation over Madrick felt he could do no more to prepare Tung. He also thought he had done enough to convince Tung how necessary he was. He was beginning to think that this pact might actually work. Not because Tung was trustworthy, he certainly was not, but Madrick knew he really was indispensable, for now.

"Right then, let us make magic. It is time."

"Right Rick, let's do it."

It would merely waste time to describe Madrick speaking the Finale Spell. It is enough to know he spoke it. Tung was kind enough not to ask about the tears in his eyes as he performed his last ever act as a wizard. When the deed was done Tung felt something immensely powerful surge into the scroll which he still clutched to his chest. It was at that instant he knew the old man's story was completely and absolutely true.

"Remember well what I have told you," Madrick said once he had recovered. "Now it is time for you to do what you must do."

Tung unrolled the scroll and stared hard at the first character on the manuscript. As he concentrated, the character began to swirl on the page, it rotated and twisted, faster and faster, and then it disappeared just as Madrick had described. Tung moved his eyes to the next and he repeated the process. Then the next, and the next, until the parchment appeared completely blank to him. As the last character disappeared there was a deafening roar in the very centre of his brain followed by a blinding flash inside each of his eyeballs. He fell backwards and was unconscious moments before his head crashed onto the stone floor.

Madrick watched Tung carefully as he 'spoke' the spell. Tung certainly had an aptitude, in that respect Madrick had been lucky. He could have ended up with an unwilling listener, or someone unable to understand, or someone devoid of the necessary concentration. He could have ended up in a cell on his own. Maybe he was not the sorriest, unluckiest human being alive after all.

He looked at Tung as he lay on the ground. He was a sorry example of a human being. He offended all the senses. He smelt bad, he looked awful, he sounded like a pig in heat; and touch and taste were two places Madrick certainly did not want to go. But he had listened and he seemed to have managed to say the spell.

If Madrick had not drifted off into his own thoughts he might have reacted quickly enough to prevent the high velocity collision involving Tung's head and the cell floor. That was going to make the massive spell-headache even worse.

Madrick examined Tung's face as he lay, still as the dead, on the cold stone. He placed his hand on Tung's forehead, it was warm and wet. With his thumb he raised one of the eyelids and, as the lid was pulled up, the other eye flicked open. Tung was conscious.

6

International Investment Bank of Europe

The International Investment Bank of Europe had a very long and prestigious history stretching back nearly three hundred years, although it roots could be traced back to Saxon times. The bank was founded in its modern form in 1715 specifically to lend money to the British government to help finance the fight against the Jacobites and the government has been indebted to them ever since.

It was listed as the eighth richest bank in the world although its true wealth was not known outside its own, very secretive, boardroom. It was, in fact, the richest bank that the world had ever seen. It had hidden assets all across the planet and was one of the few Western financial institutions that had managed to conceal vast fortunes in Chinese banks, which it secretly owned. This made the money almost impossible to trace.

Michael had first come across IIBE when Noviru installed its anti-virus software across their global network. It was, at the time, the biggest deal that the company had ever won and the job was expected to take months to complete.

Even though he was one of their newest workers, Michael had been given the lead role in delivering this highly prestigious contract. He was a rising star and the company wanted to exploit his skills to the utmost. After some serious negotiation, he was given an office in the IIBE headquarters building and for nearly four months he spent virtually every waking hour working on the implementation. This was an exceptional turn of events because IIBE was precious about its security and had never before allowed outsiders into the heart of its operation.

Michael was determined to make the project a stunning success. This was his chance to impress his bosses and this was his chance to further one of his secret ambitions. He had the chance to kill two very large birds with one stone - two big black hawks down, he thought.

Over the next few months he began to see how IIBE operated... and he did not like what he saw. These people did not break the regulations, these people made the regulations and they made them so that they were the sole beneficiaries. It is called the Golden Rule - those with the gold make the rules. And these people definitely had the gold.

He also researched the organisation on the internet... and he did not like what he found.

His research covered everything from their financial performance through to the profiles of the company directors. There was also a lot of material about a darker side to IIBE.

He read numerous perturbing conspiracy theories. For example, The One World Government claimed that some of the planet's richest people hide behind organisations such as the UN, WTO and the World Bank; and their ultimate aim is to gain control of the world's money supply therefore giving them control over everyone who is in debt, which is pretty much every government, every company, everybody.

He did not fully subscribe to any of these theories; however he felt it was no coincidence that, after a bit of digging, the name IIBE nearly always came up. He could only assume that there may be some truth in among the dross, so he logged the information in the back of his mind, just in case.

There were also well documented rumours that IIBE had a highly secretive and ruthless internal security department. It was rumoured to have been modelled on the brutal and secretive methods of the Russian KGB or the old East German Stasi... or both. That sounded a bit ironic, he thought, a communist inspired defence for the ultimate capitalist beast. Anyway, he noted that fact as well, but he

25

reckoned he was too clever to be derailed by old, cold war tactics. If only he had taken more heed of these rumours, then he might have been better prepared for what lay ahead of him.

7

I see no spell

Tung had never felt so close to death. He had all the massive pains and gut-wrenching nausea of the world's worst hangover… times at least a million. He had experienced more than his fair share of beer-induced hangovers from hell, however, this one was a special delivery, straight from the devil.

The first words he heard, or at least the first he began to understand, were Madrick's. They seemed to coming from very far away and had all the clarity of a muffled mumbler. He concentrated hard; he did not know it yet, but concentration was going to become a recurring necessity in his life.

"You will be pleased to hear that it will get less painful each time you do it. Towards the end, I was able to conjure up spells with nothing more than a twinge round the temples."

He rubbed his forehead as if to relive a fond memory, but he quickly found the bruise where Tung had punched him earlier; that stopped him rubbing and brought his mind back to the task in hand.

"Well, what is the spell? Let us see what you have created. Tell me the words you have in your head."

Tung heard, but he did not really understand. There was something alien taking up his whole mind. He could not focus on it and he could not hold it still long enough to work out what it was. It was like trying to watch floaters in your eye - you moved your eye towards them, but they moved with you and stayed just on the periphery of your vision. As he battled with it, he got the impression of three words and, through the sheer force of determination, he held them still long enough to remember. To remember that he could not read; he was totally and completely illiterate.

"This probably is not the best time to tell you, but I

suppose you'll have to know some time. I cannot read a single, damned word. I wasn't at school long enough to catch the plague never mind get an education. I don't even know the letters never mind the words."

Madrick felt a sudden panic welling up inside him. Some spells were very dangerous if they were used without care. You could easily kill yourself, and everyone around you, experimenting with an unknown spell. Without knowing what the spell was, there no way to work out how best to use it and when was the best time? The 'when' was obviously less important because, for the time being in their present predicament, the best time was almost certainly immediately. It was the 'how' that was crucial and he needed to know the 'what' before he could work out the 'how'.

Madrick summoned all his strength in an attempt to portray some degree of calmness. He had to find out what the spell was, and he needed to do it without totally spooking Tung.

"Not a problem, just tell me what the picture is. There is always a picture to illustrate the words. What do you see?"

Generally the picture would tell him straight away. That was the point after all; the picture was designed to help identify the spell. There were times when the words were needed because a picture could not easily illustrate some of the more ethereal spells. It was like Pictionary - 'dog' is easy and 'silhouette' is hard - however, Madrick knew nothing of that future problem and he had a big, present problem to deal with. For now, he just needed to know what picture this moron had in his tiny brain.

Tung tried to see what was in his head, but to do that, he had to get past the sheet of pain that was obscuring everything inside his skull. As he concentrated, the words became clearer, he could definitely see them, but that, of course, did not help him read them. Then, as the cranial mist cleared a little more, he saw it. An image of a large black stallion; the magnificent beast pawed the ground and great flares of hot breath exuded from its nostrils.

"I see it! I see it," he shouted. "It is a big black horse! It is a beautiful big black beast of a stallion!"

Madrick knew straight away what this spell was. This horse was a Pictionary 'dog' of the spell world. The interpretation was simple, but he knew immediately that it was not going to help them at all. This spell created a most majestic stallion. A stallion fit for a king, but not much use to them, given the circumstances. He realised that this great beast could not assist their escape, so they had to get it out of the way before they could move on to the next spell. There really was no option, Tung would have to 'say' the spell, create the stallion and then originate a new enchantment. There was no choice and time was running out fast.

Madrick explained to Tung how to cast the spell.

"It is much the same as using the Scroll. What you must do is stare at each letter in your head with your mind's eye. The letters, and then the words, will disappear and KAZAAM! You will have cast the spell and, once cast, you will have the power to use the Spell Spell again. And that is what we need to do right now because this Stallion Spell is of no help to us. We must use it and press on."

Tung concentrated on the words. He had never heard of his mind's eye so he very much hoped he had one. As he stared at the first character in his head it began to swirl round his brain, it rotated and twisted, faster and faster, and then it disappeared exactly as it had been with the Scroll. Tung moved his head eye to the next letter and repeated the process. Then the next, then the next until all the words in his head had vanished. Again, as the last character disappeared, there was a deafening roar in the very centre of his brain. This was accompanied by a blinding flash inside each of his eyeballs and an even brighter explosion in his mind's eyeball. He fell backwards and was unconscious moments before his

29

head crashed onto the stone floor.

Madrick watched Tung carefully as he 'spoke' the spell. Again he marvelled at Tung's aptitude. Again, if he had not drifted off into his own thoughts he might have reacted quickly enough to prevent another high velocity collision involving Tung's head and the cell floor. Again, that was going to make the massive spell-headache even worse.

"Next time, I really must try harder," Madrick said to himself, "to catch his head before it hits the ground."

As Tung crashed to the floor there was a thunderous roar in the corner of the cell and, as if by magic - which was exactly the way it had come about - a magnificent, jet black stallion appeared. It looked confused and angry; and just a little bit dangerous. It paced menacingly in its corner. Frightening as it was, Madrick knew they would have to ignore it and keep going until they had the spell they needed.

Tung was coming back to life; much quicker this time. As he opened his eyes he saw the old man and then he saw the beautiful stallion. He was overpowered by a strange sense of pride as he watched the great horse pacing in the corner; he had created it. He was Tung the Wizard. He was Tung the... very sore head indeed.

"I thought you said there would be less pain every time? The back of my skull feels like it has been bashed with a rock."

"Trust me. That will not happen again, I can guarantee it." Madrick assured him and promised himself that he would make sure that future spell telling did not result in the Tung-floor heavy impact.

As Tung regained most of his senses he became aware of the look on the stallion's face. Its dark eyes were eyeing them both menacingly. Tung was scared. Madrick was scared too and he knew time was running out, so he tried to calm Tung.

"It is more scared of us than we are of it."

"It must be pretty damned scared then!"

As if to prove Madrick right, the mighty beast lifted its tail and deposited a large steaming pile of manure on the floor. If either man had thought the smell in the cell could not have got any worse, then they realised at that very moment just how wrong they were. It was not all bad though, at least the mountain of brown sludge added some colour to the drab greyness.

"Time for the next spell," urged Madrick. "Get the Scroll. Read the words. We must be quick. We have to create a spell which will help us. I know it is in you somewhere. It is just a matter of time, but we do not have much of that left. It will be morning soon. They will be coming for me... I mean us."

Tung reluctantly reused the Spell Spell scroll and, just as Madrick had said, each time he used it, it did become less painful. Certainly he no longer got that dreadful, crushed-by-an-avalanche sensation in the back of his skull - thank you very much Madrick!

He created, and used, the Banquet Spell and the Weather Prophecy Spell. They now had a magnificent feast set out before them although it seemed entirely out of place in the dank cell. The stallion seemed pleased though and was much calmer now as it munched its way through some of the luscious fruit that had appeared.

Neither of them could work out the point of the Weather Prophecy Spell, but at least they knew that tomorrow was going to be bright and sunny.

As each useless spell was created and dispelled; Tung and Madrick became more and more despondent. Tung in particular was becoming very dejected, he was suffering plenty of pain yet it seemed that his suffering was not bringing the prospect of escape any closer. Maybe he was destined to create one useless spell after another until the guards came and dragged him off in the morning.

Madrick tried to keep his spirits up, but making motivational speeches was not one of his stronger points. No one who knew him would call him inspiring.

"Do not worry. It could be the next one. In fact, I am certain that the next spell will be the one. I feel it in my very bones. When I was spelling for Mifal, there were many useless spells, however, things always came good in time… well until the last time of course."

He realised he had rather spoiled his little pep talk so he added "So let us go forward. Trust me. This will definitely be the one!"

"That's what you said last time."

Tung reluctantly opened the Scroll one more time and went through the enchanting motions, he was actually very proud of himself because he could do it quite quickly now. Without an initial hitch, the next spell appeared in his brain. There were the words, but as he searched for the picture, a mounting panic engulfed him. Where was the picture? There was no picture. His mind's eye searched the empty space where the image should have been. He tried everything. He closed his mind's eye and opened it again just as you would with your real eyes when you cannot believe what you are seeing, or in this case, not seeing. Still there was nothing.

"I can see the words, but there is no picture."

"There must be a picture. There is always a picture if you concentrate hard enough. SO CONCENTRATE."

Tung tried again, hard. He concentrated harder than he had ever concentrated before in his life although that was not saying much because he had never been particularly strong in the brain department.

"There is nothing. Nothing at all. There is no picture," he said as his mounting panic had arrived at the blind level - 20:20 blind panic.

For at least a minute Madrick did not react at all, at least not visibly. Inside however, he felt an immense pressure building in his brain, it was surely going to explode. He slumped heavily to the floor. Why could this buffoon not see the picture? There was always a picture. No picture meant no hope. Maybe he could teach Tung to read in the next short while. That was ridiculous, he realised quickly, the futility of the situation was clouding his thinking. Tung could just say the mystery spell and they could see what happened. That could be extremely dangerous, for example, a misdirected fireball would have horrifying consequences in this confined space. He had to face up to it, no picture meant his life was over.

Then it came to him in a blinding flash of revelation. There was no picture; nothing to see. Yes, yes. There was nothing to see because with this spell there was nothing to see. It was the Spell of Invisibility, it had to be. How could they be so fortunate? This surely was the perfect spell to aid their escape.

"You are a genius," cried Madrick as he began a strange little dance around the cell. His fancy footwork had to avoid all the banquet food and the stallion; and a few other things that Tung, and the stallion, had created along the way.

"You are the perfect keeper of the Scroll. You have done it! We are as good as free! You have created the Spell of Invisibility! It is a fantastic spell; you just have to see this one to believe it."

He laughed at his own little joke.

Madrick closed in on Tung who backed off because he thought there was a hug and a kiss on its way. He was right, but he had moved fast enough to avoid both of them. Madrick did not notice the snub. He was now thinking how best they could use this great spell to make good their escape.

From his memory he dredged up everything he knew about the workings of the spell. He thought back to the classes in the Sorebun Academy where day after day they had been subjected to endless lectures about every spell known to wizardkind. He must have listened more than he thought because he was actually recalling quite a lot of detail about this particular enchantment.

He remembered that the spell would make the sayer vanish, along with any number of people who were touching him at the time of saying. He remembered that only the body was affected so they would have to be completely naked when it was spoken. At least it was going to be bright and sunny tomorrow, he thought to himself. And finally, he remembered it was a relatively short lived phenomenon, lasting only a few hours.

He devised a simple plan. He knew the simpler the plan, the more likely it was to succeed, particularly if he had to rely on an idiot like Tung. In his mind it went something like this - they would strip naked, hold hands and stand close to the door; tight against the cell wall. Tung would say the spell and the invisible pair would merely have to wait for the guards to come for them. When the door was opened they would slip out in the confusion, and there was going to be plenty of confusion. That sounded perfect, it was flawless in its straightforwardness. It could not be simpler so surely it was bound to work.

He was well satisfied with himself so he began to explain how the plan would work. Tung was immediately unhappy when Madrick started with 'we will strip naked and hold hands'. Madrick ignored his discomfort and finished describing the escape.

"It is perfect. We have the supreme escape plan and once we are free we will get far, far away from this castle. Once we are out there, we will have plenty of opportunities to steal some new clothes and maybe a few other bits and pieces as well. That should not be a challenge for an accomplished thief like you. Especially an invisible one!

"Then we can ride off into the sunset, if we steal some horses, and fulfil all our dreams. Together, you and me, we will become legends." Madrick ended with a flourish that would have reminded you of an over-acting actor at the end of an over-scripted performance.

In Madrick's head however, the speech was designed to remind Tung of the importance of 'together' - to remind him of the importance of Madrick.

Tung pondered for a few moments. His newly discovered, and now overused, mind's eye walked him visually through each step. It seemed like a sensible plan, it really felt as though it had every chance of succeeding. Then his face dropped and his stomach turned a somersault as he realised there was one massive flaw.

8

First day inside

Michael arrived at just after seven forty-five, well before his prescribed nine o'clock start time. When he walked into the main reception area he was, as usual, completely taken aback by the over-powering opulence. He had been here on many occasions while working for Noviru, however, the lavishness of this entrance hall never failed to grab his attention and impress him. The unbelievably shiny, Italian marble floor reflected more gilt than Midas could have wished for. Imposing, white marble pillars dominated the panorama. A magnificently ornate painted ceiling oversaw the whole scene; the combined effect was truly incredible.

The most prominent feature by far was on the wall that faced the entrance… giant, three-dimensional, golden letters, which he later found out were 24-carat gold, spelled out 'International Investment Bank of Europe' and underneath in smaller letters, their strap line read 'Serving Customers, Serving You.'

"Yeah right," he thought. "'Swindling Customers, Swindling You.' would be nearer to the truth."

He was sure the point of all this was to intimidate everyone who entered this building. Without a doubt it was designed to put even the most confident visitor on the defensive. He was awe-struck, but he was not threatened by this display of power. He had prepared himself well; he knew what he was going to do to this organisation. He had nothing to fear, or so he thought.

He walked towards the reception desk which was tucked away at the left side of the giant foyer. He likened it to an eastern-bloc security station as it was totally enclosed in thick glass and manned by four rather intimidating looking men in paramilitary uniforms. It was certainly not very receptive and not very welcoming. As he got closer, a rather pretty girl popped into view at a small opening in the glass. With more than a little relief he ignored the uniformed guards and reported to her.

"Hi. My name is Michael Phillips, and I'm *(a hacker – don't say that out loud!)*... I'm starting here today, I'm joining the computer support team. I was told to report to reception. I know I'm a bit early. Here's the letter I was sent."

She smiled and took the letter.

"Hi. I'm Faith. I was told you'd be starting today. Hold on while I check a few things out," she smiled again and began typing speedily on her keyboard. She quickly found the relevant entries.

Her brown eyes (yes, he did notice) darted across her screen as she took in all the information. He wondered what they had written about him; he would find out later once he had access to the systems.

"Yes. Here we are. Apparently you're to be fast-tracked through the induction process. Lucky you."

She smiled again. He was really taken with her and there was something about that smile that captivated him. She called over one of the uniformed men and, after a short discussion and a few pointed looks, Michael was directed to a large door just to the right of the reception desk area.

The door had a very sophisticated looking card-key entry system. He had no card-key, so he waited for it to be opened from the inside. He heard a heavy metallic clunking sound as solid, electronically-operated bolts slid to unlock the door. He was ushered in and, once the door had clunked shut behind him, the guard led him to a secure room where they photographed him, processed his forms and eventually printed out his new identity pass/card-key. He was half expecting a full strip search, but that was just his over-imaginative brain working over-time.

After about forty-five minutes, they felt they had done

their job. However he knew that they had merely helped him with his first step to steal mega-millions from this immoral organisation. Michael did not think of it as real stealing, he felt he was just getting the public's money back… albeit he planned to keep most of it for himself.

9

Best of three?

Tung just stood frozen on the spot and stared at the old man. How could he not have seen the problem, he asked himself, why was it up to him to sort out the mess? This guy was meant to be the wise one. He was supposed to be wiser than a barn full of owls so how did he miss something so bleeding obvious?

"Your plan has a great big hole in it. You really haven't thought it through at all," he berated Madrick. "The escape bit is fine, but we were supposed to use the Scroll to get rich, be deliriously happy and attract hosts of girls."

He wondered whether that should be 'hostesses of girls' before he realised he had lost focus. That happened a lot because he had the attention span of a gnat. He began to think about other times when he had drifted away from the important topic... then he gave himself a mental slap and snapped back to the matter in hand.

"We were even going to change the world at one point in our imaginings. Your plan may get us out of here, but what about the Scroll? We'll have to leave it behind us. You said only our bodies become invisible, so we will have to leave everything behind - our clothes, our shoes and the Scroll - we have to leave everything we have in this god forsaken dungeon.

"We will be free but we will be miserable paupers who won't even have the clothes we stand up in! We will be a pair of destitute, alms people who will never be free of the shackles of poverty and will always be on the run from Mifal's henchmen. What happened to the dream?"

He realised he was being a bit melodramatic so he stopped talking. When he thought about it, he would be happy just to escape and get away from the torture and execution, but he had bought into the dream. He had been handed a wondrous gift only for it to be snatched away before he could even unwrap it. He was distraught and he sunk his face into to his hands to emphasise the fact.

Madrick quickly realised that Tung was absolutely right. He had completely forgotten about the Scroll. They could not just carry it out in their invisible hands; that would be ridiculous. A flying scroll would undoubtedly attract attention. There had to be an answer.

They both sat in a dejected silence as they pondered their predicament. They had gone from despondency to joyousness and back to despondency in the space of a few minutes. And then, as if by magic - and this time it was brain power not magic - the answer dawned on both of them at exactly the same moment.

One of them would have to secrete the Scroll inside their body. It was a small scroll, but it was still too large to hold in the mouth or swallow. They both just stared at each other as they realised there was only one other option. Tung was the first to speak.

"It is not going to be me. I have already gone through enough pain for this escape. It's not going to be me, no chance."

Madrick tried to muster an argument even though he realised that Tung's point was more than fair. Having said that, he did not care much about fairness, particularly given the consequences of this rather delicate situation.

"I know," he said hopefully. "I know a just and fair way to decide. Rock, Parchment, Knife. We will play Rock, Parchment, Knife... best of three?"

Tung was having none of it. He loved a gamble and he was quite skilled at the game, but he was taking no chances.

"It is not going to be me. I have already gone through enough pain for this escape. Not me, no chance," he repeated his argument pretty much verbatim and, as if to indicate the end of the discussion, he began to chew on a chicken leg he had grabbed from the banquet remains that were strewn around them on the floor.

Madrick thought some more, but could not come up with an argument which was likely to change Tung's mind; Tung seemed adamant.

"You are taking advantage of an old man. Have you no pity in your heart?"

A plea for sympathy had to be worth a try. Tung just ignored him and continued to gnaw on the chicken bone.

"All right, all right. You win. I will be the bearer of the greatest pain and suffering so we can take the wretched thing with us," conceded Madrick reluctantly. "But you must remember this moment well. You must remember how it was me that gave us the opportunity to fulfil our dreams.

"I will conceal the damned Scroll. Turn your eyes away and do not listen," he said firmly as he took the Scroll and lifted up the back of his robe.

Try as he might, Tung could not help hearing the grunts and squeals of the old man as he struggled to secrete the tightly rolled Scroll. This was definitely not the fate anyone had envisaged for the magic parchment and it was clearly not designed for this.

When the moaning and groaning had largely subsided, Tung looked round and immediately felt full of remorse. This was the second time Tung had seen tears in the old man's eyes in the space of a few hours. This time he completely understood, this time he felt the tears were totally justifiable.

The rest of the plan ran smoothly and without a hitch; at least it did at first. As morning approached, they undressed and, just to confuse the guards even more, Tung hung Madrick's robe over the stallion's neck. They held hands and Tung said the spell in his head. The pair disappeared and there was a loud cracking sound as Tung's invisible head crashed against the rock hard floor.

"That was not my fault this time," thought Madrick as he felt the floor to find his invisible partner.

When Tung came to, he looked around and was delighted to see neither Madrick nor himself. He was proud of himself again, however, there was no time for back patting even if he could have found one to pat.

"Press yourself against the wall. We do not want the guards to accidentally bump into us."

Tung did as he was told.

"I am getting good at this," he said as he felt the cold against his back. "I have a skill to be proud of. I wish my friends could see me now!"

He smiled as he smugly concluded that his invisible joke was much better than Madrick's.

Shortly after they had vanished, the guards burst in. All they found was a magnificent stallion gorging on what appeared to have been a sumptuous banquet. There was pandemonium... how were they going to explain this to their chief? Someone's head would roll - probably literally.

In the ensuing confusion, Tung and Madrick, quietly and without difficulty, slipped out of the cell. They heard the shouting behind them as they moved silently along the corridor that led out of the dungeon. It was all going well until Tung saw Bildon and Tad, the two jailers who had tormented him mercilessly during his short stay in the cell. He could not resist a little mischief on his way out.

Tung reached under the table and squeezed Bildon hard in a place that made him double over like a bear trap snapping shut. His face smashed into the table and he yelped like a little girl, although the same attack would not have hurt a little girl in quite the same way. His reaction was surprisingly swift; it certainly surprised Tad who suddenly found Bildon's dagger plunged deep into his shoulder. Blood poured from the wound; curses poured from his mouth. The two men then just stared at each other with black hatred in their eyes;

neither had any idea what had inspired the other to initiate their attack. Neither of them was going to take the time to find out.

Bildon was quicker and more deadly. Before Tad had a chance to react, Bildon yanked the dagger from his shoulder and stabbed him in the chest. He immediately dropped dead to the floor. Bildon heard soldiers coming down the corridor so he quickly hid the knife in the pot of grey sludge that sat in the middle of the table. He then threw himself onto the floor holding his head and pretending he was nearly unconscious. He was definitely not going to own up to this killing.

Suddenly the soldiers arrived and there was utter confusion. They saw the stallion, which had now escaped from the cell, prancing around Tad's dead body. A bunch of jailers running about like headless chickens only added to the mayhem. The captain who led the squad of soldiers tried to bring order, but it was a losing battle. No one would ever work out what had happened here.

Tung giggled silently to himself, he was very proud of his handiwork. He and Madrick slipped out of the dungeon complex and up the stairs to the main castle. The last thing they heard as they left that dreadful place was one of the jailers shouting.

"Bildon killed Tad. Look, there's his dagger hidden in the pot of semolina.

"There's the proof," he screamed. "It's in the pudding."

What an idiot, thought Madrick as he raced up the steps, the proof is always in the eating.

10

That dreadful night

Michael was obsessed with his plan; he had been since he was eighteen years old. He felt no pangs of guilt whatsoever because he genuinely believed his planned fraud was for the greater good. He fervently believed that it was perfectly justifiable to do bad things to bad people - his father had drummed that into him from an early age. He began to think back over his life and what had brought him to this point, and what had given him the moral compass of which he was so proud.

His first clear memory of putting points on his compass came from his early schooldays. He remembered being surprised by his father's support for him when he had been called to the school to be told of Michael's attack on another pupil.

His father abhorred violence, however, after he had heard the school's account of the incident he asked for private time to hear Michael's version. Michael described weeks of sustained bullying led by the 'victim'; the more he heard the more upset he became about the nastiness of the campaign against his son. He did not in any way condone the retribution Michael had taken on the other child, it was definitely over the top, but he understood and subsequently refused to allow the school to punish him. He spent weeks fighting attempts to discipline Michael and eventually won through after the school fully investigated the bullying allegations and expelled the other child.

Michael had greatly respected his father's perseverance on his behalf and the incident did a lot to cement the strong bond with his father. That dogged pursuit of what was right was just one of the multitude of lessons he had learnt from his father. He had inherited much, much more from him, not least of which was to treasure kindness, an attribute that had been consistently demonstrated to him all through his childhood. Both his mother and father had always stressed the importance of being true to yourself regardless of the consequences. They emphasised the good in people, however, they did not allow him to view life through rose-tinted spectacles. They made him acutely aware that there were some very bad people in the world; indeed they described some as truly evil.

He had loved his parents dearly and had, most of the time, listened to the advice and guidance that they shared with him.

In particular, he thrived on the encouragement given to him when it came to technology and computers. His father had been a manager in a well known insurance company and was only exposed to low levels of technology. Even though he had never got into the nuts and bolts of computers, he was smart enough to realise that understanding Information Technology was an essential skill for a young man with aspirations towards a well paid career.

Michael flourished in the knowledge that he was growing up in a secure and loving environment. He treasured his growing accumulation of happy memories. He loved his rock solid certainty about his inherited moral compass. He knew he was a good person with a true heart.

Sadly, his life changed dramatically the evening his uncle arrived at the door accompanied by a serious looking policeman and policewoman. His comfortable and cosy world was about to be horribly shattered on that awful night. They told him that his mum and dad had died in a car crash. It was many years later when he found out just what a horrendous car crash it had been.

His uncle took him to stay with his family and he lived there for the next year and a half. Michael was just eighteen at the time, and even though that was now more than three years ago, it still hurt him deeply when he thought about it.

He still often reflected on the sinister events which had led up to that tragic day. His mother and father had been fighting constantly about something to do with his work. That, in itself, was very strange because they generally did not have rows.

It seemed that his father had uncovered a serious fraud within his company, something to do with phoney policies set up for one of the country's leading banks. When he reported his findings to his manager, she had brushed them off as a figment of his imagination. Unfortunately his sense of doing the right thing led him to investigate more deeply. The scale of the fraud he uncovered was apparently absolutely mind blowing. Tens of millions of pounds were being sucked out of policy funds set up for their 'ordinary customers' and transferred though dummy accounts into the coffers of an organisation that was already too rich to count its money. It was yet another example of the rich getting richer at the expense of the ordinary man in the street.

He gathered his evidence and reported it all to the financial authorities.

That was when the menacing phone calls had started; menacing voices late at night threatening the whole family. His mother had told him to drop the matter, but he had insisted that, if the financial authorities were not going to deal with it, he would go to the police.

Even though it was impossible to prove that the car crash was not an accident, Michael knew, deep down, that this was not some unconnected tragedy. He did not believe in coincidences. He could never shake off the belief that powerful people had conspired to kill his father and they had no problem with his mother becoming collateral damage. The outcome of the crash would have been uncertain; they could have survived, had some of the circumstances been different. They were wearing seat belts, but they were unlucky to have spun off the road at a place where there was a thirty foot drop and it was incredibly unfortunate that the car had landed on its roof; they may have lived had it landed right side up. Maybe it was intended as another warning, Michael had often thought, but the outcome was that both his parents died and he was just eighteen and alone.

He knew he could never find out who was responsible, but he remembered his father's perseverance in protecting him as a child so he put some serious effort into tracking down the guilty. Someone needed to be punished even if he could not work out exactly who the culprits were.

He trawled through the evidence that his father had painstakingly gathered. He could put his finger on anything definite. He could see that the big account holders were consistently the winners while the 'man in the street' accounts were consistently the losers. No matter where he looked there was no concrete proof, so he was left with a smouldering resentment for big banks and a dogged antipathy for their fat cat owners.

The whole experience had definitely been a major force in shaping his adult life. In particular, his animosity towards the super-rich coupled with his ingrained sense of goodness combined to create his overwhelming desire to strike back. He knew it sounded a bit grandiose, but he wanted to become a force for good and change the lives of the small fry at the expense of the big sharks.

He needed to develop a plan.

11

Escape

They crept out of the prison basement and eventually out of the castle. They moved quickly through the narrow streets which criss-crossed the inner ward of the great stone fortification.

The castle stood on a hill and towered over Thamesius, the largest town in Mifal's kingdom. It was a massive structure which could be seen from everywhere in the emerging city. It was a magnificent stone construction with thick granite ramparts and high defensive towers at each corner of the pentagon-shaped outer walls. It had the reputation of being impenetrable so, to date, England's various invaders had avoided it and got on with conquering the rest of Britain. The Normans did come later and chose to form an uneasy alliance with Mifal rather than tackle the daunting defences. Thamesius therefore attracted thousands of rural dwellers who were routinely terrorised by invading raiders. It was still a sanctuary so the immigrants kept coming.

Thamesius was a bustling settlement, but it was a grey, cold place. Its cramped houses on badly cobbled streets made it unwelcoming. The town was growing dramatically partly because of the thriving commerce but mainly fuelled by waves of scared Britons who had fled from the surrounding lands. This influx of inhabitants made for a very dangerous environment. The immigrants were resented by the locals and many of them lived rough on the streets. There were just too many people and too few houses. This led to a homeless underclass which would do anything to survive, so robberies, beatings and murders were commonplace. These were the streets where Tung had grown up and learnt what few skills he had. Now he was running for his life in those same streets - literally and invisibly.

As Tung and Madrick weaved unseen through the throng, they accidently bumped into a few folk, but it went unnoticed in these crowded streets. People just did not bother to look round to see who had bumped them. They were either too lazy or scared that it could lead to confrontation in these dangerous streets.

Tung took the opportunity to punch a few passers-by in the face just to see what happened. People could ignore a bump, but not a punch in the face so it invariably led to a fight. The victim assumed he had been hit by the nearest person and retaliated by thumping the unsuspecting innocent. It escalated from there. So Tung left a trail of brawling strangers in his wake and this amused him enormously. It took a while for Madrick to realise what was happening and when he did he was furious - why would this idiot jeopardise their escape for a silly bit of fun?

Suddenly Madrick saw one of Mifal's courtiers who had been a thorn in his side since the first day he arrived in the castle. Maybe one bit of silly fun was acceptable he thought as he punched the courtier square on the nose. It did not go well from there. The man somehow reacted quickly enough to end up with an unbreakable grasp of Madrick's invisible arm and he was tugging hard at it and screaming. He had no idea what he had hold of and he was absolutely certain he was not going to let go until, that is, he got pounded by Tung's double handed, invisible rabbit punch to the back of his skull. He collapsed as if he had been pole- axed.

"Run. We need to get out of here. Head for the village," yelled Tung, proud of his work.

"Right behind you, wherever you are," muttered Madrick, not so proud of what he had just done.

They moved more quickly now that they had both stopped accosting various unsuspecting souls. They wanted to leave the mayhem they had caused far behind them as soon as possible and they also hoped that a bit of speed might warm them up. They were both very cold, naked as they were, and it was dull and cloudy rather than bright and sunny. Weather forecasts - some things have always been wrong.

✿ ✿ ✿

King Mifal was furious when he was told of the pandemonium in his dungeon. He ordered that the head jailer be locked up forever for his incompetence and for murdering the other jailer, he added as an afterthought. He also deliberated long and hard about the crazy scene that his captain had described for him. He wrongly believed that his people looked to him for divine guidance. He assumed they needed his wisdom to explain the inexplicable. In fact, no one cared what he thought or said, although no one was ever going to tell him that.

Within an hour or so, he had managed to rationalise the situation. He believed he had solved the puzzle.

He decreed that Madrick had magicked himself into a black stallion and that explained the robe around the horse's neck. It also explained why Madrick was nowhere to be found. He could not explain why he had done it. Based on that reasoning, he further decreed that the horse was to be duly tortured to death and, in that way, Mifal felt he would have his vengeance on the wizard who had refused to do miracles for him. Nobody, particularly Mifal, cared what had happened to Tung so the matter ended there. Everyone was happy except, of course, the horse.

Actually, if the truth be told, which it never was to Mifal, one of the jailers had secretly led the great black stallion out of the prison and kept the magnificent animal for himself. The fabulous beast now grazed in a nearby muddy field surrounded by three adoring mares. So actually, everyone was happy - including the horse.

✿ ✿ ✿

Tung and Madrick made their way out of the main gate and headed for the sprawling town which nestled all around the great stone walls of the castle. They constantly whispered to each other when they thought there was no one within ear shot. They did not want to lose each other; not at this stage anyway.

They were hit straight away by the difference between the streets inside and outside the ramparts. The smell was the most noticeable distinction. Out here, they could smell the smoke from wood burning fires and the more nauseating smell of a largely unwashed population. They sneaked past the little wooden houses eyeing each one for signs of danger; in particular, they were worried about dogs. Many residents kept fearsome mongrels trained to protect their properties from intruders. Dogs would pick up their scent and would probably attack them even though they could not be seen. What a strange sight that would be - definitely one to be avoided.

Madrick watched for danger, as he always did, while Tung scouted for opportunities to steal what they needed. Clothes were the first item on his agenda. He had a well practiced eye so it would not take him too long to find what he was looking for, but they had to time things very carefully. They could not just lift the first outfits that they found, not if there was someone around to see the garments fly through the air, held by their invisible hands. Neither could they wait too long or they would reappear naked in the middle of this town and that would draw plenty of unwelcome attention. That would be enough to get them arrested and that was the last thing they wanted; an early return to Mifal's dungeon.

Eventually Tung spotted the ideal opportunity. He caught sight of a family preparing to leave their house. It was a rather grand building by the standards in this part of town. They were carrying quite a lot of stuff so it seemed likely that they would be away for some time. In fact, as they got closer, they overheard the family's plans. They were off to visit the castle and would be gone for hours. This should give the invisible men plenty of time to poke around the house and find everything they needed for the being-visible world. They would also be able to reappear in the privacy of this accommodation and, once visible, they could dress, cover their indignities and make good their escape. And so it was, more or less.

They timed their move perfectly and snuck inside before the door was secured. After a little rummaging both men found outfits, of sorts, which looked as though they would fit. They were not clothes that made a fashion statement other than 'this person neither knows nor cares about fashion'. As a bonus, Tung's well honed thieving senses had sniffed out the family's life savings hidden in a jar above the blackened, stone fireplace. Tung counted his loot while he warmed himself in front of the dying embers of the log fire. It was a decent haul, he thought, which would keep him going - sorry, them going - for some time. He had to keep reminding himself that he needed to keep Madrick content until it was the right time to abandon the old fool.

Meanwhile, Madrick used the seclusion of the dingy kitchen to retrieve the Scroll from its secret place. It was a weird sight, the scroll appearing very slowly out of... nowhere. He washed it off in a pot that already contained some foul smelling liquid - apparently it was bone soup for the family's meagre supper - and he guessed his Scroll cleansing was not going to improve the smell; or taste. He was very pleasantly surprised how easily the ancient manuscript cleaned up. Maybe it had been designed for this sort of unusual journey after all.

With the cleaned parchment in hand, he joined Tung by the fireside. He could not see him, however, he could see the coins he had stolen floating spookily in the air.

"Here is the Scroll, clean as a whistle. It has survived the journey, as have I, thank you for asking."

He handed Tung the Scroll and told him how he had

cleansed it in the soup.

"It won't do them any harm. I remember eating poo once as part of a bet. I lost the bet. I said I wouldn't eat it."

Invisibility had many advantages, for example, Tung could not see the very strange look that Madrick gave him.

About half an hour later both men gradually became visible again. It was a weird sensation to see yourself slowly take form, but they both felt it was great to be back.

"Nice to see you again. To see you again… nice."

"That would make a good catchphrase for a court jester," said Tung.

They dressed quickly and agreed that their best bet, in the immediate short term, was to get themselves lost in the crowded streets, markets and taverns of the bustling town centre. Before then, they decided to take a little time relaxing in the relative safety of this 'borrowed' house. They threw some more logs on the fire and pulled a couple of stools in close. They gazed as small flames started to encircle the new chunks of firewood.

"What did you actually do to end up in Mifal's dungeon? I never got a chance to ask you. I was so keen to tell my story so we could escape, I never heard what had happened to you."

Tung had learnt from an early age never to tell anyone anything about your life or your crimes. Every time he had ignored that lesson and shared his secrets, there had been bad consequences. So, as usual, he forgot everything he had learnt and started to tell Madrick the whole story.

12

Hard times

"I have had a very hard and very sad life," began Tung.

He was gazing into the fire and reminiscing in his head. There was so much tragedy in his short existence that he did not know where to begin. He supposed he should start by answering the question about how he had ended up in the dungeon and fill in the detail around that if there was time. He felt he would probably not be good at telling his story because he had never done it before. No one had ever been interested in hearing it. He realised that Madrick was fast becoming a sort of father figure to him; a father figure minus the ale, the gambling and the cruel beatings.

"I think you already know that I have been stealing stuff since I was about twelve years old. It started after my mother died and there was no other way to get food because my father was never around. I was left to fend for myself and my younger sister. Her name was Spring. She was a couple of years younger than me and the sweetest little person you could ever hope to meet. She was too young to do anything for herself so she relied on me for everything. And I didn't mind that. In fact, I rather liked it because it gave me some purpose and a sense of worth.

"Without my sister I had nothing really. My friends all called me a lying loser. Actually that's not even true, because I didn't have any friends. I've never had any proper friends."

He did not mention that he had no idea what had happened to his mother. His father said she had died, whereas he believed that she had, in fact, run away. There was no point in complicating the story because that would just raise questions which he could not answer. He also chose not to mention that his father was never around because he was drunk all the time. There was no point in wasting time talking about that waste of space.

"The first thing I ever stole was a fat man's coin pouch. He had far too much money for his own good so I reckoned he deserved a good thieving. I was very proud of that one and not just because it was my first time. They say you always remember your first time and I definitely remember mine well.

"I planned the whole thing carefully and, when the day came, it went off without a hitch. Well, there was a small hitch, but I won't bore you with the detail. The bottom line is I got some money and I kept the pouch as a memento of my first great success. It was probably the first thing I had ever got right in my life. I felt like I had discovered a hidden talent and it sort of set the direction of my life.

"I spent all the money on some 'very ripe' fruit from the market which I ended up giving to my sister because she was sick at the time, so she needed it more than me. She died soon after that and I still wonder to this day whether there was something wrong with the fruit. Did it poison her? Did I poison her? The thought that I might have killed her haunts me to this day."

"You should not blame yourself. You were doing your best for her. The fruit was clearly an act of kindness."

"Killed with kindness is still killed. And it leaves you just as dead as any cruel act would. I loved my sister dearly. She was the only good thing I've ever had in my life."

Madrick saw that Tung was drifting into a depression so he tried to snap him out of it by encouraging him to continue with his tale.

"Yeah, like I was saying I kept the pouch as a memento. I never used it, but I thought it was worth keeping. Many years later I came across it in a drawer when I was looking for something else. I had totally forgotten about it and now that I was much older I could see it was a rather classy little item; top quality leather with a nice gold design on the front.

It probably cost a lot more than I ever had to put in it. I dropped in all my money, a handful of coins, and stuck it in my pocket.

"I actually felt quite pleased with myself. I reckoned I had been very smart to keep it. I was looking forward to showing it off and impressing people with my new found style. No one was ever impressed with me or with anything I did so this was a chance to get some admiring looks. What an idiot! I'm such an unlucky idiot. That is the story of my life."

Madrick saw the depression creeping up again and gently prompted him to keep the story going.

"About three or four weeks later I was arrested for causing a small disturbance in the church. They preach forgiveness, but the priest was not very forgiving when he caught me taking a couple of leptons out of the collection box. And he hit me first. I hit him back naturally. Then one of the congregation got involved. I hit him with the collection box. Then the soldiers arrived.

"Anyway, I was brought to the magistrate who said I could pay a fine or go to jail."

"So you ended up in the dungeon because you could not pay a fine?"

"No. It was much worse than that. And it shows you just how unlucky I am.

"I had enough to pay so I pulled out the pouch and, before I had a chance to count out my fine, the magistrate started screaming at me. He grabbed the pouch and looked hard at it, then he looked hard at me and I looked hard at him. Even though it had been a long time since I had robbed him, I recognised him. He was my first ever victim. I think he recognised me, but he definitely recognised his pouch. What I thought was a pretty design turned out to be his initials and the magistrate's crest. It went downhill from there.

"He called me a dirty thief. I called him a dirty harlot grabber. He slapped me. I punched him. He kicked me. I hit him with a chair. Then the soldiers grabbed me. And that was it. The magistrate sentenced me to death by torture, because he could, and I was hauled off to the dungeons."

"Wow. So basically you are here because you stole a magistrate's purse when you were a child? That is harsh."

"Yeah, and I guess hitting him with the chair leg didn't help me much - nor the hatchet! Did I mention the hatchet?"

Suddenly there was a noise at the front door. Someone was coming into the house.

13

Spring roll

They both froze when they heard the sound of the front door opening. Before they had a chance to react, three big men entered the house and they were all looking evil daggers at them.

"Who are you people? What are you doing in my house? You are thieves and we are going to hurt you bad," shouted the biggest man.

He was enormous and made out of pure muscle; there was not an ounce of fat on the beast. His thick black beard added to the frightening image. His two bearded companions looked equally mean even though they were only about half his size. Nonetheless, this was a formidable fighting team.

Tung's instincts kicked in and he took control. He did not take his eyes off the three bearded figures as he hurriedly whispered instructions to Madrick.

"Go. You need a head start because you can't run as fast as me. I'll cause a diversion. You grab our things and sneak out the back door. Make your way to the market quarter. We'll meet up again there."

Madrick scooped up their possessions and backed slowly away from the approaching men towards the back door. Tung lifted two logs from the fireside and threw them at the, now very angry, men. They looked even angrier as the logs smashed into the furniture behind them. Another two logs followed; this time he hit one of them square in the face and the men backed off a little. Angry did not describe the men's mood now. They were deranged. Their faces were the colour nature had only intended for plums and they made noises that only bears had a chance of understanding.

By this time, Madrick had slipped away unnoticed and made his escape, but the men had penned Tung in. His route to the back door was cut off. He swung the last two logs around wildly to fend off his attackers, all of whom were now armed with various objects they had chosen with the express purpose of hurting Tung - a lot.

His spotted his last chance to escape a merciless beating. He darted for the window behind him and, without really thinking, he threw himself headfirst at it. It smashed as his head crashed into it. He flew, rather gracefully, through it and landed on the grass outside. It was as if he had practiced this means of exit many times because he performed a surprisingly stylish roll before he sprung to his feet and ran free. The three men were left stunned, all they could do was watch him run for his life and disappear into the maze of alleys that led away from the house.

Tung was delighted with himself. He quickly made his way through the back streets to the busy market quarter where the inns and eating houses were. It was teeming with people so it took him an age to find Madrick. Eventually he found him cowering in a small doorway near the main square. It was a good place to blend in because the place was packed with revellers watching the open air entertainment.

He slipped in beside Madrick and excitedly described his daring escape.

"And it ended with a beautifully timed spring through the window followed by a graceful roll when I landed."

Those who might have seen the escape would have been quite impressed; anyone who listened to this wildly exaggerated tale would have been in awe, had they believed half of it. Madrick listened carefully although he took the story with an extra large pinch of salt. He was just very glad to be reunited.

When they had both calmed down a bit, they agreed it was time to eat even though they both still had plenty of dungeon banquet fare in their bellies. More importantly, they decided that they needed a drink.

They left the comparative safety of the doorway and started to walk around the shops and stalls that made up the central market. They kept their eyes peeled for the three bearded men because they had no idea whether they would have tried to follow them or whether they would have cut their losses and stayed at home to clear up the mess.

They entered the first tavern they came to. It was called The Black Bear and it seemed vaguely familiar to Tung. That was not surprising as he had imbibed in most of the town's less salubrious hostelries. Tung was immediately filled with nostalgic, mainly imagined, recollections of happier times as he led Madrick through the crowded tables and up to the bar.

He ordered two flagons of the best ale and paid for them out of his recently acquired ill gotten gains. When the drinks arrived he took a deep swig from one and then handed it to Madrick, but the old wizard was too busy trying to spy out a seat to notice. While Madrick looked for a table, Tung surveyed the room. It was filled with a motley assortment of human lowlife. My kind of people thought Tung happily as he took a long swallow from his own tankard.

There was an empty table towards the back of the room so the pair quickly took up their places at it. It was marvellous to be sitting in a reasonably comfortable chair, in a comfortably warm room with an adequately cool tankard of ale. Surely life could not get much better than this thought Tung as he downed half the brown liquid in his jug. It had been a long time since he had had good food in his belly, a drink in his hand and money in his pocket. Life was good and he felt that it was only going to get better from here on in.

By the time they were half way through their third pitcher they had formulated the next few steps in their plan. They had already reserved one of the four rooms which the barkeeper had available and they agreed that, after one or two more drinks, they would retire to the room and create the next spell. They would then get some well earned sleep and hopefully, when the morning came, they would have an idea of how best to use the new spell to their maximum benefit.

It seemed like a good, solid plan however, it did not take account of the fact that Tung's 'one or two' more drinks actually turned out to be eight or nine - and the Scroll in the hands of a very drunk man was not a clever combination; not clever at all.

14

Home sweet work

Michael was escorted by his own personal security guard to the third floor which was to be his new working home. The guard shepherded him to Mr Toner's secretary; apparently she had been tasked with settling him in and getting him started. Toner was the Chief Technical Officer and Melissa was his secretary; although the little plaque on her desk said 'Personal Assistant to the CTO'.

Michael was glad when Mr Scary Uniform headed back to the lift and left him alone with Melissa. There was something very threatening about the security man. He was definitely from a military background and he looked as if killing people was just a normal part of his day. He reminded him of the immortal line from one of his favourite films, 'City Slickers'. Billy Crystal asked Jack Palance if he had killed anyone today and Jack replied in his gravelly voice, 'Day ain't over yet.' That security guard was definitely a 'day ain't over yet' kind of guy.

It starts now, he thought, as the guard walked away. He wanted to impress everyone he met on his first day. He knew that it was a very old cliché, but 'you never get a second chance to make a first impression' was definitely true. He knew he had to become one of IIBE's most treasured people assets, so step one was to make sure that people liked, admired and respected him from day one.

By working ostentatiously hard he planned to make IIBE view him as the oil that kept their applications lubricated, the glue that held them all together and the trusted custodian of their precious systems. These great digital creations enabled them to screw enormous profits out of each and every one of their clients so they were effectively the beating heart of the beast - and he wanted to be thought of as the trusted cardiologist. He wanted to be their technology superhero until, that is, he became their ultimate nightmare.

"Hi Michael, I'm Melissa and Mr Toner has asked me to get you settled in. He's got back to back meetings up until about two o'clock and he said he'd see you after that. In the meantime, I'll be able to show you around and get you acclimatised. First, we'll meet a few of the people you'll be working with. Follow me."

Before he had a chance to exchange any pleasantries she was off, so he just tagged along behind her as they started to wend their way round the enormous open-plan office. He knew he would not remember all of the names initially, however, he would try and make sure that they remembered his.

Every introduction was much the same.

"Hi John, this is Michael Phillips. He's joining the computer support team so he's the man to ask if you have any problems with the system. You'll be talking to him a lot if past performance is anything to go by."

She had the same dig at 'the system', as she called it, over and over again. She was clearly not a fan.

"Michael, this is John Kerr. He looks after the wages so he's an important man!"

After an hour's worth of introductions, handshakes and small talk he eventually ended up at his new desk. The oak veneer desk and large faux leather chair were actually very impressive, however, they were not particularly important in his great scheme of things, what mattered to him was the PC. It was his window into the heart of this banking beast. As it turned out, they had given him a good, powerful PC with three 32 inch monitors. That gave him plenty of desktop real estate to play with, although 'play with' was the wrong term because this was no game.

"Let the games begin!" he whispered silently to himself thinking about the Roman 'games'. They were brutal affairs

- Christians and lions; gladiators and slaves. This was going to be brutal too, but in a very different way.

Melissa left him with a pile of chunky manuals which documented the main systems for which he was going to be responsible. He was actually looking forward to getting stuck into them because technical reading had always been his passion and these manuals would hold some of the information he needed to get right inside the bank's systems. They were his guide books, but he was not going on holiday.

Michael settled into his new chair and tried to give the impression that he was casually surveying his surroundings. There were lots of people clicking away at keyboards, talking on fancy phones and furiously scribbling notes on their IIBE notepads. Not one of them was looking at him. Not one of them suspected that he was the man who was going to destroy their cosy world.

He was in and he was ready to infect.

He started reading the manuals and was surprised to find how badly written they were. Very little time had been spent on them and it showed. They were over simplistic and clearly had not been updated for some time. He knew from his Noviru days that the bank had some very complex systems. These manuals implied that the systems were in fact, very simple. Maybe they were originally, but it was the lack of simplicity that kept computer specialists like him in jobs - they created complex systems that did not work to replace simple systems that worked just fine.

Shortly after two o'clock Malcolm Toner returned from his rounds of meetings. After about ten minutes he called Michael into his office and introduced himself. Toner ran through his standard welcome and motivational speech, and then he made it very clear that he was in charge.

"If you play ball with me then I'll play ball with you. But always remember - it's my ball."

Michael was motivated. He returned to his desk more

determined than ever to destroy this place, and he was going to have a ball doing it.

15

You are chicken

The more Tung drank, the louder he became. The louder he became, the more people noticed them. The more people that noticed them, the more nervous Madrick became. He tried to shut Tung up, but he was at least two tankards too late.

It was about to get a whole lot worse. Soon Tung was starting to engage with the groups of revellers around them. It was not long before they had been joined by a ragged bunch of fellow drinkers and Tung seemed determined to become the centre of attention. There must have been at least forty boozers in the immediate party when Tung pulled out the Scroll and made an announcement.

"I am going to show you the best trick you have ever seen in your miserable lives."

Madrick had to stop him. He knew this was heading for a Vesuvius scale disaster. Unfortunately, the more he tried to get close to Tung, the farther he got pushed out to the edge of the crowd. He was utterly powerless to stop what was unfolding, so all he could do was watch helplessly from the back of the ever growing throng of spectators.

Tung was now on the table and he had the unrolled Scroll in his hands. He was staring at the parchment, he was saying the spell. The crowd was baying.

Madrick had one last chance to stop him. With all his might he hurled his tankard full force at Tung's head. He missed by a gnat's whisker, but he missed nonetheless. The last chance was gone as the tankard smashed against the head of an unsuspecting bystander. He crashed unconscious to the ground. At least, now there was one less pair of eyes watching the spectacle.

That was it, all his options were exhausted. He had

nothing left to try. He resigned himself to accepting that this was going to end in whatever disastrous conclusion the fates decided. And it was undoubtedly going to be disastrous.

Tung finished the Scroll words, crashed off the table and landed squarely on the back of his head. The hard floor, combined with falling from a height, would definitely conspire together to give Tung, yet again, the monster of all headaches.

"Not my fault this time," said Madrick to no one in particular, "and it serves him right. I did try and stop him. What a stupid idiot."

The crowd were still laughing when Tung came to. As far as they were concerned, the 'best trick ever' seemed to be this fool staring hard at an old parchment and then falling off the table onto his head. Not the best trick ever, although it was certainly funny enough to keep them entertained for a while.

Tung regained his senses, tucked the Scroll safely into his jacket and climbed back on the table. The crowd cheered in the expectation of seeing him fall off again, but Tung had other plans.

"I'm back, people. That was just a slip of the Tung."

He laughed loudly at his own joke. It got no response from the audience because it was not a particularly funny joke and anyway, virtually no one knew that his name was Tung.

He ignored the lack of laughter because he really did not care. He was here for the money, not the laughs. He believed that this was going to be a big pay day so he tried to focus on the new spell image in his head. If he could work out what it was then he could construct some sort of bet around it. On top of that, if he could work it out without Madrick, then he could dump the old man and make his own way in the world.

His befuddled brain could picture himself making a fortune in taverns all across the land. The drink had definitely clouded his judgement; he had completely forgotten how powerful some of the spells could be. Some of them clearly had the potential to make him rich beyond his wildest dreams, but in his booze fuelled state, he was happy to gamble it all away for the sake of a handful of coppers and a few free drinks.

He concentrated on the image in his head. It was taking longer than usual; maybe it was a dull spell, but probably the ale was the culprit. The haze cleared long enough for him to see something; it was a chicken. He was sure it was a chicken; nice brown feathers and a bright red comb on the top of its head. It had a hand touching its back but that bit of the image did not make sense, so he decided that the best thing to do was to ignore it.

"I," declared Tung at the top of his voice "will create a chicken out of the thinnest of thin air. If I perform this fantastic, magical feat I demand that everyone who is watching must buy me a tankard of this house's finest ale. Hands in the air if you agree."

He swayed a bit as he watched all the hands around him rise into the air. Only Madrick kept his hands firmly by his side, only Madrick had a terrified look on his face. He watched in horror as Tung said the spell in his head. Only he knew the inherent dangers of an amateur trying to interpret the purpose of a spell, never mind a totally inebriated amateur.

Tung fell backwards off the table and landed squarely on the giant bump that the last fall had caused. He had enough beer in his belly to ensure he felt very little extra pain. He climbed back on the table as the crowd howled with laughter. He looked around for the chicken. There was no chicken to be seen anywhere. All he could see was the crowd in hysterics, and at the back, Madrick jumping up and down mouthing the word 'NO' over and over again.

He could not understand why the spell had failed. He could only surmise that maybe he had used up all the power, perhaps he was now flat-lining spell-wise. That was disappointing, he thought, no fortune to be made today after all.

He decided to get off the table more carefully than his last two dismounts, so he gingerly leaned forward and placed his hand on a nearby shoulder. The man he touched immediately turned into a chicken. At first the crowd cheered and clapped, although this quickly turned to panic as Tung touched more of them and they too turned into chickens. Everyone fled frantically from Tung and soon there was virtually nobody in the tavern apart from Madrick, who was trying to keep a healthy distance. Apart from Madrick there were about ten plump, inebriated hens doing excellent impersonations of headless chickens... but with heads.

Madrick counted the chickens and found that there were in fact eleven.

"Touch that sleeping drunk in the corner," he screamed as he backed away. "You need to make a dozen chickens to complete the spell."

Tung wobbled unsteadily over to where the unsuspecting drunk slept. He touched the top of his head and the sleeping man immediately turned into a sleeping hen.

"And they say you shouldn't count your chickens," said Madrick as he grabbed Tung by the arm and dragged him out of the tavern.

They fled up the dark entry that ran alongside the old inn. They ran and ran until the noises of men shouting and women screaming died away. After running for what seemed like an eternity, the pair eventually collapsed exhausted in an empty barn just outside the town. Almost immediately they both fell into a troubled sleep, Madrick from the exhaustion and Tung from too much booze.

Back in town, the excitement was frenzied as the assembled crowd animatedly exchanged stories and experiences of the unbelievable happening. Everyone who actually saw the event grossly exaggerated their own part in the incident;

claiming to have been a mere whisker from the poisoned touch. Many who did not see it pretended that they had been there in the midst of the action. And everyone was desperate to find out who the chickens had actually been. These people were not going back to their family nests in a hurry.

The town's grapevine was buzzing and soon some of the more fantastic stories reached the ears of henchmen of the rich and powerful. From them, word went out in three different directions; to Mifal, to the Order of White Wizards and to the Order of Black Wizards. Soon all these powerful entities would be searching for the pair of strangers who had, like one of the chickens, flown the coop. Madrick and Tung did not know it yet, but they were about to become the targets of three separate, massive manhunts.

Meanwhile, the barkeeper was feeling pretty pleased about the night's events. He may have lost twelve of his regular customers, but he had been able to round up eleven of the hens so now he would not have to buy any meat for tomorrow's stew. Also, beer sales had risen dramatically since the incident because everyone wanted to lubricate their throats as they shared their individual adventures with anyone who would listen.

So everyone in the tavern was happy except, of course, the chickens.

16

Have a little Faith

After only a few days, Michael had already impressed legions of IT illiterate folk. The place was absolutely coming down with them. It had been so easy and, actually, he was not at all surprised. He had always expected to make an impact very quickly because he was extremely good at what he did. As he always said, 'if I can't fix it then it ain't broke'.

He was, however, continually surprised at just how little the average Joe (or Jane) knew. Even the really senior guys, and they were all guys, knew much less than the typical schoolboy. He solved umpteen user problems that really boiled down to recurring 'pilot error' as he liked to term it. Put simply, no one round here knew how to use a computer properly. Indeed, very few knew how to use a computer at all. It was great for him though because even the simplest problem solved added to his growing reputation.

Michael also started to make a few decent work friends. They all seemed to be of the female variety, which tended to be the way with him. He defined 'work friends' as people you like to spend time with in work, although they were not the sort of people with whom you would share your own time. He had also made one very special friend.

He had definitely hit it off with the pretty girl he had met on day one at reception. Her name was Faith and she had been with IIBE for nearly four years; an old timer in terms of this company. Most lower-level people seemed to stay for less than two years before moving on. Most of them seemed to use IIBE as a CV builder or maybe they left once they started to realise how corrupt this company actually was.

She had seemed to latch onto him from that very first meeting. Now, she always went out of her way to welcome him when he entered the building, no matter how busy she seemed. She was interested in what he did, what his job responsibilities were and how he had learnt to be 'so clever', as she described him on more than one occasion. She was very hard not to like, particularly for someone with an ego like his.

She was twenty and she was supremely pretty, far and away the most beautiful woman he had ever known; classically beautiful by anyone's standards. She had short dark hair, a swarthy complexion, bright brown eyes and high cheekbones. On top of that, there was something extraordinary about her. It was not so much that she was easy to look at, but more that it was impossible not to stare at her. She drew your eyes towards her, but as you looked you could not quite pinpoint why. Or was it just him, he wondered?

She also had the strangest of accents, a confusing fusion of London English, North American with a hint of Australian; he was totally intrigued by the way she spoke. In summary, she had everything that attracted him and a lot more besides.

He had been out for after-work drinks with her a couple of times and already he was certain there was some bubbling chemistry between them, nonetheless he was not going to rush things. He was convinced she liked him a lot, after all she had told him so on more than one occasion.

Once he had taken her to a rather intimate boutique pub near the office. He chose it precisely because of its intimacy. He wanted a proper talk, not the stilted and stifled shouting exchanges that they had been forced to endure in some of the other busier places they had been to.

They chatted about families, friends, enemies, previous relationships (that brought up enemies again!), work, childhood, likes and dislikes. He was sure that no one had ever been so interested in him. She was continually asking questions about his background, his aspirations and what he thought about work. He loved it that she took such an interest in him and everything he did.

There was only one thing that seemed to bug her - she did not like his facial hair, but then again, neither did he. The hair was part of the plan and he was not telling her about the plan... yet.

She shared little intimacies, like the story of how her parents had tried for ages to have a baby. They had been frustrated by phantom pregnancies and two miscarriages. They had tried all the old wives recommendations, they had used medical interventions and they had prayed for help. They were on the verge of giving up when her mum got pregnant and ran to full term. When the day that she was born finally came, apparently her mother had cried relentlessly as she held her in her arms. She had never been so happy.

"This is our perfect reward. Our prayers have been answered. All we needed was a little faith. A little faith," her mother had said through the tears. "That's what we shall call her - our little Faith."

Michael also loved her sense of fun. She did not really tell jokes as such; she just kept on saying things which he found endearingly amusing. He remembered telling her once that she should smile more because he loved her smile so much.

"It would hurt my face if I smiled every time I felt like it. Honestly, I'm a really happy person. I just don't show it... or feel it," she smiled widely. "Only joking. I know you can see how happy you make me."

She sometimes wore her sense of humour on her chest. He loved her taste in amusing t-shirts. His favourite read 'Six out of seven dwarfs are not happy'. He felt it was doubly funny when she was beside him because he was just over six feet tall and she barely scraped the five foot mark. The day she wore it, she told him that he made her the one out of seven, and that made him happy too. She was Happy one and he was Happy two.

They found they had quite a lot in common and when it was time to go home she told him she had never felt as close to anyone else after such a short time. This was really promising, although he knew it could potentially be a problem later because she seemed to really like IIBE. He was not sure where her loyalties would lie when it came to the crunch. And there was going to be a mighty crunch sooner rather than later.

That was a problem for another time. There were, of course, much more complex problems to be solved in the short term; difficult technical problems which taxed him to his limits. The bank had massive international networks and any small disruption to the millions of transactions which ran round the wires set off system alarms all over the place. His primary role was to fix the breaks, reinstate the systems and keep things running smoothly. Even the smallest interruptions in the service could cost the bank hundreds of thousands of pounds. The faster he fixed problems the more money they made and the more they valued and trusted him.

Mr Toner, the Chief Technical Officer, had certainly taken a shine to him. He understood most of the complexities associated with the bank's technical infrastructure so he definitely respected Michael's skills and capabilities. To prove the point, he had told him he was in line for a significant salary increase if he kept up the good work. He had also intimated that he could be in for a number of big promotions over the next few years.

"Play your cards right and you could have my job before too long."

Toner was in for a very nasty surprise indeed. He would probably be changing jobs sooner than he thought, but it was not going to be by way of the promotion he was hoping for.

17

Run

Madrick was the first to rouse. His first thoughts, futile hopes really, were that the bar, the crowd, the drunken spectacle and the chickens had all been a horrible nightmare. It did not take him long to realise it had all really happened. This was a complete disaster. They had engineered a near perfect escape and now it had been jeopardised by this idiot who still slept noisily beside him. Their freedom had been put at risk by this cretin who was completely oblivious of his stupidity.

He tried to wake Tung by screaming maniacally into his ear. It was loud enough to waken the dead, but it did not waken Tung. He tried again by poking the massive bump on his head and he poked it hard. Tung screamed with pain and began a slow, throbbing ascent back into consciousness.

Madrick ranted and raved about his stupidity, although he realised very quickly that Tung was suffering too much to pay any heed to his chastisement. He was too busy being crushed by the pain of a fierce ale hangover compounded by two headfirst floor collisions; not to mention the 'normal' headache resulting from spell saying.

It was going to be some time before there would be any sort of sensible conversation so Madrick pulled him to his feet, dragged him out of the barn and supported his weight as they started to put as much distance as possible between them and the town.

He knew that they had to flee because it was certain that Mifal would have heard about last night and he would have sent out teams of his soldiers to capture or kill them. What he did not know, and this was even more frightening, was that both the Black and White wizards had also dispatched specialist hunters to track them down.

Being Mifal's prey was a frightening enough prospect so

Madrick put all his effort into helping this dead-weight fugitive run away, although walk away fast was a better description of their clumsy getaway. Tung was still in no fit state to travel under his own steam so Madrick had no choice other than to cart the semi-conscious lump along the dirt track. He tried everything, starting with 'carroty' encouragement followed quickly by 'sticky' scare tactics.

"Move yourself Tung," he badgered. "They are on our trail and woe betide us if they catch us. We must make haste and keep distance between us and those evil men who pursue us. I do not want to be back in that dungeon. I, for one, do not want to be a plaything in the hands of Mifal's torturer."

It had little effect on Tung. After more than half an hour and less than half a mile, Madrick realised the futility of this mode of escape. He released his hold on Tung who promptly slid to the ground, fell backwards and smacked his head hard on the only protruding rock for yards around. Madrick had decided that they needed another spell and they needed one that would help get them out of here fast or, at the very least, a bit faster. The Stallion Spell would have been perfect now, however, knowing their luck, they were more likely to end up with a plague of rats or an everlasting lantern.

☼ ☼ ☼

Back at the castle, the king had been told of the strange goings-on in The Black Bear tavern the night before. He knew it was probably Madrick and the thief however, he could not be seen to accept that explanation. That would show his subjects that he had been wrong about the stallion and he never ever admitted to being wrong. He believed that his people thought he was infallible, but he was wrong about that too. He definitely had to find an alternative story. If he said it was Madrick who had been at the centre of the chicken incident, the people would surely hate him even more because he would have tortured an innocent horse to death. Torturing a guilty horse was barely acceptable.

So he decreed that an evil pair of demons has visited themselves on the townsfolk and played chicken with them. As the great defender of his subjects he, Mifal, would send a squad of his best soldiers to slay these devils and make his people safe again. He knew that would make him popular with the populous so the squad was assembled, briefed and duly dispatched.

✿ ✿ ✿

At the Sorebun Academy, which was the headquarters of the Order of White Wizards, word had filtered through about the magical incident in the inn. The Great Grand Wizard and the six Under-Grand Wizards met to decide what, if anything, they should do about it. From the stories it was clear that there was a scroll in the hands of a buffoon and that posed many dangers as evidenced by the chicken debacle. Equally important, there was a scroll which needed to be tracked down and brought to the White Library.

They discussed the spell. It appeared to be a minor scroll, the Chicken Transformation Spell, it merely metamorphosed men into chickens for forty-eight hours. The men would be back to normal soon and they would remember little of their ordeal. Nonetheless every scroll was important and every scroll they had was one less for the Black Order.

They discussed how they would track it down and eventually decided they would send Gravalar, one of their top stalkers, to find the idiots and retrieve the scroll. So he was summoned to them, briefed and duly dispatched.

✿ ✿ ✿

At Devil Lair Keep, which was the headquarters of the Order of Black Wizards, word had also filtered through about the weird chicken happening. A meeting of the Council was hastily convened and the members concluded that there was something very curious about the incident and, while it seemed to centre on a minor scroll, their gut feel told them there was something more out of the ordinary involved here. For that reason they decided to send Stanverital and Devligrate, two of their top assassins, on the trail.

They were treating this happening with unusual urgency because their instincts told them that this was an epic event. They also knew that the Whites would be on the trail too and they wanted to beat them at all costs. So, without any undue delay, the assassins were summoned to the Council, briefed and duly dispatched.

✿ ✿ ✿

Never before in recorded history, or unrecorded history for that matter, had so many frightening and skilful individuals been sent on the trail of such ordinary and rather pathetic common folk. This would have been the most unfair of all contests... were it not for the Scroll.

18

Ten types of people

Michael had settled seamlessly into the routine at IIBE. His feet were well and truly under the proverbial desk. He had a strong and growing reputation; he had engaged with every one of the important people he had targeted and, without exception, they all now trusted him to get the job done. They all, to a man, and they were all men, openly praised his contribution to the organisation. He had done everything he could have done in his first few weeks to become liked as well as respected.

It was the same everywhere, but people did not generally tend to become friends with the computer support geeks because they knew too much and were usually a bit strange. To counteract this he had developed a range of techniques to ingratiate himself with his 'using' public. For example, he loved to trot out stock phrases which he knew the non-technical folk appreciated. Things like 'Computers should work. People should think.' and 'A computer will always do what you tell it to do, but rarely what you want it to do.'

He knew that these phrases, and ones like them, made people feel good about themselves and made them feel less threatened by the mysterious systems that seemed to have become such an integral part of their lives. It was important to recognise that the average person was intimidated by computers so he felt it was part of his job to make 'the system' seem more friendly.

He still liked to do the geeky things so the geeks liked him as well. He had a notice on his desk that read 'In this world there are 10 types of people, those that know binary and those who don't.' The geeks got it, but he had a layman's explanation which made the other folk laugh too.

"In binary one-zero represents the number two. It's

because there are only two states in binary - one or zero, on or off.

"Or to put it another way - binary is either stupid or it is not."

"Stupid!" they invariably replied and felt better for it.

That usually did it. He reckoned that made him smart and likeable, a win-win in anyone's book, or technical manual, depending on who he was talking to at the time.

He had adopted lots of other different approaches to make people like him, for example, he had done a number of homers for a select few - fixed their personal PCs, made their home networks work or helped them choose the best printers to buy. Things like that were easy for him, but always seemed terribly difficult for the average Joe. It was another Homer who had warned, many centuries before, 'beware of geeks bearing gifts'. They did not take that advice back then and he hoped no one would feel that way about him now.

Not only did the average employee like him, the bosses also liked him. He had concentrated a lot of his efforts on impressing them. He knew the more important the person, the more of his time they deserved; after all they were the ones who could give him what he needed. They were the ones who could, and indeed already had, elevated his security rating so he now had access to pretty much any system within the organisation.

He had been able to check his own personnel records. They had made a few candid observations about him, although there was nothing in the files for him to worry about. He actually made a few undetectable changes to his records, for example, he now had a verified university degree, a PhD no less, and a long history of voluntary charity work. He also upped his salary, just to prove to himself that he could.

His new higher level security clearance also meant he could come and go at the times which suited him. This was important because it meant he had more privacy and it was much less likely that someone would notice as he invaded their systems.

As well as creating the necessary reputation, he had, in parallel, put many of his plan's fundamental building blocks in place. He had disabled specific parts of the Noviru hacking protection system and that had enabled him to invisibly add little modules of his own software. These modules gave him secret entry points into the key systems which, when the time came, would let him begin to manipulate the swathes of money that swished through the bank's network.

It was all going very well and he had achieved everything which he had set out to achieve. He was definitely in a position to initiate the next phase of his plan.

He would soon begin to siphon off relatively small sums of money into random bank accounts all over the world. The clever part, he thought, was that these bank accounts did not belong to him so, when the problem was highlighted, the full force of the security department would rush off in pointless directions to try and work out who was benefiting from this fraud.

When this happened, when they were completely distracted, he would go in for the kill.

19

The flight

Madrick knew deep down that they were in serious trouble and that they had to put a decent distance between them and the scene of The Black Bear incident.

"We need the next spell."

"Let me sleep for a while. I need some rest. I cannot take any more pain," complained Tung. "Making spells still hurts me bad. My head feels like it has been mashed by a landslide."

"Your head has indeed taken a pounding, but not all of it was due to the spell making. I can tell you that much of your pain was self inflicted through your own stupidity," said Madrick unsympathetically. "But that cannot be helped now. You must create a spell that will help us get many miles from this place. You must do it now because I can guarantee that Mifal's men are hot on our heels. And it is because you are an idiot. Your idiocy has put us in great danger. You need to make things better."

Tung reluctantly pulled out the Scroll and slowly went through the routine. As the spell infiltrated his being, his body flopped like a rag doll and, this time, Madrick caught his head as he fainted and laid it gently on the ground. Then he had a change of heart, so he lifted Tung's head a few feet off the ground and dropped it roughly.

"You deserve that," he said to the unconscious face that lay below him.

Tung drifted back into consciousness and hardly had time to feel the throbbing pain in his head before Madrick was badgering him to describe the picture.

He searched his head. There was a lot of pain in there and there was an image as well. It was an image of a golden goblet filled with red liquid.

"That is an easy one. It is just a golden wine goblet, not of any interest to us. You need to create it now so that we can move on and create something useful"

Tung dutifully followed his orders, he knew he was in no state to argue. He said the spell and, to Madrick's credit for not holding a grudge too long, he caught him properly this time as his head headed for the hard earth.

Tung was still unconscious so he did not see it. There was a blinding flash and a magnificent, golden goblet appeared a few feet away from them. It was filled with a luscious red wine, fit for a king. Madrick knew there would be wine in the goblet and he also knew that it continually refilled itself. This was exactly what they did not need right now so he dropped it surreptitiously into the ditch by the road before Tung was alert enough to work out exactly what was happening. That simple act was going to have very serious ramifications later on that day. Had Madrick only taken the cup with them then the world might have ended up being a much happier and safer place.

"Next spell," demanded Madrick. "Come on. There is no time to waste. Next spell please."

Over the next couple of hours Tung created six more unhelpful spells. It was like being back in Mifal's dungeon; they were under severe time pressure and the useless spells just kept on coming.

Then, as before, their luck changed. As Tung described the image, Madrick became more and more excited. Tung did not know what he had created, but he knew it was good and he punched the air while he waited for Madrick to explain how his latest inception was going to be their salvation.

Madrick could not contain his delight and he started that strange little dance again. This time he was not restricted by cell walls, strewn banquet food or a mad stallion. This time he had room to express himself and so he did; with gusto. It was even stranger than before; it was bordering on the bizarre.

Eventually he calmed down. The dance stopped and he hugged Tung.

"You have done it again, my friend. This time you have created the Wings Spell. This enchantment will give you the wings of a giant eagle, the wings of an angel, wings that will allow us to fly away from this place. Once you lift off into the sky, the wings will be with you until your feet touch the earth again. We can be miles from this sinful town and our pursuers will have no trail to follow. We will be gone without a trace."

"Gone? Great, where are we going to go to?"

"We will know when we get there," said Madrick rather profoundly. "Anywhere is better than where we are right now."

They did not know how close the hunting teams were. The three separate groups of pursuers arrived at their take-off spot almost simultaneously - well, the two groups plus Gravalar. They all got there less than twenty minutes after Tung grew his magical wings and lifted off into the sky clutching Madrick to his chest.

As they swept through the air, Tung and Madrick marvelled at the sights below them. It was spectacular as they glided high over the trees and soared above the great lakes. They thought they had made a clean getaway. They would soon find out just how wrong they were.

20

Just good friends

Faith and Suzie lived together in a small flat in North Acton, a relatively nice commuter suburb of London. It was quite a trek into the city centre where she worked, but it was very close to a tube station which brought her, without changing trains, to Bank station and it was just a short walk away from the IIBE headquarters building. She could have found a place that was handier, but she was delighted to have the opportunity to live with her best friend.

She had lived with Suzie for about four months now, but they had been friends since childhood. They had met at secondary school and hit it off more or less immediately. They had a natural affinity because they were two out of only three children who received free school meals. They both came from very poor families so they never had the latest fashions, accessories or gadgets. In fact, they often came to school in hand-me-downs and they were teased mercilessly about it.

There was one incident, very early on in their relationship, which had cemented the friendship. Suzie was being tormented by a group of older children in the playground after school. That in itself was a fairly common occurrence and the girls had agreed that their best defence was to ignore the unpleasantness as much as possible.

The ring leader was an extremely nasty boy called Brian Clarke. He had led the harassment over the last few months and had directed the attacks which had become ever more offensive as time went on. It had progressed from unpleasant teasing to overt bullying. It had only been verbal up to this point; on this particular day it turned physical.

Clarke had started pawing at Suzie's clothes. He was pulling at them with his finger and thumb, turning up his nose as if he held something dirty between his fingers.

"Tramp, tramp, tramp," he began to shout in her face.

The watching children joined in the chant. Spurred on by the support, Clarke pulled hard at her cardigan and it ripped as he tugged it off her. She tried to hold on, but the harder she resisted, the more he pulled and the more it ripped. Eventually she let go and he held the tattered garment above his head like a trophy. Suzie completely lost it and, without thinking, slapped his face, very hard. He reacted immediately and punched her full force on the side of her head. She fell to the ground while Clarke stood over her, posing like a victorious boxer. The crowd of onlookers were silenced. They were shocked by the violence and felt it had gone way too far this time, however, they were all individually too afraid of Clarke to do anything. No one wanted to speak up in case they became the next victim.

Faith had arrived just in time to witness the punch. She pushed her way through the crowd and hurried purposefully towards Clarke. She was approaching him from behind so he did not see her although he may have sensed the mood change in the crowd of spectators. She had no idea what she was going to do - until she got to him.

She pulled hard at his trousers and they, along with his underpants, came down past his knees. He stood stunned, still in the boxer pose with his fists above his head. It was now a ridiculous stance - a boxer with no boxers. The crowd erupted with laughter. The girls pointed and the boys jeered. Clarke's face turned a strange puce colour; the colour of deep embarrassment tinged with rage. He pulled up his trousers and without even reacting to Faith, pushed his way through the crowd to begin the futile search for his dignity. As he left he heard the crowd cheering and laughing. He knew he would never again command the respect he had gained through his bullying.

As he walked away he vowed that he would get those two

girls though, he thought, it would be all in good time and in private.

Faith helped her friend up and they were both surprised how warmly all the watching children treated them. It became obvious that their resentment for the bully was only suppressed by their own fears. Now that everyone realised how much they hated the bully, there was a completely new dynamic. Faith and Suzie became widely accepted and no longer figures of fun. They both made lots of other friends although none of them ever rivalled their own special relationship.

Brian Clarke was expelled shortly afterwards for stealing homework books from Faith. She had reported him to her teacher and that just fuelled his growing resentment. Because of his appalling record, no school would take him so he ended up being home tutored which meant he had too much time on his hands. He hung about outside the school every so often, looking for an opportunity to hurt Faith, but she was always with friends - she seemed to have so many friends now. Maybe school was not the right place, but he knew his time would come. He could wait.

Even though it had worked out well for the girls, they realised how much they hated being different. They realised how much they hated being the underdogs. They realised how much they hated being poor. They decided that they were going to do everything and anything to change things. They wanted money. They were determined to become rich.

That was a long time ago, but it had paved the way for them to be best friends for more than eight years now. Faith's recent travels had meant they had not seen much of each other for the last few years. Even though they had kept in touch via email, it was no substitute for having regular girlie chats about love, life and everything.

"Tell me about the new man in your life."

"OK, if you promise not to make fun of me. This guy is

special.

"His name is Michael Phillips. Well, you knew that already. He's one of the computer experts at the office although he's definitely not a geek. He knows a lot of technical gobbledegook but he's not a bore about it. He's a real whizz-kid and he does really cool... whizz-kiddery stuff.

"We've had some great times together already and we actually have lots in common. I'm getting to really like him... a lot."

"Has anything happened yet?" asked Suzie with a mischievous wink.

"No. This is a proper platonic relationship. You know, love from the neck up."

"I'm really happy for you, I am. It's great that you've found someone special, but don't you dare forget about me. I missed you when you were away and I don't want to lose you again."

"Don't worry, we're friends forever," said Faith.

"Friends forever," said Suzie as she gave her a warm hug.

They talked on for ages. Faith listed some of the things that she and Michael had in common, like their taste in music, food loves, their sense of humour and their attitude to relationships. She always liked to chat to Suzie about things that mattered to her and she had missed that desperately during her travels. She liked the fact that she could tell her friend anything and she knew Suzie felt the same way. Since they were children the pair had shared everything and they had never kept secrets from each other; until IIBE.

Faith had described her job in IIBE as a boring receptionist. She said it was the fact that she could be posted anywhere in the world that kept her interested and excited about it. It seemed a little strange to Suzie because a receptionist job was never going to make Faith rich and she knew just how much she wanted that. Making money had obsessed her since the Brian Clarke incident, but as always, she accepted without question what her friend told her.

Faith justified not sharing the other 'little details' about her job with her friend by telling herself she was not lying, she was merely leaving out telling her about some of the extra duties she performed. She also left out just how much she was earning.

These were not the first things that she had held back from Suzie and they would not be the last.

21

Long eye

The pursuers had all followed much the same route. Mifal's men had started at The Black Bear tavern where they had bribed and threatened the locals until they found out the direction in which the pair had fled. They had to endure many fantastical stories from drinkers who all claimed to be key players in the previous night's events. Most of the men sampled the wonderful chicken stew before they moved on. It was tasty, but unusual in that virtually every meat on the planet tasted of chicken, yet this tasted of something that was just a little bit different.

The wizards independently and surreptitiously watched the proceedings by mingling in the crowd, although wizards did not mingle well. They were very noticeable, however, years of experience had told the man in the street to completely ignore them, otherwise you could end up with an outbreak of warts or pig's ears, or something a lot worse.

So mingle they did, 'unnoticed' by the crowd, while they watched. There was no point in putting themselves out, they thought, if Mifal's men were doing the work anyway. Anyway, who wanted to talk to this rat bag of humanity?

From the tavern, they had used all their senses and skills to follow the trail to the barn where the pair had slept. Then, using logic and a little bit of trial and error, they had tracked them the short distance to this spot where they all now stood.

The three groups arrived at the spot from slightly different directions and they eyed each other suspiciously as soon as they realised they were all after the same thing. In particular, the opposing wizards stared at each other with intense malice, but they knew that a battle was not in any of their interests. Not yet anyway. Mifal's men had no idea who these strangers were, but some deep instinct told them that they were not to be messed with.

Independently they all surveyed the scene.

Mifal's men made very little sense of the landscape. In fact all they noted was a pile of charred clothes and the burnt out patch of grass by the roadside which had been the result of an ineptly used Fire Spell. Mifal's captain, who was commanding the soldiers, wanted to abandon the search and go home. He knew there was something very dangerous about the strangers and he wanted to get out of there as quickly as possible. He told his troops that the hunted men must have accidentally set fire to themselves and burned to death. After a very quick search of the nearby area, they decided there was no more to see so they left the scene to return to Mifal with their report.

It was different for Gravalar, Stanverital and Devligrate. They appraised the scene with much more educated eyes. They quickly spotted the golden goblet and the endless flow of wine that spilled onto the ground from it. They noted the hoof prints made by a large herd of cattle. This was very unusual because generally there were no cattle in these parts. They observed the luscious corn field that was so out of character for the area. In fact, they identified the evidence of at least eight spells. They realised that this was no ordinary scroll they were chasing; there were either multiple scrolls or, unbelievably, it could be the mythical Spell Spell scroll.

The two Black Wizards huddled for a tactical discussion. The trail seemed to end here so, they agreed, now was the time to employ some more magic. Stanverital took out a faded scroll from his cloak and read the spell quickly. It was the Long Eye Spell which gave the caster a short period of extraordinary vision. He scoured the ground and within a few seconds he spotted a gathering of peasants cowering in the distance, they were clearly avoiding the scene while the wizards were there. They were probably going to move in and see if there was anything valuable to plunder once they were gone. There was corn and a herd of beef for starters. He moved on with his sweep and had soon scanned three hundred and sixty degrees around him. There was no sign of the thieves.

Then he turned his eyes to the sky and searched the heavens. Again he began to scan three hundred and sixty degrees to make sure he missed nothing. There, far in the distance, he saw the flying men; one with great white wings and the other holding on for dear life. He called Devligrate and directed his gaze to the fleeing flyers. All he could see was a tiny speck in the sky, but he understood immediately what Stanverital wanted him to do. He pulled out one of the two scrolls he had safely stowed in his jacket.

He selected the Thunderball Spell, one of the offensive spells he had been given to aid their crusade. He cupped his hands in front of him and said the spell. A throbbing and humming thunderball appeared; he had to use all his strength and concentration to restrain it in his trembling grip. He carefully aimed at the dot in the sky and then released the tiny ball of concentrated sound. It soared, at the speed of sound naturally, towards the fleeing speck.

Tung and Madrick were blissfully unaware of what was happening on the ground behind them. They were enjoying a view of the countryside that few people had ever seen and congratulating themselves on their escape. By the time they heard the cacophonous roar of the thunderball it had already grazed the tip of one of the great wings and had sped off past them high into the atmosphere.

Tung immediately lost control and began to spiral to the ground. He flapped furiously to stay aloft, but the turbulence had broken Madrick's grip on him and the old man started to slip away. Tung knew that he could let the old man drop and quickly regain control and keep fleeing. He could be gone and free. Or he could risk his own safety and grab the old man.

Even Tung was not sure why he decided to save Madrick; it was totally out of character. Maybe this old fool meant more to him than he realised. Maybe he was becoming the father figure that Tung had always craved. Or maybe he realised that he would quickly kill himself with the Spell Spell if he did not have Madrick there to guide him.

Tung grabbed Madrick's arm just as his clutching fingers slipped from his torso. The manoeuvre completely unbalanced the aerodynamics and again the pair started a gravity dictated spiralling descent towards the hard ground. Tung regained some control before they hit the ground; it was enough to break the fall and stop them from breaking their bones.

After the beauty of flying high over the green earth the touchdown was not a graceful affair. The very moment that his feet hit the ground, his marvellous wings retracted instantaneously into his body and this further unbalanced him. He performed an extremely ungraceful somersault over the top of Madrick and bashed his head hard on a protruding boulder. He was getting used to these head smashes so he recovered surprisingly quickly. His recovery would have been even quicker had he not been hindered by the dreadful ale hangover and the old man who was still half clinging to his chest and arm. Both men slumped thankfully, albeit awkwardly, onto terra firma.

They had no idea what had shot them out of the sky. They both surmised that it had to be something to do with their pursuers. They thought they had flown free, after all, there were now a good few miles between them and the feather filled tavern, but they had clearly not shaken off their hunters. At least the flight had given them some breathing space so they had a decent head start. They picked themselves up and ran.

Stanverital watched the scene in the sky with his Long Eye and described it to Devligrate. He congratulated him on his accuracy at such an extreme distance. Gravalar had heard the commotion and was now standing close by, listening to the conversation. They all knew that their prey was miles away and they had flown over a great lake which would take many days to go round. At least they had slowed them down for now and they had an idea of what direction they were headed. They also knew that they would need more men and resources if they were to track down and capture these fugitives. If they had the Scroll then they were much more potent enemies than had first been thought. They had powerful magic at their disposal and they knew how to use it.

As the reality dawned on each of them, they stood in awe contemplating how close they had come to winning the prize of all prizes for their respective sides. They gave each other a final eyeing before heading back to report to their masters.

Just before he left, Gravalar secretly concealed the golden goblet under his robe. No point in letting a good thing go to waste, he thought as he swigged the best wine he had ever tasted in his life. This unfortunate act, along with too many more swigs on the journey home, meant that the Black Wizards got back to base well before Gravalar. This gave them a crucial lead in devising a cunning plan, the consequence of which would shape the world for the next one thousand years.

✿ ✿ ✿

When Mifal's men reported to the king and told him what they had found, he pondered for a while. He knew he needed a good explanation to satisfy his people. He was a bad king, but he was a clever man and he eventually devised a story that he knew would work. He decreed that the two demons that had turned some of his subjects into chickens had been so petrified of his righteous vengeance that they panicked as his men approached. They were too scared to fight so they self-combusted because that was the only way they could escape back to hell and avoid his retribution.

94

The pieces fitted. The story explained the charred clothes, burnt grass and the fact that there were no demons to be found. It played well with the subjects and all was well in the kingdom. The people were happy that these malignant spirits had been dispatched back to hell. Everyone slept easier in their beds that night and Mifal was satisfied that the Madrick matter was finally, finally at an end.

✧ ✧ ✧

It was a very different story at the Devil Lair Keep where Stanverital and Devligrate were making their report in the tiniest of detail to the Council. They explained how they had tracked the pair with little difficulty. They told of their skill and cunning, omitting that they had piggy-backed on the hard work of Mifal's men at The Black Bear.

They described everything they had observed at the place where the trail had disappeared. They shared their observations and thoughts about the evidence of spell use. They boasted about their cleverness in spotting the flying men and the incredibleness of their long distance thunderball shot. They concluded by telling the Council that Gravalar had been at the site at the same time so the White Wizards also knew what they knew. The Council pondered everything carefully and, unlike Mifal they did not jump to any hasty conclusions.

Their deliberations went something like this. There had been multiple instances of magic. That fact was indisputable. The scroll user in the 'chicken incident' was clearly an untrained imbecile. That fact was even more indisputable, if that was possible. No one who was as stupid as that could possibly gather up more than one scroll. Therefore, it was distinctly possible that, what he had in his possession was indeed the fabled Spell Spell scroll. There were clearly two renegades and, to make up for the buffoonery of the 'chicken' user, the other must have had some training in the use the magic.

They debated the issue for many hours and could not find a reasonable alternative to their original theory. The Spell Spell existed and they needed to find it. Something as powerful as that could not be left in the hands of an idiot.

"This threatens the very fabric of the universe," declared the Black Grandee. "We must track it down. There is no time to lose.

"I believe that this is too important for us to handle on our own. I recommend that we offer a truce to the Whites and pool our resources so we can remove this danger from the planet.

"Of course, once the Scroll is secured we will terminate the truce and seize the Scroll for ourselves. This plan could be the foundation stone for our final victory over the Whites."

And so it was. The Black Grandee, accompanied by Stanverital and Devligrate, set off on the short journey to the Sorebun Academy. Sadly for the White Wizards, and more crucially for the world, they arrived long before Gravalar returned from the original quest.

22

Here be trickery and deceit

The bumpy crash-landing from the flight had shaken both men so they were not able to run far before they needed to stop for a rest. Being shot out of the sky had dented their confidence, and their butts, but they were sure they had little time for the luxury of sleep. They did not know that their pursuers had temporarily given up so they could have taken a decent break to charge up their energy and their spirits.

They were just outside of a town that lay nearly ten miles away from their crash site. Madrick knew that this gave them a decent start over their hunters. He hoped it was enough for their trail to grow cold.

Their big worry was, what had knocked them out of the sky? It was clearly some demonic magic, but how had Mifal's men deployed it? Had Mifal employed a new court wizard and was he now part of the hunt? That would be a worrying development because magic was the only thing that had kept them ahead of the pack. If their trackers were now using magic as well then that could neutralise their advantage.

Madrick had some idea about the local landscape and he knew they were not too many miles from the boundaries of Mifal's kingdom. He reckoned it was twenty miles at the most. He believed that once they crossed into the adjoining land they would be relatively safe. Mifal could still send spies to track them, but why would he bother? They were not all that important, given he did not know about the Scroll. Some of his logic was spot on, but some of his conclusions were very wrong.

Tung wanted to get some sleep, however, Madrick wanted to plan their next steps. All in all they had been very lucky so far, but they would need to be extremely careful if they were to stay ahead of the chasing pack. Madrick was sure that Mifal would still be after them so he would have been delighted had he known that the king had actually called off the hunt. He would, however, have been horrified to learn that it was the infinitely more dangerous wizards who were now on their tails.

"Create another spell," he said to Tung. "We need more distance between us and Mifal."

There was no reaction whatsoever because Tung was fast asleep. This was becoming a very annoying, recurring situation; Madrick was talking to a comatose Tung. Eventually, with a lot of hard shaking, he managed to rouse him from his stupor.

"Create another spell," he repeated. "We need to get more distance between us and Mifal."

Tung, although only half awake, obliged. Here we go again. Read the Scroll. Say the incantation. Collapse to the ground. Madrick catches the head.

This time, it was a great example of exactly how it should be done. This time, it was nearly perfect.

"What do you see? What is the image?"

"My head is full of flames. This is really frightening! I need to get this out of my head. NOW."

He started slapping the sides of his head with his hands.

"Don't panic. It will be the Fireball Spell. Just say it, but point your arms at that ring of trees. That is where the flaming ball will hit."

With some difficulty Tung fought through his head fire and found the words. He 'spoke' the letters and an enormous ball of fire crashed from his hands and engulfed five of the twelve magnificent oak trees which had dominated the landscape there for nearly a hundred years. The five trees burned vigorously and crashed to the ground in a smouldering heap. It was horribly awesome. Tung regained his senses in time to see the last of the trees vanish in the super heated firestorm.

"That was scary. That fireball is definitely not something you want to keep in your head any longer than you have to. I'm ready for the next spell. I need to put that last one a long way behind me."

He went through the routine again. The new spell materialised and he stared into the depths of his head and saw water. He tried to focus more, but no matter which way he looked at it, it was just water; lots of water.

"I see water," he said rather sheepishly. "Lots of water."

"Water," pondered Madrick. That was either the simple 'water to drink' spell which had been created to help travellers parch their thirsts as they crossed some of the vast deserts that used to cover the landscape. Or it was the spell which caused a great expanse of water to part so there was a safe and dry passage through it. He had no way to determine which one it was; not without the words. Worryingly, he was also not sure what would happen if the sea-parting spell was used when there was no water around. He really did not know, but he felt it might be extremely dangerous so he did not want to find out.

He decided the best thing to do was to continue to travel south, directly away from Mifal, and only use the spell when they came across a decent sized body of water. That was wise and sensible, he concluded. So they set off, at a decent pace all things considered, heading south.

Hours later the villagers congregated to stare at the semicircle, as it now was, of trees. That was all that remained of the great circle of oaks that had been there longer than anyone could remember; certainly much longer than the village. Five trees were gone. The elders agreed they would have to rename their town. 'Twelve Oaks' no longer made sense!

Tung and Madrick eventually came to a small lake. It was serenely beautiful and very secluded, being completely surrounded by a forest of luscious pine trees. This was the right place to find out which spell they had so Tung spoke the spell and, unspectacularly, a small cup of crystal clear liquid appeared. Tung was disappointed because he had wanted to feel the power of parting the lake. They were, however, both grateful when they started to sip from the magical cup of the cleanest, freshest, sweetest water they had ever tasted.

Rested and refreshed, they set off again on their southerly journey, making the short detour around the lake because the magical shortcut had unfortunately failed to materialise.

"Create another spell," Madrick demanded as they set off. "You should be able to do it on the move now that you've had a bit more practice."

The saying ritual was repeated over and over again on their journey southward. Many, many spells were created and used. Very few helped them, but some had the unfortunate consequence of leaving behind magically created landmarks which would act as pointers for their pursuers. The ever burning camp fire and the giant pillar of salt were two good examples of the signs that would tell informed observers that magic had passed this way.

They had now been on the road for more than six days and, as each day passed, they both felt slightly safer. The longer they travelled, the more likely it was that the pursuers would give up, particularly as they were coming very near to the boundary of Mifal's kingdom. Once they crossed into the adjoining kingdom, surely they would be safe?

They eventually reached the town that lay at the edge of the kingdom. It was a small settlement built around a substantial wooden castle which nestled beside the river that marked the southern boundary of the Mifal's lands. There was a ferry to take people across the river, but the villagers resented paying the high fee which the ferryman charged; he had a monopoly so he could charge what he liked. The villagers had no choice other than to accept his prices, but they hated him for his greed.

It was an interesting coincidence that Tung had the Bridge Spell in his head when he arrived. He decided he would gift it to these people.

He said the spell and watched as a fantastic bridge snaked its way across the river. Tung and Madrick were afforded the privilege of being the first to walk across the bridge as they made their way out of Mifal's kingdom and continued their journey south. A small group of the locals watched this amazing sight and they clapped loudly as the pair crossed the bridge and walked away.

Hours later, all the villagers congregated to stare at their wonderful new bridge. The elders agreed that they should have to rename the town - they would call it Tungbridge.

Everyone in the town was happy except, of course, the ferryman. His business had been destroyed in one magical fell swoop.

Madrick knew that the river crossing was an important milestone in their journey because they had now escaped from Mifal's jurisdiction. They still did not know that they were, in fact, being trailed by a group of highly motivated and stealthy wizards and not by Mifal's soldiers. They would have been rightly terrified had they known.

✧ ✧ ✧

Five days earlier, the Black Grandee, accompanied by Stanverital and Devligrate, had arrived at the Sorebun Academy. Initially the White wizard guards had panicked, they had no idea why the supreme Black Wizard would be approaching their headquarters with only two men and a white flag. Was it an evil deception, they wondered, or was it a genuine surrender?

After much discussion and debate, the Black Grandee was eventually granted permission to meet the hastily convened assembly of the White Order. They listened suspiciously to what he had to say.

He recounted the story of what Stanverital and Devligrate

101

had done and seen. He explained the conclusions of the Black Council and the potential catastrophic danger of the Spell Spell scroll being outside the control of the Orders. He freely admitted that he wanted the Scroll in the arsenal of the Blacks, but he granted that he would prefer it to be with the Whites rather than in the hands of the common folk.

"The elite must remain the elite," he concluded. "We must unite to ensure the common man does not get powers beyond his station. Otherwise, they may rise up and threaten our privileged existences. It is our collective duty not to allow that to happen."

After careful deliberation, the White Council reluctantly agreed. Almost unanimously they decided to accept the Black proposal and create a small joint force of their best men to hunt down the Scroll. It was to be Stanverital and Devligrate joined by Gravalar, if he returned within the next day. The Whites would also send Nextar, he was their finest young scroll finder and his skill of distance hearing would be invaluable to the team. Four junior wizards would reinforce the magical contingent of the task force.

Gravalar arrived a few hours after the momentous pact had been formed. He was too late to affect the decision, so he did not try. He knew that had he reported to the Council before the Black delegation had arrived, then this dangerous pact might never have come into existence.

He could have reported that he had overheard whispered conversations between Stanverital and Devligrate which did not bode well for the pact. He could have advised them of his observations which showed the treacherous nature of these bad seeds. He remained silent however, because he did not want to admit his theft of the golden wine goblet. He did not want to tell of his weakness for the endless supply of wine. He did not want to tell them that he had partaken of this red nectar all along the journey home. In fact, he had partaken to the extent that his return journey had lasted a day and a half longer than it should have. Most of all, he did not want to give up his treasured goblet. He was not going to share anything with the Council. He was not going to share the goblet or the story. He therefore accepted the decision, in silence, and prepared for the mission that had been assigned to him.

The next day the joint task force assembled midway between the Lair and the Academy. Stanverital, Devligrate, Gravalar and Nextar eyed each other suspiciously as they shook hands. They had, at their command, the four junior wizards and about fifty scouts and serfs. Under their direction, this small army would scour the ground for clues as to the whereabouts of their prey. They would question those they met, and trade threats or small rewards for useful information.

The four senior wizards had each been given some spell scrolls, carefully chosen to help them with their search and ultimate capture of the fugitives. Unbeknownst to the others, Stanverital had been given a special extra spell; one that would help him snatch the Scroll from the others, so he could return the priceless treasure to the Black Order.

23

Get thee behind me, Stan

Madrick and Tung had started to move with much less urgency since they had left Mifal's kingdom. They had a little celebratory dance when they reached the new land, but they were not going to let themselves become too complacent, Madrick would see to that. After a few more days travelling they reached the sea and that put a stop to their southerly trek. They needed to decide whether to head east or west. Madrick had made all the decisions so far. This time Tung decided it was his turn. He made his first major decision of the journey.

"We have seen no sign of any pursuers for ages. We have left Mifal and his men far behind. Now, we are probably running from shadows. It is time to rest and if you don't want to, you can go off on your own.

"There is an inviting alehouse over there. I, for one, am staying there for a break."

Five days later they were enjoying their fifth day's stay at a very pleasant little, secluded seaside tavern. It was not terribly busy and, as time passed, they felt increasingly at home and safe.

They had traded some silver spurs, which Tung had created, for seven night's board and all the food they could eat. Madrick had wanted no ale to be included in the package, but Tung had insisted and so far there had been no problems. Eat, drink moderately and be merry was the order of the day.

Unbeknownst to the happy revellers, their pursuers were now a mere hour away. They had followed the remains of spells, traded silver for information, threatened when necessary and used their inherent tracking skills to get ever closer to their fleeing prey.

Even though it had been a long and arduous trek, their

combined skills had kept them going in the right direction. They knew the gap was closing and believed that only a day or two separated them from their quarry. They were about to discover that they were an awful lot closer.

As they approached the tavern which entertained Tung and Madrick, their only thoughts were about a resting place for the night. They did not realise that they were about to encounter their prey, face to face, for the first time.

✿ ✿ ✿

Luckily, Madrick had succeeded in convincing Tung that he should have the next spell up his sleeve. He had enchanted the usual batch of useless spells which he had subsequently dissipated. And then he created the ultimate escape spell. The spell that was perfect should they be cornered by their pursuers. Tung had the Time Shift Spell in his head.

"This spell will transport us both, if we are touching, into the future," explained Madrick. "It could be a matter of days, or weeks, or even years; but whatever time period it takes us to, we will confound our enemy and be long gone, literally."

One small problem, he explained, was that the spell only time-travelled the bodies. They would end up naked in their new time zone. And, nothing would travel with them unless it was contained within the body.

It was déjà vu. Again, one of them would have to secrete the Scroll within their body. They both just stared at each other as they realised there was only one option. It was the same option as before.

Tung was the first to speak. "It is not going to be me…"

Madrick was having none of it this time.

"I did it last time and I'm not doing it again. It's your turn."

"No chance. I have to suffer the head pains. I'm not suffering pains at the other end as well."

They gave each other hard looks, but it was obvious neither was going to crack. Madrick broke the deadlock.

"This time we will leave it to skill and chance. This time, we will play Rock, Parchment, Knife - best of three."

Tung had had a few ales by this stage so he reluctantly agreed; after all, he knew he was rather skilled at the game so he should beat the old man.

The pair faced each other and clenched their fists.

One, two, three - Rock, Rock.

One, two, three - Rock, Rock.

One, two, three - Parchment, Parchment.

One, two, three - Rock, Parchment. First blood to Tung.

One, two, three - Parchment, Knife. Tung wins!

So it was decided that, once again, Madrick would hide the Scroll. Tung handed it over and Madrick slipped it in his pocket and hoped that he would be ready when the time came. It was deeply unpleasant, but at least he knew they had prepared themselves well for escape should the worst come to the worst. And it did come, sooner than either of them expected.

✿ ✿ ✿

From nearly a mile away, Nextar, using his extraordinary hearing skill, heard the happy hubbub which emanated from the tavern. He steered the small army of wizards and serfs in that general direction. It was Gravalar who first spotted the lights of the secluded inn.

"There it is," he pointed, "we will stay there for the night and make our plans for tomorrow."

Only the wizards, of course, would stay in the inn; the rest of the entourage would camp nearby in makeshift tents. Serfs and common people had no place indoors as far as the elite brethren were concerned.

As the eight wizards entered the tavern, they saw Tung and Madrick almost immediately. They froze. Tung and Madrick spotted the new strangers at exactly the same time. They had no idea who they were, but they knew they spelled trouble with a capital 'T' - well, Madrick knew about the capital 'T'.

They also froze.

"Run," screamed Madrick. "We must get out of here. We must get to our room."

The wizards reacted like lightening. Three set off through the crowd after the fleeing pair while the others ran outside to organise the serfs.

Madrick and Tung pounded up the stairs and dived into their room.

"Barricade the door," Madrick ordered as he pulled out the Scroll and prepared himself for the pain.

Using all his strength, Tung managed to push the great four-poster bed against the door just in time. From outside, he heard bodies slam against it, but it held fast.

"Give yourselves up," shouted Gravalar through the thick wood. "We only want the Scroll. We do not care about you people. We will do you no harm."

"Have mercy on us," shouted Tung trying to buy some more time. "If you spare us we will happily give up the Scroll. I will get you the Scroll now. It is here. Let me get it for you."

There were shouts outside the window as the serfs made sure there was no escape by that route. The wizards pounded on the door. Stanverital, the biggest of the wizards, shoulder charged the door, but the thick oak with a large bed behind it was too formidable a barrier.

"Get thee behind me, Stan," cried Devligrate as he prepared to use the Thunderball Spell again.

Stanverital jumped out of the way in the nick of time. Devligrate had said the spell at super fast speed and suddenly the door, and most of the bed, exploded in a thunderous blast of splinters. This spell was a lot more offensive when it was used at close range and in a confined space.

Despite the chaos, their quick thinking had bought just enough time. Madrick had suffered the pain and humiliation of concealing the Scroll yet again and now he grabbed Tung and screamed.

"Quickly, use the spell now. RIGHT NOW."

"Right," said Tung slightly disoriented, "I guess there's no time like the present."

And then, there was literally no time like the present... there was just the future. Tung and Madrick were catapulted into the twenty-first century.

24

Gone but not forgotten

The wizards just stared at each other after they watched their prey disappear in a puff of nothingness. Gravalar and Stanverital blocked the door while Devligrate ran to block the window. There was no way out, so if the pair had become invisible they would not escape. It was rumoured that they had used invisibility when they mysteriously broke out of Mifal's dungeon and the wizards were definitely not going to allow that to happen again here.

When Nextar, the other senior wizard, and four serfs arrived, they searched the room thoroughly. It was empty except for the piles of clothes which now lay untidily on the ground. They patted their way around the room, feeling every corner and crevice. Nextar also used his extraordinary hearing skill, but he picked up no trace of the thieves. There was nobody hiding anywhere in the room. There was nothing. It was clear that the pair had not become invisible; there must be some other explanation.

The discarded clothes meant it was not the Transportation Spell - a spell which moved the subject to a place up to five hundred miles away. Had it been that particular spell then the clothes would have gone too and there would have been the smell of burnt wood. No one knew why, but that smell always accompanied a magic transportation.

The wizards all put forward various scenarios. Despite the wide range of theories, they only came up with one plausible explanation. The pair had invoked one of the major spells and had time travelled. They were now somewhere, or rather sometime, in the future.

They discussed what they knew of the great spell and agreed that conventional wisdom suggested they could have jumped anything between five hours and ten years - it was inconceivable to them that it could have been nearly a thousand years. They could re-appear anywhere within a hundred miles of their departure point so the task facing the wizards was nigh on impossible.

After further debate they decided it was prudent to remain in camp while they planned their next step. They searched everywhere for the Scroll because they knew it should have been left behind. Unless, of course, they had done the unthinkable! Their search produced nothing.

After waiting in the area for five days, to see if the pair turned up, they decided that they had no choice other than to report back to the Black and White Councils and let the wise ones decide what to do next. They left twenty serfs at the inn to maintain the vigil even though they knew, deep down, that this was a futile gesture. The fugitives and the Scroll had gone for good or, at least, gone for a very long time.

✿ ✿ ✿

The expeditionary force returned to report to the joint Council of the Black and White.

They bragged about how they had successfully followed the trail to the secluded tavern. They described the brief moment of contact.

"They were there in front of us. We had them cornered and then… they were gone."

They held up the ragged clothes they had retrieved from the scene. They described the detailed search of the area and how they had waited and watched in case the time leap had been a short one. Finally, they told them of the team of watchers who had been left in place.

The Council members listened carefully. The more they heard, the clearer it became that the Scroll had time travelled with the pair; the same way it had travelled with them when they had used invisibility to escape from Mifal. They agreed they should strengthen the party which was waiting at the tavern. They accepted it could be a very long wait and the pair would not necessarily turn up in that place, although it was the most likely point of re-entry.

The Council comprised the wisest wizards in the land so they knew more about spells than anyone else. They knew a lot about the Time Travel Spell and they understood that the time leap could be up to two hundred years, much longer than the ten years that the younger wizards believed. They knew they would have to play the long game. They had no idea just how long. They certainly had no idea that this was going to be a thousand year game.

After many hours of deliberation they collectively decided that the only way to be certain of retrieving the Scroll was to be there, in place, when the Scroll arrived. Not just a bunch of serfs, but a well disciplined, well resourced organisation. This needed to be a very special organisation because this was the most important of all the scrolls and they now knew, for certain, that it existed.

They therefore initiated a secret society which would pass on its remit from generation to generation. It would perpetuate the story of the great Scroll and how it had fallen into the hands of two thieving common folk. The sole purpose of the Society would be to find the Scroll. They decreed that the Society would be in existence from that day forth so, by the very nature of time, it would be in place when the time travellers arrived. Through the Society, they would be waiting.

Stanverital, Devligrate, Gravalar and Nextar would be the founding members so they were to be entrusted with recovering the Scroll. The leader of this new Society would be titled the Great Grand Master and the first of these was to be Gravalar.

The Council armed the four founders with resources beyond the dreams of the masses and they demanded total secrecy. The Society would be named the secret ones or, to give it its formal title, the Occultus Populous.

And so it was.

Over the centuries, the secret was never discovered. Sometimes some 'genius' from the common people would feel very clever when he exposed a secret society such as the Freemasons, the Hashshashin, The Knights of the Golden Circle or the Illuminati. But these 'geniuses' had all been tricked by an on-going deception because these other societies were merely smokescreens created by the Occultus Populous. It had ingeniously established these other societies to conceal its own secret until the Scroll and the travellers appeared.

As decades turned to centuries, the Society's aims became more and more blurred. There were still the writings about the Scroll, but after so many years, the stories had become somewhat myth like. It was no longer clear if the Scroll actually existed and the story of the time travellers took on the qualities of a fable. The Society's purpose evolved into one that protected the standing of the elite and kept the commoners in their place. Over the centuries, it expanded far beyond its original roots and became truly global.

Using its vast wealth and trickery, it gained authority over most of the world's money and it had virtually total control over everyone who was in debt. In order to maintain the cloak of secrecy, it deluded the masses using distractions such as unnecessary work, pointless study, mindless entertainment and sport.

By the time the twenty-first century rolled around, the Occultus Populous owned the majority of the world's most powerful financial institutions. Virtually every Government was trapped in debt and many were forced to sell their own Nation's assets, lose sovereignty and place their citizens in poverty to repay their crippling debts. The rich got richer and the poor got poorer; that was how the Society deemed that things were meant to be. Everything was going well as far as that plan was concerned.

The Society had gradually lost sight of the very reason it had been created all those centuries ago; its raison d'être had shifted. The Occultus Populous had largely forgotten about the Scroll, and its members were now focused on their own selfish power and greed.

That would all change very soon.

25

New age travellers

Tung and Madrick appeared as instantaneously as they had disappeared. They hurtled into the twenty-first century naked and confused. Both men crashed heavily to the ground. Tung hit it head first, as usual, but amazingly there was no pain because, this time, he had hit sand. The pair had landed on a beach somewhere.

They gradually regained their senses and surveyed their surroundings. There was the sea on one side and a row of very small wooden houses, all facing the sea, on the other. They were extremely colourful and looked well constructed, but they were very small and very close together. It was incredibly cold, just beginning to turn dark and, luckily, there was no one else around. Their good fortune was holding; for now.

They both felt very uncomfortable in their nakedness; the last time they had been in this predicament, they had been invisible. They needed to get indoors and dressed as quickly as possible.

They quietly and stealthily crept up to the nearest of the houses. They quickly worked out that it was unoccupied, even though it had no windows at the front for them to look through. There was no sound and the double doors were bolted and padlocked on the outside. After a short search, Tung found what he needed to prise open the lock. In no time at all they were inside.

"You are very skilled at that."

"Years of practice," said Tung as he pulled the doors closed behind them.

They rummaged around the single room dwelling and found a few clothes - enough to restore some semblance of dignity. They also found some blankets and a bag of sickly sweet biscuits - in their time, sugar was almost unheard of so, the biscuits tasted superbly unusual. As they searched, they both marvelled at the quality of the furnishings and the strangeness of many of the items they found. Having exhausted their scavenging, they moved on to the house next door and then the next. They gathered more clothes, a pair of shoes each, some food provisions and a good handful of silver coins.

Madrick studied the coins; he noted a lady's head and a year; 2008. She looked very regal with her crown, but surely a woman could not be the one in charge.

The coin was well worn, so today's date was probably later than the 2008 shown. Unbelievable - Madrick calculated they had travelled nearly one thousand years into the future. He decided that that was impossible so deduced that the number on the coin was not the year, so it must mean something else, but for the life of him he could not think what. Then again, as far as he knew there was no limit to the length of time that the spell leapt - maybe it was a thousand years. A thousand years, he mused, if that was truly the distance of their time jump, then things were going to be mightily different. They were the epitome of strangers in a strange land.

They decided to stay put for the night. This place seemed quiet and safe and they needed time to recover and get their bearings. Tung slept while Madrick browsed through a selection of books he had picked up during some of their break-ins. The language was a little strange, but he quickly adapted his reading to cope. The books showed amazing pictures of wonderful foodstuffs, great cities, fantastic machines and people in strange costumes. He read prolifically while Tung snored noisily in the corner. It soon became too dark for him to make out even the pictures so he reluctantly gave up and joined Tung in sleep.

It was an uneasy sleep because his dreams constantly reminded him of the wondrous things about which he had read. He was wide awake at first light and wasted no time in getting back to his studying.

One book was particularly engaging and enlightening. It was a most amazing history book which charted Britain through the ages. He started at the beginning and saw many things that he recognised from his day; things like the Danish Invaders who ravaged parts of England and descriptions of some of the towns they had built. It was a bit frightening to see pictures of ancient ruins; ruins of buildings which he remembered as newly built. This would take some getting used to. Fascinating as this was, curiosity got the better of him very quickly and he skipped to the end of the book and started reading backwards. Every page held a new wonder. This was an absolutely incredible world into which they had arrived.

Madrick was totally transfixed by what he read and saw, but he was not overawed. His training as a wizard had introduced him to the most fantastical phenomena. These modern things, which now surrounded him, were amazing, but they were no more amazing than some of the things he had seen in wizard school. He knew he could adapt quickly to his new environment. He was not so sure about Tung.

He found a chapter on inventions. It began with a quote under the heading 'Clarke's 3rd Law' which read 'any sufficiently advanced technology is indistinguishable from magic.' That was a fascinating thought - eventually science would catch up and explain all the things he had been taught were magic. And it seemed that that was the law. Maybe it had caught up already; maybe they already had an explanation for the Scroll. That is highly unlikely, he thought, and he read on.

He was particularly intrigued by the inventions because he had always loved machines and contraptions. He read about steam power, motor cars and electricity.

What a fantastic discovery it was, he thought, as he leafed through pages of incredible gadgets all powered by the rather mystical force that was electricity. He looked around and immediately recognised the light switch. With a little trepidation he flicked it down. The room was instantly bathed in a soft, yellow light. He clapped his hands as he played with the switch - off, on, off, on, off, on - he could do this all day, although all night would make more sense. If only he had discovered this last night he would not have wasted the hours of darkness sleeping.

Eventually he returned to the book and read the captions under the pictures of other electric machines. As he read he spotted some more of the illustrated gadgets in the room around him. He worked out how to plug them in - it was obvious because the plug fitted the socket precisely. He plugged in anything that had a plug and turned knobs and pushed buttons. He could not make the radio work although he had more success with the toaster. It certainly got hot, however, he realised too late that the slots were not for warming your hands. He had a lot to learn and that had been a painful lesson. The burns did not dampen his enthusiasm as he moved towards the plug in the corner of the room; the plug on the television.

This was Madrick's first great modern-day success. He got the television to work. It came on showing a twenty-four hour news channel. He watched the moving pictures and was totally fascinated, at first by the images and then by what the world had become. He could contain his excitement no longer so he woke Tung and got him to watch this miracle. They 'oohed' and 'aahed' as story after story mesmerised them.

Weather forecasts regularly interrupted the news stories. Neither of them understood the mystical symbols which peppered the map, but it was nice to see that at least one of the old spells had survived. Madrick's thoughts drifted back to the 3rd Law. Maybe, one day, science would explain how it was possible to forecast the weather but that, like an explanation of the Scroll, seemed highly unlikely. Also, it appeared that the accuracy of the forecasting had not improved since they had used the spell all those years ago.

All in all, this was a brilliant introduction to the twenty-first century, all achieved in the safe seclusion of their little beach hut. Tung adapted better than Madrick had imagined. Maybe his crash course (and he had crashed many times) in spell casting and spells had prepared him well for accepting the miraculous.

In parallel with their TV watching, they planned for their eventual excursion into the outside world. It was probably just as well that they never discovered how to change channel or they might have been there forever.

They also created a variety of spells until they had one which would be useful once they left the safety of this sanctuary. The owner of this little wooden house would be excited by the remnants of some of the spells. For example, the ancient parchments would fascinate, the great silver sword would definitely be a talking point and the scattered gold coins would clearly enrich him in every sense of the word. There were going to be a few happy owners because Tung had insisted they leave some coins in all the huts they had raided. He understood what being poor was like and these people were clearly not well off given the tiny size of their dwellings.

They had been there for three days, watching the TV and systematically raiding the adjoining huts. They rested, learnt about modern life and fed themselves on a variety of very strange foods. They might have stayed longer had it not been for the banging on the door and the voice shouting strange words.

"Barry. Barry. Barry," the voice cried.

It was funny how the same word, or name, said over and over again with no change in tone or volume sounded really bizarre.

"Barry. Barry. Barry," the voice cried, still in the same monotonous manner.

Tung and Madrick panicked. They grabbed their valuables, actually they were mainly someone else's valuables, and crouched behind the only two bits of furniture big enough to hide them. They made no noise as they listened to the pounding on the small wooden doors.

"Barry, are you in there?" asked the mystery voice. "We've had our hut broken into. It looks like a lot of the huts have been robbed. I can see the TV on, are you in there?"

The voice belonged to the owner from two huts down. He had come to collect some odds and sods from his holiday house. He had found the lock broken and when he went inside he could see that the place had been searched and a number of items stolen. There had been nothing of real value there, but it was still very annoying to know that someone had invaded his private little retreat. He had not yet found the gold coins which Tung had left him.

As he banged on the door, he realised that the lock there had been broken too. It was not immediately obvious because Tung had managed to pry it open with very little damage. The man, who was no hero, suddenly became very anxious.

"I've called the police. They said they'd be here in a few minutes. Are you in there?"

He had not really called the police. He knew from experience that the police would not come. There had been break-ins here before and it had always turned out to be a tramp or homeless person trying to grab a night's sleep and a bit of warmth. There was no point in prosecuting them so the police felt there was no point in investigating.

Tung's survival instincts kicked in and he came up with a rather pathetic plan which he whispered to Madrick. It sounded ridiculous but it was all they had.

"The back window. Out the back window," shouted Tung as he smashed the small window at the rear of the hut. This was merely a distraction tactic because the window was far too small for either man to get through. There would be no spring-roll, dramatic escape through that little opening.

They could not believe their luck when they heard the man run to the back of the hut. In reality, he was scared and had scarpered back to his own house. He was not about to tackle one tramp never mind more than one. The instant they heard him racing from the door, Madrick and Tung bolted out the front and ran for their lives; here we go again, they thought, as they headed for the trees.

They hid in the shadows and peered out to see if they were being followed. There was no sign of anyone and the voice had disappeared. They crept away, constantly listening and checking for pursuers. Luckily, no one seemed to be after them, which was a welcome novelty. They soon began to relax a little and enjoy what was effectively a quiet walk in the woods. After a few hours they knew for sure they were not being followed so they took a break to assess their situation. They had clothes, food and some modern coins so things were actually pretty good. They also had the 'never empty' gold coin pouch which Tung had magicked up and a useful spell in their arsenal in case things took a turn for the worse. They kept walking, away from the huts and heading inland. They hoped they would come upon a town soon so they could get lost among the townsfolk there. Madrick knew that being amongst modern people would throw up all sorts of new challenges. They would just have to adapt. They had no other choice.

This was actually very exciting, they were in a strange and fascinating era so there was going to be an awful lot to explore.

Let the new adventure begin, thought Madrick.

26

The Ritz cracker

Eventually they left the small forest and found a rough track which they followed to a larger road. There, they soon encountered their first motor vehicles. They had seen these machines on the television, but nothing could have prepared them for the effect it had on them. They were overwhelmed by the speed, the smell and the noise. These machines were truly frightening.

After a few close encounters of the very near kind, they realised that the vehicles went on the black bit of the wide track so they, as walkers, needed to stay at the edge of this dark torrent of roaring madness. Before long they also had the chance of a real conversation with their first modern man. He had stopped his car and asked them for directions - this modern world was no different to their own because that 'directions request' always came when you were a stranger. As usual, the asker was already tense and exasperated so the conversation was short and not so sweet. It was clear from this exchange that some of the most offensive swear words from their time had survived and were alive and doing very well.

They walked for miles and eventually came to what looked like an enormous, indoor street market. The massive sign above the entrance confirmed this - SUPERMARKET it proclaimed.

"Let me do the talking," said Madrick. "We will pretend to be from a land far away and we will say that we are unfamiliar with the customers here... I meant customs. We are unfamiliar with the customs here."

It went surprising well. Everyone had a large basket on wheels so they got one for themselves - imitate and blend seemed to be a good strategy. They gathered food provisions and a trolley full of useful items such as backpacks, warm coats, a torch and a couple of very sharp knives. They queued behind other shoppers who seemed to be waiting to pay for their goods. When their turn came, everything was passed over a glass window which beeped as each item flashed by. The 'shopkeeper' smiled and asked for a meaningless sum of money; meaningless to them that is. After having their modern coins refused as being insultingly insufficient, the manager was called and the two were hauled off to his office. They explained they were not from these parts, but the manager was in no mood to deal with these tramps, as he saw them. He threatened to call the police. He lifted a strange, bone shaped object from his desk and started to punch buttons. Madrick was frightened because the last thing they needed was a brush with the authorities. Mifal may be long dead, but there was undoubtedly some other equally cruel, modern dictator to contend with. So, as a last resort, he offered one of the gold coins as payment.

The man thumbed the beautiful coin and, within an instant, his attitude had changed dramatically. Not one to miss an opportunity, the manager offered them a hundred modern day pounds for the coin. He could spot value when he saw it. Once the deal was done, he led them out of his office and helped them through the check out process.

They left with their purchases and some modern paper money. They were very pleased with themselves, but they knew they would have to come to terms with modern money and modern ways of shopping, sooner rather than later.

They kept walking along the road and came to a small cluster of shops. One displayed a glistening array of jewellery in its window and had a little notice on the glass that said 'We Buy Gold'.

"We should try and get more of this modern money. I will try and sell another coin. I want to know if others will give us one hundred of their pounds again. Maybe the man at the market was a fool to pay so much.

"You wait here. Don't talk to anyone."

Madrick went in alone and showed the man one of the gold coins from the 'never empty' pouch. The man examined it though a strange eye glass and became quite animated and excited. He offered five hundred pounds which Madrick immediately accepted; that was so much better than the hundred he had been given in the supermarket.

"That was great," he said to Tung as he left the shop. "We now have plenty of today's money so we should find it easier to fit in. We need to hide though and the best place to hide is among lots of people. We need to get to a big town where we can be anonymous. That will give us space and time to make a plan."

As their confidence grew, they began to ask passers-by for directions to the biggest town around. London, they were told, was as big as they came so they headed for it. They followed the directions and their instincts. Things got busier - more people, more houses, more shops - so they felt that they must be getting closer. They kept asking for London and eventually someone very kindly offered them a lift.

They rode in the back of the car, wide-eyed and silent. There was no need to talk to the driver because he was separated from them by a glass window. This was fantastic - the speed and the comfort were amazing. Eventually they stopped and the driver opened the door for them.

"Forty-seven pounds please."

Madrick was surprised by his request. He decided not to query it because he thought it would be best to go along with, what was clearly, a modern custom. He handed the driver three twenty pound notes.

"Thank you very much," he said as he jumped back in his car and drove off. There was to be no change for the strangers.

They looked around and found themselves in the heart of

a sprawling metropolis.

"So this is London," said Tung. "I'm frightened."

"Don't worry, we'll manage. We've made it this far after all. We were told that we should find a 'hotel' because that's the modern equivalent to an inn. Once we get a room of our own we'll be fine."

They set off in search of a hotel. This place was so big there must be plenty of them around. After wandering the crowded streets for an hour or so, they saw it; The Ritz Hotel.

It took a while, and a few 'we are strangers in this land', to get checked in. They also struggled with giving names. Madrick was reluctant to give his real name but he had blurted it out before he could conjure up an alternative.

"Mr Madrick, welcome to the Ritz."

"No. Madrick is my first name," he said before he could stop himself.

Now the man behind the big desk wanted a second name. This time Madrick was a little more prepared and gave Tide as the surname. He was definitely not going to give his real name; he hated to be reminded of it and had not used it since entering the Sorebun Academy. His real family name, Zabarus, carried a damning stigma that he did not want to divulge to Tung; maybe someday he would share that secret, but today was not that day. His mind drifted back to the task in hand and he realised that he should probably not have given Tung's real name either, but it was too late. After a few more 'we are strangers', they were registered as Tung and Madrick Tide - father and son. Tung felt surprisingly comfortable with that and it felt right to Madrick as well. There was definitely a growing trust and friendship between them.

They were accompanied to a small box room with no windows. There was no bed and it was distinctly claustrophobic when the metal doors slid shut. The hotel man who was carrying their backpacks pressed one of an array of buttons and suddenly their whole room began to judder. This was awful! This was not what they expected from a hotel - a tiny room that shuddered, had no windows and they had to share it with a stranger.

The judders and shudders stopped as suddenly as they had started. The doors slid open but they were not where they had started. It was like the Transportation Spell in a box.

"Follow me please," said the man with the bags.

They walked down a long corridor and the man opened one of many doors and ushered them into a luxurious suite. This was more like it. They were stunned as they looked out of the windows and realised they were high above the ground. They both marvelled at the expanse of the city below. Massive buildings with vast facades of shiny windows, mazes of streets thronging with cars and crowds of people rushing to who knows where.

It did not take them long to settle in and feel at home although neither of them had ever known a home like it. This place was fabulous. It had a large living area, a separate bedroom and a bathroom which actually had a toilet in it. The whole place was warm, the beds were incredibly soft and there was an enormous television which, over the next while, they would watch avidly. There was a cold cupboard which held little bottles of drink and there was a mysterious speaking device which allowed you to name any food you wanted and a man would come to the door bearing that very food... it was magic!

They ventured out a number of times and, as their confidence grew, each outing became a little longer and a little more adventurous than the previous one. They were adapting well although they were frequently flabbergasted by the miracles they saw around them.

Madrick was impressed with the way they had coped so far. They seemed to be safe and secure in their new environment so he thought that now was the time to use the spell that Tung had in him, the one he had had in his head for quite some time. They had kept it for protection, just in case their pursuers had caught up with them again. He felt that they should use it now, because now that they had no modern chasers and they had left the original hunting party a thousand years behind.

"Let us use your spell," he suggested to Tung. "It will be a little dangerous, but we can do it if we are careful. It will allow us to create other spells which may be more useful to us now that we are free of pursuit."

Madrick had already explained that this spell was another either-or spell. He could not tell which one it was without the words. He had tried to get Tung to describe the letters but that had defeated him. So the spell was either NOISE or Siren Shriek. They were similar and he reckoned either would have helped them gain a tremendous element of surprise, enough surprise to allow them to escape had they been in danger of capture.

Madrick reminded Tung that he would not hear the mind numbing noise whether it came as a massive explosion of sound or whether it came out of his mouth in a directed, ear piercing scream. Tung nodded and said he knew what to expect.

Tung went out onto the balcony while Madrick took shelter in the bedroom, wrapping thick blankets round his head and pressing pillows against his ears for extra protection.

Tung spoke the spell and crashed forwards into the rail. At least he bashed the front of his head this time - sweet relief. Even before he had hit the ground, the most deafening noise ever exploded in every direction.

Thousands of people within a quarter mile radius were totally paralysed by the incredible sound. Once they recovered from the initial shock they looked all around expecting to see complete devastation from some kind of dreadful explosion. All they saw were other startled people looking around in bewilderment. Many exchanged animated, embarrassed chatter as they tried to work out what had just happened.

Tung peered over the balcony and was astounded to see the chaos he had caused. Hundreds of people stood rooted to the spot, many more had fallen over, cyclists had been floored and there were multiple, traffic pile ups caused by motorists who had lost control when the sound wave hit.

That spell would have worked fine if we had been cornered, he thought to himself as he re-entered the suite. Madrick was emerging from the bedroom; he was shaken even though his preparation and expectation had shielded him from the worst effects.

"Noise Spell!" remarked Madrick stating the obvious. "That was astounding."

Tung held his forehead. Blood oozed from where he had hit the balcony rail.

"I've cut myself," said Tung stating the bleeding obvious. "But no real damage done… to me that is."

They could hear people panicking and screaming in the corridors and the adjoining rooms. It seemed to be chaos out there. They smiled at each other because they were the opposite; they were calm and were settling into the comfy chairs in preparation for another session of television. They had been fairly sure it would be impossible to pinpoint the source of the almighty sound blast and it looked as if they were right.

Suddenly there was a loud, insistent knocking on the door. They looked at each other, trying to work out what to do. Madrick put his finger to his mouth. Tung understood and stayed totally silent. They tried to ignore the banging but it became louder and more persistent.

"Get ready to run," said Tung as he crossed the room and opened the door cautiously.

A hotel porter was standing breathless in the corridor. He looked as if he had been running for miles.

"Are you all right Sir?"

"We are a little shaken but we're fine," replied Tung as casually as he could. "What on earth was that dreadful noise?"

"No one knows, Sir, no one knows," replied the porter as he turned away and walked to the next room. "I'm just checking with all the guests to see if anyone needs any help."

Tung closed the door. He smiled and winked at Madrick.

"That is yet another win for the good guys. It is clear that no one knows what happened... except us!"

"And we are not going to be telling anyone," said Madrick settling deeper into his chair.

✿ ✿ ✿

In one of the grandest old buildings in the business quarter, four men discussed the rumours about some ancient coins which had apparently started to appear in various locations around the city. The rumours told of a strange old man who seemed happy to part with the coins at way below market value. They were trying to decide whether they should try and gather some of the coins so they could determine their origin.

They were musing this over when they heard the most enormous KABOOM. It shook the building. Even though they were nearly half a mile from the Ritz, the sound was still loud enough to make everyone freeze on the spot. They gave each other puzzled and enquiring looks as they tried to work out what had just happened.

As soon as they recovered their composure, and it took them a good few moments, they all went to the windows. They expected to see evidence of an explosion. They expected to see flames, smoke or collapsed buildings. There was nothing to be seen.

"What just happened? Can anybody see anything?"

"I can see nothing. I fear this may be another mystery for us to add to the questions about the coins."

They started to solemnly discuss this latest strangeness. Was this another extraordinary occurrence that might demand their urgent attention? These were powerful men and it was a very unfortunate day for anyone who became the subject of their urgent attention.

27

Dictation

Those without true knowledge would tell you that there is a prophecy, long written down, which foretells a momentous happening that is to befall the whole world. They say the predicted happening is supposed to banish evil and replace it with goodness. Neither the nature nor the time of the happening is known. The happening's name is Valdeus Calambonus.

These unknowing scholars and intellectuals dismissed the prophecy as pure nonsense because of its complete lack of detail; they likened it to an arranged meeting that does not have an agreed place, time or purpose. They argued that such a prophecy had no merit as it could claim nearly any eventuality and hail itself to be the truth. That is the nature of prophecies and predictions, from Nostradamus to the great Holy Books. They try to convince the world of their cleverness and veracity. They are self-promoting entities which people love and hate in equal measure.

Those with true knowledge however, understand that Valdeus Calambonus is not in fact a prophecy. It is a dictacy; a set of forced circumstances created by a great spell. It is much more controlling than a prophecy because it forces the event to happen rather than merely predicting it.

This particular dictacy came about when a powerful Black Wizard used a powerful spell to wreak the ultimate revenge on his enemies. Through this primordial magic he would force the universe to create a momentous event which would shape the future of all the people on the planet.

Back in the mists of time, when the Black and White Joint Council dispatched four wizards on a joint mission to retrieve the Scroll, they gave each wizard a set of spells to help them with their pursuit. One of their number, Stanverital, was given a special extra spell; one that was intended to help him snatch the priceless Scroll for the Black Order. Few knew of this spell, neither its existence nor its power.

When the mission failed, the Joint Grand Council established the Occultus Populous to snare the time travellers and reclaim the Scroll. They appointed Gravalar to be its leader and the first Great Grand Master. Stanverital was the more senior wizard so he believed it was his destiny to lead the Society. He was furious. He hated Gravalar for usurping him but more so, he hated the Council for overlooking him as the rightful leader.

He did not realise, and he would never find out, that the Black had very special plans for him. These plans would have written him a vaunted place in Black history, but he was too annoyed and impatient to think of anything other than revenge.

He acted as an Under Grand Master in the organisation for a few months, but his jealousy and ever growing resentment were so destructive that eventually Gravalar was forced to expel him. Stanverital's boiling fury became volcanic and his life became a seething quest for revenge. He began plotting his vengeance on all those who had wronged him.

Gravalar did not care, for he was just one wizard with a few minor scrolls at his disposal. He could not harm the power of the Occultus Populous - it was invincible. What no one realised was that Stanverital had not returned the special spell to the Scroll Library. He was now a very bitter man with very dangerous potential.

He had the Spell of Dictacy. This was one of the most powerful, and dangerous, spells in creation. It allowed him, the sayer of the spell, to create a set of circumstances which would be forced into existence by the core power which was embedded at the centre of the universe. Only one dictacy could exist at any point in time because the Universe had made it that way to eliminate the possibility of dictated contradictions. This meant that Gravalar, and Gravalar alone, had the power to change the world.

The circumstances had to be very simple and carefully scribed so there was no ambiguity because the Universe tended to mess with man's wishes if she was given the chance. The spell demanded that the dictacy be precisely ten words written in the ancient Salatin language.

When he was originally given the spell, Stanverital had agreed secretly with the Members of the Great Black Council to wait until the joint mission had reclaimed the Scroll. He would evaluate the situation and create a simple dictacy which would allow him to steal the Scroll for the Black Order. It was long recognised that it could be ineffective, or indeed perilous, to create the dictacy too far in advance as this could lead to unforeseen, potentially catastrophic, consequences.

From the very first day of his expulsion, Stanverital spent every waking moment, and some of his sleeping ones, plotting his revenge. He dreamed up elaborate ways to extract his retribution, but each time, he realised that he was making it too complicated. He knew that 'too complicated' would be used by the universe to thwart his retribution so he had to simplify things.

Eventually he thought he had devised the perfect plan. He would create a tide of goodness which would destroy the Black Order forever and take down the Occultus Populous too. That would be the ultimate degradation for the Black; to be destroyed by goodness.

It was a profound irony that a man of such malevolent intent should set out to destroy the biggest evil on the planet by employing the power of good. However, as the planet would discover, the power of good does not necessarily create a better world. The planet would discover that too much good is a very bad thing indeed.

Once Stanverital had his idea he dedicated himself to drafting and crafting his words. The words of the dictacy that he committed to the spell were, of course, written in the Salatin language of magic. These are the words he wrote.

'Certamen duos valde voxonum universum pro bonus atterus duco malum'.

The translation from the ancient language is never simple. This is one reason why scholars down the centuries failed to understand the dictacy. Over the years there had been many iterations of the translation process, each with its own inherent weaknesses. One of the better versions the intellectuals came up with read as follows.

'Combine two great powers for good and destroy the influence of evil.'

Stanverital was pleased with his words. He felt his logic was sound. There was only one 'influence for evil' on the planet and that was the Black Order. He did not want to name them specifically as there may be loopholes for some of those he wanted to punish, for example, members of the Occultus Populous. Also the unambiguous Salatin definition for the Order was five words whereas 'influence of evil' was only two.

His logic continued. There were only two great powers for good, namely the White Order and some of the great spells which had been exclusively created to promote goodness. So bring together the White Order and a great good spell, and the evil influence of the Black Order would be destroyed.

To cement his revenge in eternity he burned the dictacy scroll so that no other wizard could ever use it to try and reverse his legacy. As he watched the parchment smoulder, he felt a profound sense of calm as if his true destiny had been realised.

He had no idea that the Universe had already conspired against his intention. She, to defend herself from the influence of man, was always taking preventative measures to minimise his power. These were things of which he knew nothing and they led to consequences he could never have predicted.

The first event, unknown to him, was the spontaneous combustion of a Fire Spell right in the heart of the new combined Great Library. It was the Library that held the scrolls that the Black and White Orders had gathered over the centuries. The spells were never meant to be collected and stored. It had been bad enough when there were two separate libraries, but when the two Orders came together and combined their scrolls, they created something that was totally unacceptable. It was against the natural order to have so many spell scrolls gathered together in one place.

The Universe had created magic in the first place. She had allowed a limited number of scrolls to be brought into being, but she had never intended that man should accumulate them for the furtherance of his greed.

That problem had been sorted. Now, all that was left were the few spell scrolls which had never been found or those that lived in the collections of kings and emperors. They were mostly minor scrolls and, over the course of time, many of them would be destroyed by a variety of universe-instigated events. Of course, the Spell Spell scroll was not in the library, so as one of the few remaining major spells, it had now become one of the most valuable artefacts on the planet.

As a consequence of the loss of all the scrolls from the Great Library, there was no real point or purpose for the Orders to continue to exist. On top of that, the invading Normans had targeted both Orders because they wanted to secure scrolls for their king in France. Without their magic, the wizards could no longer protect themselves from the invaders so they were constantly under attack. Within fifty years the Order was dissolved so Stanverital could merely have waited, had he lived long enough, for their demise and basked in the belief that they had been punished for deceiving him.

The second thing which Stanverital could not have known was the fact that the Universe would wait a thousand years to enact his dictated incantation. And he could have no vision of that time. He could not have understood the impact of his dictacy in a world where the Black Order had been replaced by many other 'influences of evil'. He also could not have known that no spells for good existed in this new world, except those that might be created by the Spell Spell. He could not have predicted that one of the many powers for good, in that time long in the future, would be an ordinary human being with an extraordinary desire to destroy one of the great immoral behemoths of the twenty-first century.

Nearly a thousand years after Stanverital had died, his dictacy was about to change the world forever.

28

Champagne and stories

Michael's relationship with Faith had flourished over the last few weeks. They had seen a lot of each other and Michael was beginning to think that he was falling in love for the very first time. She was everything he wanted in a girl; beautiful, clever and really interested in him. She was continually asking him questions about his life and his aspirations. He had not shared his real plans for IIBE, but he had decided that he would soon. He was falling in love with her so she deserved to know the truth.

Michael had decided to push the boat out and treat Faith to a fabulous lunch somewhere. He was not considering any of their usual haunts; he wanted to go somewhere really special. He was mentally going through the various posh places he had heard about when suddenly it came to him; it came out of the blue as if the thought had been forced into his brain. He decided they would lunch at the Ritz.

They arrived shortly after one o'clock and were shown to a table near the large windows that ran along one side of the dining area. Michael had not made a reservation so they were lucky to be given such a nice table. In the current economic climate, even the Ritz found it hard to fill the room, but they were still incredibly busy given the prices and circumstances. They settled in with a glass of wine and held hands across the table while they perused the menu.

Michael looked around the plush restaurant and congratulated himself on his choice. The place was alive with affluent looking couples, ladies doing lunch and businessmen oiling the wheels of multimillion pound deals. Everyone looked as though they were rich enough to dine in the Ritz every day; everyone that is, apart from the odd looking pair at the next table.

Michael wondered what their story was. They looked distinctly odd. What was this very old, bearded man doing here with the black haired youngster? They did not look comfortable in these surroundings; they did not look like a pair who could afford this sort of thing. Little did he know that they had access to more money and power than everyone else in the restaurant put together.

Conversely, Madrick and Tung felt totally at ease because they had dined here every day; breakfast, lunch and dinner, for nearly a week. They absolutely loved the food and the service; this century certainly had much more to offer the stomach than the one they had left far behind.

Michael did what he often did when he was out and about. He tried to construct little stories in his head about the people he saw. He had just started to think about Fagin from Oliver Twist when Madrick caught him looking at him. He was used to quizzical looks so he just smiled his best smile and got on with his food. Michael looked away guiltily and returned his attention to Faith. The imagined story of the strange pair would have to wait.

Michael was determined to make this a very special day for his relationship with Faith so he ordered champagne and asked if he could pop the cork himself. It was an unusual request, but always wanting to please his customers, the sommelier agreed. When the bottle arrived in its ice bucket, the waiter left it discretely on the table and backed away smiling. Michael lifted out the bottle and made a show of removing the gold foil and the wire cage.

Twist the bottle not the cork, he reminded himself. POPANG! The cork slipped out of his grasp and exploded out of the bottle. It travelled at lightning speed across the short distance to Tung's head. Fortunately, Tung was looking away at the time so his eyes were out of danger. Unfortunately the cork hit him hard on the tender, bruised part of his skull which was just beginning to get over all the previous impacts. Tung crashed off his chair and onto the floor. There was that split second when everybody froze and, as usual, it seemed to last forever. Then Michael and Faith broke their trance and rushed to see what they could do to help; Michael through fear of a law suit and Faith through compassion for a fellow human being. The sommelier watched from a distance and made a mental note not to agree to any self-opening requests in the future.

Michael and Faith rounded the table towards the stricken body. No one knew at the time, nor would they ever know, that this meeting had been brought about by a dictacy cast nearly a thousand years before.

"Are you OK?" asked Michael as he bent to help Tung to his feet. "I am so sorry, it just slipped out of my hand."

Faith took his elbow and helped guide him back onto his seat.

"I am all right. That was relatively painless compared to what my head has gone through over the last few weeks."

"I can't apologise enough," Michael persisted. "The thing just went off in my hand."

"Don't worry, I am all right… really. To tell you the truth I am well used to this sort of thing. I actually have not been struck on the head for a few days now so I was beginning to miss the sensation."

"At least let me treat you to some of our champagne," offered Michael, still keen to make sure this did not end badly in some sort of unpleasant legal dispute.

Neither Tung nor Madrick had sampled that particular liquid delicacy so this seemed like the ideal opportunity to try something new. Michael signalled to the waiter with the traditional shaky 'C' hands and, as soon as the extra glasses arrived, he filled them with sparkling wine.

"No hard feelings," proposed Michael.

"At least nothing harder than that cork, please," added Tung.

"And to meeting new people," said Faith to complete the toast.

The four clinked glasses and they all took a long sip.

"This is the fizziest, most wonderful drink I have ever tasted," bubbled Tung as the froth tickled the inside of his nose. "I thought beer was unbeatable but I just love this. We must have some more because a bottle doesn't seem to go very far.

"Unlike the cork!" he added with a chuckle.

He immediately called over the waiter and ordered a bottle of their best champagne. He had found that ordering 'the best' always got them terrific service and, after all, money was no object to the pair who had a seemingly endless supply of valuable gold coins.

"Careful," warned Michael. "That'll probably cost you over three hundred quid. This stuff is not cheap - particularly in this place!"

"We have plenty of money," said Tung slightly smugly and he ordered yet another bottle just to reinforce the point.

Madrick was slightly put out by this show of bravado. He hoped it was not going to lead to another unfortunate incident like the one in The Black Bear tavern all those years ago. But the champagne did taste good so another bottle or two would definitely go down well.

Long before the three bottles had been consumed, the group had pulled their tables together and, the way tipsy folk typically do, they were loudly making unrelated statements in opposition to having a conversation.

"Champagne for my real friends. Real pain for my sham friends," toasted Michael.

"Too much of anything is bad for you but too much champagne is just right," chirped in Faith.

"Here's to the champagne and caviar lifestyle. You just can't get enough of it, but I bet we'll feel that we had too much of it in the morning," shouted Michael wondering if they should order some caviar.

Before Michael had time to finish his thought about what they were missing from the champagne and caviar lifestyle, Tung had ordered four portions of the 'best caviar in the house'. This was definitely going to be a day of excess.

Tung felt the urge to add something to the banality. He decided to repeat Michael's clever toast - as best as he could remember it.

"Shampoo for my real friends. Real poo for my enemies."

They continued to drink until the waiters politely declined to bring more bottles. At that point Tung invited his new friends up to his suite and ordered a case of champers, as he had now learned to call it, to be delivered there as soon as possible. Michael and Faith gleefully accepted the offer and the four made their way to the lift.

"When we first arrived, we thought this was our room!" giggled Tung as he hit the button for the seventh floor.

They arrived a few minutes before the champagne so had time to settle into the comfortable leather chairs that littered the suite. A porter wheeled in twelve bottles each housed in its own ice bucket. The hotel had assumed the bottles were for a party - rather than just a party of four. There was trouble looming but no one was sober enough to notice. Not even Madrick, who had vowed after Tung's best trick in the world debacle, that he would never let Tung get drunk again; not even he could stop the booze inspired insanity that was about to ensue. He could not stop it because he was a willing participant in the fizzy madness.

They drank champagne until the early morning and, with each bottle, they talked more and more. The conversations were fun and helped them become ever more comfortable with each other.

"It's an unusual name you have, Tung, where does it come from?" asked Faith.

"It was my father's idea of a joke." Tung said. "Not only

140

was he a cruel, totally selfish and unloving drunkard... he gave me this appalling name. Some joke. Thanks, dad."

"I don't understand. How's it a joke? If it's just a silly name then it's just a silly name. I don't get it," chipped in Michael.

"Our family name is Tide. That makes me Tung Tide - tongue tied - ha ha."

"Oh right, that's quite funny actually. But I suppose it is a little bit mean. Why did he do it?"

"He felt he had no choice, at least that's what he always told me. His name was Hans - Hans Tide! Stupid family tradition, stupid family, stupid names."

"It could have been worse, you could have been called Low," smirked Michael.

"That is my middle name," said Tung as he downed the rest of his glass.

"I have spent my life listening to people making fun of my name. If I had a lepton for every time I'd heard 'Oh look the Tide's come in' then I'd have... a big pile of leptons."

His story had petered out a bit but he felt he had made his point. He hated his name. He hated all his names.

That was typical of the level of conversation, but as the evening wore on, and the champagne ran down, they began to share more intimate details... and some secrets.

Michael told of his aspiration to be super rich and, in the process, he was going to make the world a better place. He did not say how he was going to do it. Something stopped him. He was not sure why he did not share his plans for the bank. Was it the fact that Faith was there? Was she giving him a strange look or was that just his imagination?

Faith totally lied about her aspirations; she said she wanted to fall deeply and completely in love, she wanted to have at least five children and she gazed into Michael's eyes when she said it. She also said she was not interested in money, all she wanted was happiness. She suddenly felt a pang of guilt about lying and tried to deflect attention from herself by reverting to small talk.

"I heard a great quote once," she said. "'Burgundy makes you think of silly things, Bordeaux makes you talk about them, and Champagne makes you do them.'"

They all laughed a little even though Tung and Madrick had no idea what Burgundy or Bordeaux were. There were many things in this modern world that they still could not rationalise, in particular, the size of the world and the wide variety of countries and cultures. They were learning gradually because of the television, but the various regions in France that produced different wines would have been a wobbly step too far for now.

Madrick decided to follow on from her 'happiness' conversation so he told them that he just wanted to enjoy everything life had to offer. He nearly talked about how this century had so much more than the one he had come from, but he held himself back. Like Michael, he was not sure what had stopped him telling his tale. He need not have bothered holding back because Tung was about to open an incredibly wiggly can of worms and spill the beans.

Without any preamble, Tung launched into his story of Mifal's horrendous dungeon and the sorry life that had led him there. He described meeting Madrick and learning about the Scroll. He got really excited as he illustrated their adventures with florid descriptions of invisibility, the chase, flying, thunderballs and time travel.

"And here we are now," he concluded.

Madrick and Faith were soundly, and in Madrick's case noisily, asleep long before he got to the escape from Mifal's dungeon. Michael, on the other hand, managed to stay partially awake for the whole tale. However, he was so befuddled with champagne that the whole evening took on a dream like quality, but there was something about Tung and his saga that was going to stick in his mind.

This could be bigger than my IIBE cyber-raid, Michael

mused - although mushed was a more accurate description. Unfortunately, however, he was not going to remember much of this in the morning.

"This could be the most exciting thing that has ever happened to me" was his final though before he passed out on the plush leather sofa.

29

The morning after

They all woke up the next day dreadfully hung-over and feeling absolutely horrible. Madrick was the first to waken and he, very sensibly, ordered breakfast for four. By the time room service had arrived, everyone was conscious; more or less.

They all re-introduced themselves and reflected on what they remembered from the night before. They spread out the breakfast and all started to enjoy the relief that the fruit juice, assorted toast and fried food offered.

Madrick, Michael and Faith all showered (individually) while Tung dozed some more. By the time midday rolled around, everyone was feeling relatively human again. Each one of them was trying very hard to remember what they had said the night before, and what the others had said.

They collectively decided that they had thoroughly enjoyed their party experience. They were, however, too fragile to enjoy this inevitable morning after.

"I feel like the proverbial newspaper in the birdcage of life," said Michael trying to lighten the mood.

Tung and Madrick looked at him as if he was speaking a foreign language. Michael had no idea that neither understood the concept; no one had pet birds back in their day and, even if they had, they certainly would not have put something as valuable as paper in the bottom of their cages. Michael assumed that the hangovers were dulling everyone so he let it lie.

"We definitely overdid it last night. What started off fairly calmly ended up in a massive binge. We're all hurting a bit. I guess you could say we've all suffered minor binjuries."

No one even smiled. Maybe they are major binjuries, he thought.

With no encouragement from anyone in particular, they happily decided to meet again that evening, in the Ritz restaurant, to see how a more sober encounter would work.

On that note, Michael and Faith headed off to work. Madrick settled in front of the television to absorb more of the twenty-first century and Tung, naturally, went back to bed.

✿ ✿ ✿

All the way to the office, Michael and Faith talked excitedly about the evening of champagne, partying and chat. They were in no doubt that they should go back to the restaurant and meet again with the two, rather strange, individuals. It had genuinely been fun and Michael sensed that there was something intriguingly interesting about the pair. Neither of them had any memory of the incredible tale that Tung had told them although there was some remnant of the story in Michael's head; a remnant that he could not pin down. It had the evasiveness of a half remembered dream and the more he tried to recall it, the more it faded away.

As it turned out, Faith decided that she was far too ill to go out that night, indeed she left work early complaining of 'food poisoning'. However, Michael had an intense gut feeling, which was not food poisoning, that he should meet them again, so he decided to go alone.

He arrived at the Ritz shortly after six o'clock. His new friends were nowhere to be seen so he settled into a large leather armchair and ordered a coffee. Tung and Madrick arrived before the coffee did. They nodded awkwardly at each other because everyone was a bit unsure how this was going to pan out. They decided to adjourn to the restaurant and get some food under their belts before they started to dig too deeply into the night before.

After the small talk that accompanied the meal, Madrick launched into a short spiel about how they were strangers in these parts. It was a well practiced speech which had served them well up to now. He added that they had no close acquaintances here and that there was no one they could fully trust. They wanted to forge some lasting friendships otherwise, he explained, it would be impossible for them to 'fit in'. He did not expand on the reasons why. He did not want to share that for now.

Michael said he was honoured that they should consider him as a potential friend after such a short time. He confided that he had very few close friends that knew him intimately. He did not expand on the reasons why. He did not want to share that for now.

As the conversation progressed they shared more and more about each other and their aspirations. It got to the point where Madrick and Tung looked at each other and nodded conspiratorially.

What Michael did not know was that Madrick had remembered enough from the night before to believe that Michael might have a guilty secret about his intentions at his work place. He had discussed it with Tung and they had agreed that Michael had, possibly unwittingly, started to share an intimate confidence with them. They felt that if Michael had his own secrets then maybe he was a good person with whom to share their secret. They needed to get some allies in this new century because, deep down, they both knew they could not survive forever hiding in the Ritz. They needed to take a chance and if it went wrong they would just move on.

"Come up to our suite, we would like to tell you a bit more about us," said Tung. "We have secrets and surprises which will blow your head."

He meant 'blow your mind'. He was trying to pick up the more modern way of speaking, but he was not always successful.

"I'd like that," said Michael. "I have something I'd like to share with you guys too."

What Madrick and Tung did not know was that Michael

had some deep down residual memory about Tung's champagne inspired story and he wanted to find out more. Also, he had grown to quite like the pair.

When they arrived in the suite they settled into the leather furnishings and decided they would chance a glass of champagne; there was plenty left from their last party. Madrick spoke first, adopting the storytelling tone he had used when he first met Tung.

"We have decided to trust you with an incredible secret. It is all true but you will not believe it. Tung will tell you our tale because he is a bit more entertaining than me."

That surprised Tung and he was glad because he did find Madrick's story telling technique to be a bit dry and boring. So, in a repeat of the night before, Tung launched into his story of Mifal's dungeon and the horror of what lay before him.

"And then the horror came to pass. I met Madrick!"

He was enjoying telling the tale and saw no reason why he should not pepper it with a little humour. Even Madrick smiled.

He talked about the Scroll and described some of the spells he created.

"The stallion was magnificent. The weather forecast was pointless and wrong."

"Still the same today," agreed Michael. "But you don't need a weatherman to know which way the wind blows."

Michael half said and half sung the last bit. Bob Dylan would not have been overly proud but he would not have disowned his song on account of this rendering. Madrick and Tung looked at him as if he had lost his mind.

"Blowin' in the Wind," he said before he realised that he was merely compounding the problem. He signalled Tung to continue.

"Then I totally cracked it. I created the spell that could make us invisible."

He paused for effect before he continued to describe the chase, the chickens, bird man, thunderballs and the time-travel.

"And here we are now," he concluded.

It was like a very weird déjà vu for Michael; even though he felt he had heard it all before, he had no idea what was coming next. It was a strange feeling, however, the fact that he already had this incredible tale stored somewhere deep in his subconscious made it, for some reason, more believable. Well, less unbelievable maybe.

Michael stared at Tung and Madrick. He was not sure what to make of what he had just heard. He felt it was best not to ask any questions until he had absorbed it a bit. So, he decided to share his story.

He started to tell them about his skill with computers, but it became apparent very quickly that this made no sense whatsoever to the pair. He simplified his story.

"I work in a bank. It's the richest bank in the world. I plan to steal all their money."

"Where will you hide it? How will you carry it all?" asked Tung who was immediately interested in the theft even though he had absolutely no need for money now they had the pouch of gold.

"It's not actual money that I'll steal," he began, however he stopped when he saw the look of confusion on both their faces. Could they really be from the past, he wondered?

"I'll explain it all some other time. Tell me more about you guys. Exactly where are you from? Or should I say when? Your story is a bit strange to say the least."

Madrick realised how astonishing their tale would sound to someone who had never come across magic. He decided that a demonstration may help convince Michael to totally believe them. He handed Michael the pouch.

"Feel that," he said. "How many coins are in it?"

Michael felt the soft leather between his fingers and

thumbs.

"Two, maybe three," he said puzzled by the change in the conversation.

"There are two," said Madrick. "Lift them out and have a look."

Michael took the money out of the pouch and was immediately taken by the beauty of the large gold coins. They were in pristine condition and had identical dates which placed them at the turn of the first millennium. He examined them more closely. They were superbly crafted and absolutely immaculate.

"These are the most fabulous coins I have ever seen," marvelled Michael. "They are in such perfect condition. I could nearly believe they are brand new rather than nearly a thousand years old."

He was fascinated by the sheer beauty and he wondered where they had got the coins. They could have come from anywhere, bought or stolen, so this certainly did not prove their story.

"How many coins are in the bag?" asked Madrick.

"None," replied Michael. "I have them both here in my hand."

"Look again."

Michael felt the pouch and was flabbergasted to find two more identical coins.

"Again," said Madrick and again Michael pulled two more coins out of the bag. He examined the bag in minuscule detail, but he had no way to explain what was happening. He knew that there was, in fact, only one possible explanation; it was genuine magic. And if this was real magic then maybe the whole story was true.

Madrick watched him as he went through the thought process of trying to rationalise their incredible tale. He knew that Michael was on the brink of belief, but he had no idea how to tip him over the edge. Maybe the brink was enough for now, he thought, only time would tell.

30

Can you believe it?

Michael felt completely confused and a little disorientated. He had been introduced to an unbelievable fantasy world yet he was convinced it was as real as anything else in his life. He knew he was going to have to totally realign his sense of the universe; he just hoped he was capable of the mental leap.

He felt he had been asked to believe something that previously, in his mind, was in the domain of science fantasy. Of course he had read tales of time travel, but come on, he thought, surely it is not possible. He had been shown real magic, there was no doubt in his mind that it was real. But come on, there's no way this can be happening, he thought. It was the ultimate dilemma, he had seen things that were patently true, however, the explanations were completely unbelievable. In fact, there were no rational explanations at all.

His heart wanted to believe because that could open up the most exciting adventure ever. His head was having none of it. His head seemed incapable of accepting what was plain for the eye to see.

After a little time to reflect, he decided that all he could do was try and fully embrace what had just happened. He would convince his head to accept what his heart was telling him. He needed to open his mind and see where things led him. If this was all true then he had an unparalleled opportunity to influence how a major force of nature impacted on the world. If this is true, he thought, this was way more important than his 'destroy IIBE' plan; this could be the way he was going fulfil his fantasy dream and change things on this dying planet. This could be the ultimate opportunity to stick it to the bad guys.

"Well, what do you think? I know this will have come as

a crazy shock to you, but do you think you can accept what you have been told?"

"I'm struggling with this. I'm a great believer that you should avoid zebra thinking at all costs."

"Zebra thinking?"

"Ignoring the obvious answer. Making things too complicated. When you hear hooves coming up behind you, you should think horse, not zebra."

He saw the confused look on their faces. His story about keeping things simple was having exactly the opposite effect.

"You don't know what a zebra is, do you?" said Michael disappointedly.

They both shook their heads.

"It's a horse with black and white stripes, but you only get them in Africa. We don't have them in England so the hooves you hear will probably belong to a horse. Look for the obvious answer."

"And what's the big difference between getting trampled by a horse and a zebra?" asked Tung.

Michael gave up with the explanation. He knew he had been lucky to get away with mentioning 'Africa' never mind the other problems.

"I'm just saying there is no obvious answer here. I need to think outside the box with this one."

"Outside the box?" said Tung.

It was Madrick who put an end to it. He realised that there were times when it was best to let some of the modern expressions fly over one's head.

"Let's take a break. We're all tired."

Michael took a quick comfort break and by the time he got back, Tung had faded and gone back to bed.

"He says he's suffering from hallucinations, but I think he's just imagining it. I think last night has got the better of him and he needs more sleep."

Madrick looked very weary too, but he was still very much

focused on Michael. He realised how important it was to bring Michael along with them.

"Do you think you can trust us? More important, do you think you can become our friend? What we have here is truly amazing and we need someone from this century to help us survive and thrive. Could that someone be you? Please, we are asking you to be that somebody."

Michael thought for a few seconds before he realised that logic was not going to help him with the answer. He had always relied on his ability to judiciously analyse all the possibilities of a situation and come up with the right course of action, but that was not going to help him this time. This was not one of those 'normal' situations. This was a zebra outside the box.

"I don't know," he said honestly. "This is a lot to take on board in one go. My heart says embrace it and, funny enough, I guess so does a part of my head. The problem is the other part of my head says this whole thing is ridiculous. The other part of my head is holding me back. I want to go with this, I do."

Suddenly, it was like some switches had flicked inside his head. There were still doubts, but the part of his head that had been stamping on this lunacy seemed to have unilaterally surrendered and given up on the argument. He felt a surge of relief and contentment.

"I am going to force myself to go with this. It's incredibly strange, just like most of life. Let's toast life's mysteries and our newly formed friendship! I'm game to sign up to this adventure wherever it leads us.

"Here's to magic scrolls and dreams coming true. Here's to us and a better world… chink-chink."

"With our combined efforts, the sky is the limit," said Madrick.

"Don't tell me the sky's the limit, I know there are footsteps on the moon," replied Michael.

He loved this expression and, for the first time, it seemed genuinely appropriate. Madrick looked utterly and totally confused, then Michael realised yet again that there was still an awful lot that Madrick did not know about the modern world. The moon landing was probably far beyond his ancient mentality for now. One small step for a man was definitely one giant leap too far for Madrick.

There was an extended pause as they waited for a change of subject and they both hoped it would change into something more comfortable.

Eventually they broke the awkward silence by chinking glasses again and settling into the comfy sofas. This was the start of something special. They knew that for certain. Both men knew that they had some exciting adventures lined up in their futures; they knew they were in for a crazy roller coaster ride albeit Madrick had no idea what a roller coaster was.

After a bit more discussion and a few more shared secrets, Michael said he wanted to have some time to himself to reflect on what he had heard and to think about what they should do next. He did not want too long to ponder, he was worried he might change his mind, so they agreed to meet again for lunch tomorrow.

As a parting gesture, Madrick gave him one of the coins so he could remind himself of the inexplicable magic and to authenticate its value if he wanted to. It was a nice gesture that helped reinforce Michael's belief that these were good guys and he was doing the right thing.

He loved the coin but decided not to keep it. After all there were plenty more where it came from - wherever that was. He decided it was important to find out if it was genuine or just a part of an ingenious scam so he dropped into a small jewellery shop he passed as he walked to the station. The man was totally lethargic about the prospect of yet another lump of gold destined for the big smelting pot. That all changed, as soon as he saw the Aethelred. He took it in his hand and fondled it between finger and thumb. He asked where it had come from. Then, before Michael had a chance to answer, he said it didn't matter. It took all his strength to curb his excitement, but he still offered a thousand pounds because he was determined to have the beautiful coin and he knew it was worth at least twice that sum. Michael had no interest in negotiating so he happily accepted. He was not there for the money per se, he was there for confirmation that the coin was indeed something very special and it obviously was.

He went home and lay on his settee thinking about the last couple of days. He knew deep down that he was already committed to believing in the madness; maybe he should be committed full stop he thought! He was a born planner so he started to carefully map out in his mind how he and the two travellers could make the most of this strange opportunity. He also wondered whether he should tell Faith. He had no idea how she would react to this incredible story so he decided against sharing it for the time being. He was not sure why. Could it be that he was just too embarrassed? If she had come to him with the same story he would have labelled her as a total nut job.

Back at the hotel, Madrick and Tung also reflected on their afternoon meeting. Madrick in particular felt it had gone well because they all had lots to gain from working together and, probably more importantly, lots to lose if they did not. He also knew that, even though they had done well so far on their own, they would not prosper in this crazy new world without help, and Michael could definitely help them.

"I think he will be back. I think he believes us."

"I hope so," said Tung, "because I sense there's trouble on the way."

31

Sixteen Aethelreds

Since the creation of the magic pouch, Madrick had used, gifted or cashed in twenty-one of the gold Aethelred II coins. These Aethelreds were bought and sold by a series of traders, each one along the chain making a very healthy profit. Eventually, sixteen of the coins ended up on a deep brown, highly polished mahogany table being stared at by four, rather sombre looking, suited men.

These were extremely rare coins and six weeks ago there were very few known examples in the world, and not one of them was in anything like this uncirculated condition. Now, within the space of a few weeks, sixteen perfect examples had turned up in the city. This was just one of a series of strange occurrences that the men were now investigating.

They examined the coins in great detail and marvelled at their beauty. They knew they had to find out exactly where they had originated and why they were now appearing in such numbers.

"We need to keep a very close eye on this," said the tallest man carefully replacing the coin beside the others.

The sixteen circles of gold were identical; they all had the same date and they were all in pristine condition. It was as if they had been taken directly from the engraver's die and stored in protective isolation for nearly a thousand years.

"Maybe a secret collector has decided to sell off part of an illicit collection."

"No, it is something different. A collector would know the value and would not have sold them all over the city for a fraction of their worth, even if his collection had been gathered illegally."

"Maybe they were stolen from a collection and the thief did not know the value of what he had stolen."

"Very unlikely because a thief would usually off-load his proceeds to a single fence. I think there is more to this than we can explain. We need to find out quickly what is going on."

They researched the history of the coins and consulted experts in the field. They checked with listed collectors, and some unlisted ones. They used their connections so they could talk to the directors of banks whose vaults contained secret stashes of gold, like Nazi gold, but no one could shed light on the mystery. They even referred to ancient manuscripts from their own extensive library in an attempt to work out how so many of these pristine Aethelreds could have turned up at precisely the same time. They came up with no logical or reasonable explanation.

This research process was becoming uncomfortable because they had been forced to contact outsiders and they never liked interacting with the outside world. It was much better to remain apart and in the background; any attention they drew to themselves was unwelcome and potentially harmful to the organisation. As much as they disliked talking with these strangers, they felt they had no choice because they had exhausted the 'easy' options. It was clear that they needed much more specific information about this treasure.

Reluctantly they sent out sixteen of their trusted agents; each was tasked with tracing a single coin back to its source. Once they knew where the Aethelreds had come from, they were confident they could decide whether they needed to take action.

Even though the agents were all loyal servants, they would not be told the whole story. They would be blinkered in their search, however, that was probably not a bad thing. That would allow them to focus exclusively on their individual tasks without the distraction of the big picture and without the pressure of knowing the importance of their mission.

"This is the right thing to do. Our agents will track down

the source. They will find out if there is more than one individual who is selling these coins. We must wait and see what they discover. It will not take them long."

The four nodded in agreement. They wanted to find a simple explanation, but they were becoming increasingly concerned about the growing numbers of strange incidents that were being reported from around the city. They knew that they had to move with great urgency because their guts told them that something big was stirring. They needed to understand everything about each event and work out if, and how, they were all connected.

They needed to gather all the detail very quickly because their boss had demanded a formal report. That demand was not to be treated lightly because their boss was the Great Grand Master of the Occultus Populous.

32

Fish tales

Madrick, Tung and Michael were enjoying yet another lunch at the Ritz. This was definitely a perfect way to spend an afternoon; except he missed Faith. He was there again without her because he had decided not to share this secret until he knew what direction things were going to go.

"Where's Faith?"

"She's still not feeling the best. Does that girl get hangovers, or what?"

"My guess is yes," said Tung.

"That was a rhetorical question," said Michael.

"What's a rhetorical question?"

"It's a question that doesn't want an answer."

"Then what's the point of asking it? That's just annoying."

"Is there anything more annoying than a rhetorical question?" replied Michael rhetorically.

"No, I don't think there is," said Tung as the joke flew silently and unnoticed over his head.

They got back to their meals and the talk began to get more serious. It was time to get down to business. By the time they had finished their main courses, they were deep in meaningful conversation. Each of them had reiterated what their priorities were. Tung wanted to live it up at the Ritz; forever. Michael wanted to destroy IIBE and become very rich in the process. Madrick wanted a quiet life of luxury. He emphasised 'quiet life' because he knew there were people who would do anything to steal the Scroll so it had to remain a well guarded secret.

They chatted easily about how they could achieve their aspirations. Michael started again to try and explain the outline of his hacking plan. Once again, it soon became clear that they were not going to grasp any of it. He decided it was better to hear what way the travellers wanted to go.

Tung, Madrick and Michael now shared an increasing level of trust. They all knew secrets about each other and that was a good building block. Also, there were true friendships developing within the group.

Madrick, therefore, had little hesitation in asking Tung, in front of Michael, to create the next spell. They had decided to leave him 'empty' for a while because Madrick suspected that constantly carrying round an active spell might cause problems. He did not know for sure, but they had seemed safe in the Ritz haven so it had definitely been a good time to let Tung's mind rest. It had worked out fine so far, but Madrick knew they could cope better with anything unexpected if they had a protective spell up their sleeves. Also, it would be the final proof for Michael and should cement his belief in their story.

Tung duly obliged as Michael watched in fascination; he was slightly disappointed in the event because nothing particularly dramatic happened. Tung merely wobbled a bit on his feet, as if he was going to faint, but then he was back to normal almost immediately.

"I see a giant fish. A great big silver fish with intense black eyes and two pointy fins on its back," said Tung without being asked.

"This is an easy one. You are going to create an enormous, delicious fish which will be so big it could feed a small village. In fact, two of these fish would be enough to feed five thousand people. It is of no worth to us so you might as well do it and get it out of the way."

It was indeed an enormous fish and actually not so easy to 'get it out of the way' thought Tung. The monster now lay in the middle of the lounge area, half of it on the floor and half of it draped over one of the leather sofas. Michael gawped, and his mouth dropped open, as he watched the magic unfold in front of his eyes. His face froze in amazement and he looked quite a lot like the fish, which must have been equally surprised by events.

"That is going to be very smelly very soon," said Tung as he prepared the next spell.

Michael watched totally transfixed as Tung formed spell after spell. He used them to create a white marble statue of a beautiful woman, a black bearskin fur coat, a small sack of gem stones, a great bronze battle shield and an elephant's foot. There had been many rather silly and pointless spells up to now, but not even Madrick could conjure up any sort of reasonable explanation for the foot.

Michael did not say anything, but he knew now, for certain, that the amazing tales of the Scroll, time travel, hunters, escape and adventure were all true. Strap yourself in, he thought, the roller-coaster is heading up the first big incline.

Michael surveyed the mess in the room and made an instant decision.

"You are going to have to get out of here before that fish rots. Why not come and stay at my place, it won't be as comfortable, but it will give us some time to work out how to keep you guys out of trouble."

After a short confab, Madrick and Tung agreed. They packed their small collection of possessions into their backpacks and said a final goodbye to their luxury room. It had served them well - the hotel staff had served them well.

Before they left, Tung put the fur coat on the statue and placed her hand in the giant fish's mouth. Also, just for good measure, he attached the great battle shield to the side of the fish. That will surely confuse whoever finds this he thought; as if they were not going to be confused enough by Moby Dick and his lady friend!

33

A land far away

After they checked out of the Ritz, they made their way on foot to the nearest underground train station. Michael bought tickets and led the way to the platform.

This was a new adventure for Tung and he became quite agitated as they descended farther and farther into the bowels of the earth. Madrick took it in his stride although his first attempt to board an escalator had not gone well. He had not realised the stairs were moving and, to compound the problem, he had chosen the up escalator rather than the down because it was less crowded. Why is no one using these stairs, he wondered, as he stepped faster and faster, but seemed to be getting no-where? When he stopped walking he was surprised to find himself moving in reverse. He toppled backwards when he came back to the top, but Michael managed to catch him before any real damage was done.

Michael led the way onto the down side and, after a bit of wobbling, the others managed to get on safely behind him. They were well before the rush hour so at least they did not have the added scariness of thousands of rushing bodies and packed trains. This was a particularly frightening experience; this train was a lot faster and noisier than anything they had ever experienced before. They both held on tightly to their seats; seats that would not have been available if it had been the rush hour.

In less than thirty minutes they arrived at the station nearest the apartment. Madrick carefully followed Michael's lead when they came to any stairs because he did not want a repeat of the earlier 'wrong escalator' fiasco. When they all eventually surfaced, it took less than ten minutes to cover the short walk to the first floor flat in a converted warehouse. It was not as plush as the Ritz by any stretch of the imagination, but it was a fantastic home for one so young.

Michael gave them a lightening tour of the place, ending up in the bedroom that would be their resting place for the foreseeable future. Tung looked disappointed - his aspirations had certainly changed in the short time he had been in the twenty-first century. He lay down on one of the beds and promptly fell asleep before he had the chance to complain. Madrick lay on the other bed and thought about the crazy turn his life had taken over the past few weeks, but he decided he was very happy and was looking forward to whatever the universe had planned for him. Soon he too was asleep; dreaming his dreams.

Michael did what he always did when he got home; he logged onto his computer and started to trawl through his emails, messages and, most important, his monitoring programs. They automatically kept an electronic eye on IIBE. They helped him keep on top of his job and told him if all the key systems were functioning as they should be. They let him know if anyone was looking for him and they identified any unusual activity on the network.

His programs also allowed him to monitor what other people were doing. He had a quick look through his boss's emails and those of the chairman and some of the bank's other senior managers and directors. Information is power, but this time there was nothing of particular interest so he logged off.

He was still fairly relaxed about IIBE because he had not activated phase two of his plan yet. That was when he would siphon off money into random accounts as a distraction for the security department and that was when he would have to start worrying. All the adventures with Tung and Madrick had put his plan on hold for the time being. Once phase two was in play he would have to spend a lot more time monitoring their reaction and taking evasive action as necessary.

Suddenly he felt ravenous so he went to his small kitchen to rustle up some food for himself and his new house guests. He chose two big pizzas because they were easy to heat and easy to eat, and they always went well with a few bottles of beer. And he felt like a few bottles of beer.

The gas oven did not flick into life - it did that sometimes. He rummaged around the 'stuff' drawer and eventually found the electronic pilot light lighter. He went back to the oven, held the tip against the pilot and hit the button. The bright blue spark jumped from the tip to the gas.

It was not a big explosion, but it was enough to singe off most of Michael's eyebrows. It also brought the others running to see what had happened.

"Are you OK? You're not out here messing about with magic, are you?"

"No," he smiled at the thought. "Just a small problem with the gas."

"What have you done to your face?"

He rubbed his hand over his face and could feel the prickly remnants of his eyebrows.

"Just a minor sinjury!" he said as he popped the pizzas into the now lit oven.

An hour later they were all in front of the big television enjoying the simple dinner. Tung had forgotten the joy of simple food, and beer, so now he was thinking that Michael's place might not be so bad after all. He used to be easily pleased, but the Ritz had spoiled him a bit - happily though, the beer had brought Mr Easy back.

The news was on in the background and suddenly it caught their attention. There was a story about an inexplicable discovery at the Ritz. A reporter was standing outside the hotel trying to describe the bizarre scene that one of the chambermaids had come across. They cut to an interview with the maid.

"It was unbelievable. I opened up the room as usual and wheeled my cart in. And there it was - a giant fish eating a statue which had a black fur coat on. I couldn't help it, I started screaming. It was the weirdest thing ever."

They cut away from the interview and showed a photograph of the room. It certainly was the weirdest thing ever. The three of them laughed out loud and clinked bottles.

"All in a day's work," said Michael. "But hold on. That's a bit strange."

"Of course it's a bit strange," giggled Tung. "I made it that way!"

"No. That's not what I mean. Look. Remember the shield? The shield has gone."

They all looked at the image. There was the scene exactly the way Tung had left it. There was the statue in the fur coat with its hand in the mouth of the big silver fish; but Michael was right, there was no shield. They started to speculate about what might have happened when the hotel manager appeared on the screen.

"Can you tell us anything about the person who had been staying in the room?" asked the interviewer.

"Well, it was actually a bit unusual. There were two of them - a father and son. They gave their names as Tung and Madrick Tide. The father, Madrick, had very long grey hair and a long grey beard. He seemed very... I don't know how to describe it... old-fashioned. The son didn't say much, but he seemed old-fashioned as well. The unusual thing was that they paid us with cash and, we've only realised now, they didn't give a home address. They told the receptionist that they were from a 'land far away' and that's what they wrote in the register for their address - a land far away!"

"And where are they now?"

"I don't know," said the manager. "They checked out earlier today and left no forwarding address. We would like to talk to them because it seems the statue and fur coat are extremely valuable. We have the items safely stored for them. We pride ourselves in returning anything our guests have left in their rooms.

"We are not planning to store the fish though," he added with a smile.

The manager was relishing this opportunity to promote the Ritz on television. He would have continued to talk about how wonderful his hotel was, but the interviewer cut him off in mid flow and turned to the camera.

"This is a fascinating story. There are so many unanswered questions. We will keep you posted about any developments, but in the meantime, please contact us if you know who these men are because we would love to talk to them. This is John Black, Channel 6 News, reporting from the Ritz Hotel in London, England. Now back to the news desk," he said and the report was over.

They watched for a few minutes to see if any more was going to be said. Michael then flicked round some of the other news channels to see if they had picked up on the story. There did not appear to be any more coverage for the time being.

"We certainly made an impression," said Madrick somewhat smugly.

"The fur coat on the statue was genius. They will never work out what happened," said Tung proudly.

"Let's hope not. Media attention is the last thing we need."

Michael was not as happy as the others and pointed out how dangerous this was. His aspiration to maintain a low profile had been spectacularly scuppered. Tung and Madrick outwardly agreed, but inside they were both quite enjoying their fifteen minutes of fame.

That evening, the Ritz restaurant had its busiest night for years because of the excitement generated by the extremely strange findings in one of their hotel rooms. The fish pie special was particularly popular.

34

An interesting time

"There is great strangeness afoot. I believe things are happening that we must understand and over which we must take control," said the tallest man.

"I agree. There have been too many extraordinary goings-on recently for it to be mere coincidence. The bizarre scene at the Ritz leaves me in little doubt of the grave magnitude of what is happening. I think we are seeing something incredible and frightening unfold."

"It is definitely an interesting time in which we live! But before we make any earth shattering decisions, let us hear the reports about the coins."

"Yes. We should have all the information available before we debate our next steps."

On his instruction, the agents who had been tracking the coins were ushered into the room and the four sombre men listened to the lengthy reports of how the Aethelreds had been traced to their source.

To date, they had successfully tracked seven of the coins. Six trails led back to an old bearded man who had traded single coins in 'Sell your Gold' and antique shops. The storekeepers had all given similar descriptions of the man and they all remarked that there was something a little strange about him; something very old fashioned that they could not quite put their fingers on.

The last trail led back to a young, very modern man. That did not fit the pattern, but all the information they could gather was important.

When the agents had left, the four discussed what they had heard. One particular piece of information linked the coins to the events at the Ritz - the description of the old man. Also the epicentre of the great KABOOM noise appeared to have been around the Ritz Hotel.

They decided that they should dedicate all their local resources to tracking the old man and his companion. They summoned the captain of the Occultus Populous agents and gave him a detailed briefing, stressing the importance and urgency of his mission. The manhunt was underway.

In parallel, the four men began a search of their extensive archives to see if there was any guidance from the past to help them solve this present day mystery. Only one of them knew precisely what he was looking for. He had researched many of the archives as part of his training when he was a young man. He was recognised as being the expert, but the annals were so extensive that no man could know them completely. There had been a plan once to computerise the records, however that had been abandoned before it had started. It was now believed that most of the chronicles were myth and mythology and the Council did not want to propagate the fantasy and deflect the organisation from its more tangible pursuit, namely the pursuit of wealth and power.

For the next three days they all leafed through the piles of old manuscripts that had been treasured by the Society since its formation. They scoured the selected parchments, searching for clues that would help them understand what was happening in the city streets around them. They hoped they would get guidance from the past to help them solve the mysteries of the present, but only one of them was confident that this was where they would find the answer.

"Here. Here is the one I was looking for. Listen to this," said the most senior of the four. "This was supposedly written by Gravalar, one of the founders of our great Society and the original Great Grand Master."

His finger rested halfway down the parchment. It was written in Salatin, a language that pre-dated, and was in fact the root of, Latin. He read out loud, translating as he went.

"We tracked them by the day and rested only when the

darkness cloaked our passage. We followed a rich trail of evidence left by their magic-making. We gleaned information from the peasants of the land. The trail led us to an old tavern that overlooked the sea. We entered and there were many people. We caught a brief sight of the thieves. One was an old man with a lengthy grey beard. His hair was long, grey and dishevelled. The other was a young man with curled black hair. I did not get more than the shortest glimpse of the thieves so my description of them lacks deep clarity."

He scanned the rest of the page and then turned to the next, muttering as he read the words to himself. At last he reached the part he was looking for.

"We shattered the door and burst into their sleeping chamber. And they were there. And then they were gone. And with them was the Scroll. My belief told me they had shifted through the time of human man. This too was the conclusion of the Great Grandee."

The men sat in silence for a minute or two.

"This is it. We must gather the Council," said one.

"I agree and we must do it immediately," said another.

"This is why our Society has been in existence for a thousand years. We are the chosen ones because the prophecy is beginning to happen as we speak," said the third.

"By all that is sacred," added the forth. "We are blessed. We are about to witness a momentous event unfold before our very eyes."

They knew what they had to do so they did it. They started the process that would lead to the gathering of the Occultus Populous Council. This would be the first time that the full Council had been convened in over two hundred and fifty years. They knew it was a colossal occasion. They knew their actions would have far reaching consequences, but they did not realise that they had set in motion a chain of events that would change the world forever.

35

ALPP119829837

Word was about to go out across the globe to the forty-eight members of the Great Council of the Occultus Populous. A Council meeting was to be convened.

This was a truly momentous occasion as the last full meeting had been at the end of 1789 when the French Revolution and other peasant unrest across Europe had greatly concerned the ruling elite. At the same time the US Bill of Rights had been adopted. The common people were getting too organised and the elite were beginning to lose control.

The Council Members were, of course, in regular contact. In the past, communication had been slow and complicated. Now, they used all the modern communication channels to keep each other informed about developments and initiatives that offered opportunities to make money. They had sophisticated electronic voting mechanisms that allowed them to agree policies and make collective decisions. They could contact each other at any time of the day or night, but they had not all been present for a real time meeting for nearly two hundred and fifty years - albeit, this time, they would not be physically in the same room.

That eighteenth century meeting had been extremely successful and great plans which shaped the future of the world were agreed and put in place. This was no less than the Members had expected, after all they were the greatest minds and most powerful men on the planet.

Within ten years, the common man was back in his place and the rightful order had been restored. The power of the Occultus Populous was undeniable, but of course, only they knew that they were in charge and making the big decisions that shaped people's lives. The rich and powerful had regained full control and again they all slipped into the background.

Each Member of the Council individually controlled his own geography. These people were the monarchs, the presidents, the business leaders, a few legendary criminal geniuses and the super rich. These people were the ones who initiated great global events, but they always pre-warned all other Members so everyone could take advantage. World Wars One and Two were perfect examples of that. Those two events alone had made eye watering sums of money for many of the Members. There had been millions killed, but as always, it was the common man who made the sacrifice so the rich and powerful could become richer and more powerful still.

Now there had been a coming together of circumstances in the United Kingdom which could threaten their power so it demanded their collective attention. It was not a mass rising like the French Revolution. This time it was much more threatening, this time there was magic afoot. And the magic was in the hands of others - not theirs.

✿ ✿ ✿

The encrypted and top secret email invitation arrived in the inbox of all forty-eight Council Members virtually simultaneously. They had all been briefed about the impending meeting and had been told when the email would hit their systems. Some had been warned about the purpose of the gathering whereas for others the email was the first detail they had been given of an impending crisis.

Each one read the email very carefully and immediately began rearranging their schedules, meetings and work commitments so they could attend the Council Meeting. Not one of them considered, not for even a second, missing the Meeting. Everything else faded into the background. The Meeting took total precedence. This had a ripple effect in some very high places around the world as crucial business meetings were put on hold, public engagements were cancelled and major plans were delayed. All the Members were very influential people so clearing their diaries inevitably had a wide ranging impact.

By way of preparation, the Members organised immediate and full briefings. They demanded to see every piece of evidence collected so far. Each Member studied what they were sent in minute detail; they all wanted to make sure they were ready for the Meeting.

While worldwide arrangements were being made, the men who sent the email on behalf of Buckingham continued their investigation into the strange happenings around their city.

✿ ✿ ✿

One man who knew all about the Meeting and the email was Sir Samuel Buckingham, the Chairman of the International Investment Bank of Europe. He had worked with the four men in the drafting of the email and he had authorised its distribution.

He was talking to a fellow bank director in his office when his message announced its arrival by beeping on his PC. When he saw the subject line he politely, yet firmly, asked to be left alone and he instructed his secretary to hold all calls until further notice.

He opened the small safe which was cleverly hidden in the wall behind him and removed the de-encryption device which he deftly hooked into his computer. He disconnected the PC from the network and leaned close to the screen on his desk. It would be obvious to any observer that this was not the first time he had used this particular device.

He opened the email and read it carefully. He was checking that it had been sent exactly as he had agreed it. He knew that precise wording was vital to ensure there was no ambiguity and no room for misunderstanding.

Subject: *Pricing Reports Now Available ref ALPP119829837*

This was the only part of the email which was unencrypted. It was a meaningless subject line to the uninformed so it should not raise any suspicions amongst the hundreds of emails which passed across the recipients' desktops. They would all recognise the secret number immediately and follow procedure, just as Buckingham was doing now.

He settled into his chair as he waited for the special device, which now hung from his PC, to do its thing. After a few seconds, the body of the email had been de-encrypted and he began to read.

Subject: *Pricing Reports Now Available ref ALPP119829837*
After solemn and due consideration, the European Executive of the Occultus Populous has deemed it appropriate and necessary to convene a meeting of the full Grand Council. This decision has been ratified by the Great Grand Master.
Magic which is outside our control has been used on at least twelve different occasions. Our research has pointed to the strong possibility that the time travellers have arrived with the Scroll.
Council members will congregate at their designated locations at 07.45 GMT 17 inst..

His eye ran down the locations, it was an impressive array of buildings; every one of them highly prestigious and iconic, including his own, the headquarters of the International Investment Bank of Europe (London).

The email was electronically signed by the four Masters of the European Executive.

He had made all the preparations he could at his end. He had all the evidence gathered and he had his speech written and practised. Even he was slightly nervous about the occasion. You did not bring together some of the world's most influential people and then fluff your lines.

He had organised that an Occultus Populous agent would work with him to ready the secret teleconferencing facility within his headquarters. He was going to make sure that the technology worked and did not interfere with their gathering.

He knew that four fellow Council members would physically join him in London for the Meeting. They would stay in the private quarters, on the top floor of the building, away from prying eyes and they would stay for as long as it took to agree their plan of action.

Buckingham reclined in his leather chair and pondered the gravity of the situation. He was well aware of all the strange incidents which were going on in London; in his City. He, as Great Grand Master, had been regularly briefed since the first suspected magic episode had occurred. The incidents kept happening and the evidence of the presence of the travellers had mounted until he had no hesitation in ratifying the decision to convene a full Council meeting. It was clearly the only possible course of action.

The call had now gone out and history was about to be made.

36

Other people's emails

The television coverage had put everyone a little bit on edge except Tung who was still secretly basking in the glory of his new found celebrity. Michael was particularly worried because he knew the reach that this type of broadcast had and there were any number of people who could have spotted them and reported the sighting to the TV station. He knew how much Joe Public valued even five minutes of fame so anyone who had seen them was likely to try and get themselves on TV.

They definitely did not want to be found because there was just no way to explain the strange objects that had been left in the hotel room. Michael had no idea how they would be treated if they were tracked down, but he knew he did not want to find out.

"This is worrying," said Michael. "You guys probably don't understand the reach that this kind of coverage has."

"But we're famous. That's got to be good."

"That is definitely not good. We don't want to draw attention to ourselves. We must keep that in our heads - low profile. Keep things simple - everything we do must be simple as ABC."

As soon as he said it he realised it was a poor choice of simile. Tung could not read so ABC was distinctly not simple.

"Low profile," he repeated. "Low profile."

Michael was also troubled because he had not seen Faith in person since the crazy champagne party. He had talked to her on the phone on numerous occasions, but the conversations had been very superficial; he had not even told her about his subsequent meetings with Tung and Madrick. He was not sure why he was keeping that a secret, but his gut told him to keep it to himself for now.

She had not been back to work since the infamous party; her hangover had morphed into a severe dose of the flu. Michael felt sorry for her, but it gave him some time and space to sort out what direction his life was going to take without dragging her along this unknown path. He thought it would be better to wait and then share everything with her once he had some sort of idea how it was all going to pan out.

He turned up at the office just before nine o'clock and got stuck into his work straight away. He was distracted most of the day, thinking about his new companions and his plan. There were no particularly difficult problems to deal with so he breezed through the day, but unusually, he was relieved when five o'clock rolled around. As usual, most of his colleagues packed up and left on the dot of five, but he waited about fifteen minutes before he followed them out. It was that last fifteen minutes that meant ninety-five percent of his workmates had no idea how late he had stayed; all they knew was he had worked later than them and that was always good for the image.

He arrived home to find Tung and Madrick in front of the television eating pizza. They exchanged a few pleasantries before he headed for his computer. He had decided that now was the time to initiate phase two of his destroy-IIBE plan. He was concerned that the antics of his traveller friends might force them all to beat a hasty retreat from the media and that might scupper his plan. He was happy to run with his new friends, but he did not want all his meticulous preparation work to go to waste.

He logged onto his computer and went though his usual routine of checking his own emails and messages. Then he checked the email accounts he had hacked into. There was one odd email to the chairman that caught his eye. It was not the subject matter that piqued his interest; its title suggested it was about some pricing report. He was curious because the body of the text was encrypted.

He stared at the encrypted email. He loved this sort of puzzle. Codes and ciphers had always fascinated him, but this one was a tricky little number. It was going to take him some real effort to crack it so he filed it away for later. He would tackle it when he had more time; it probably was not very interesting or important anyway.

It was now time to concentrate on his plan. He knew that once he hit the metaphorical 'start button', there was no turning back. His scheme would be in play. It would take on a life of its own and he would have to run where it took him. He knew he was ready, or at least as ready as he was ever going to be. He typed in the commands that started a number of little routines running at the heart of the IIBE systems. The ultra sophisticated Noviru software would not detect them because he had disabled the particular components which would have spotted this type of attack.

Thunderbirds are go, he thought as he hit the enter key.

He suddenly felt invigorated. This was the moment he had been planning towards for the last eighteen months. There was nothing more he could do until someone noticed the unusual financial activity and started to investigate. He would have to monitor things closely from now on.

He went back to other people's emails. Specifically he went back to the encrypted message to Samuel Buckingham. He stared at it and looked for obvious patterns, but there were none. He searched it for familiar number sequences that would suggest what encryption method had been used, but he found none.

The next step was to run it through the highly sophisticated Noviru intelligent analyser modules which he had 'borrowed' when he left the company. These modules sifted and sorted text, making intelligent trial-and-error decisions about the type of message. In the first pass, they could generally determine the originating language. In the second pass, they could work out the nature of the message - was it a scientific message or did it relate to financial data? Then finally, it would grind away until the message was cracked.

These were state of the art routines which security agencies around the world used regularly. What these agencies did not know was that there were even deeper levels of sophistication which Noviru did not share with anyone. These were the levels that Michael was now applying to the message.

After an hour, the Noviru analysis had made a little progress. It had determined that the originating language was English and the message contained a date and time, 07.45 GMT 17th of this month. It had also ruled out a lot of things. The message was not scientific, mathematical or financial in nature. He reset some of the parameters, widened the analysis and left it to run while he went to talk to the others about what they should do next.

This message was just a distraction anyway, he thought, maybe he should not bother with it at all; he had enough other things to be getting on with.

37

If I ruled the world

Sir Samuel Buckingham sat in his plush office and pondered on some of the strange events which had occurred in his City. There was powerful magic afoot and it brought into clear focus the truth of the ancient legends and prophecies. It also offered a stark reminder of the actual purpose of the organisation he led, a purpose that had somewhat faded over the last few centuries.

Things had changed dramatically in the short time since the strangeness had begun; other things would need to change dramatically as a result. It was clearly going to be an interesting and exciting time. Some men would be frightened by the prospect, but he was not 'some men'. His very being buzzed and his soul tingled.

What a fantastic legacy it would be, he thought, if he turned out to be the Great Grand Master who recovered the Scroll. He thought about what that could mean to the Occultus Populous as an organisation, but he spent more time considering what it would mean for him as an individual.

He was already immensely wealthy and powerful so he had no need, nor desire, for more money or any further trappings with which his wealth had blessed him. The family fortune had been amassed over many centuries, but its true origins were known only to the head of the clan. The other family members only knew that their ancestors had held a baronetcy since the title was introduced by James I in the early 1600s. They knew there had always been great sums of money, but they did not realise the true source of their immense privileges.

Buckingham, as current Baronet, had been given the ancestral tome when he acceded to the baronetcy upon the death of his father. He therefore knew the whole story, and what an utterly fantastic story it was.

The ancient book traced the family name back to the year 1360 when they adopted the surname Buckingham for all future generations. The book also mentioned the earlier years and charted their ancestry back to a great wizard, Gravalar, the first Great Grand Master of the Occultus Populous. Their lineage spanned over twenty generations and was better documented than many of the great royal dynasties. However their ancestral philosophy was to be prominent, but never overtly great. Hence they had chosen the barony in the sixteen hundreds rather than any grander title or any tight connection to royalty.

There were many benefits to a barony and it had been a wise choice which had served the family well. It enabled the heretical title of 'Sir' and officially documented their genealogy, but it kept them below the radar of most snooping commoners.

The centuries had been very kind to the family, although his family had not been particularly kind to the centuries. They had been responsible for many atrocious acts over the last millennium. These acts had been typical of the elite lineages; each act designed to enhance their wealth regardless of the consequences to others. They had caused wars, famines and global financial crises, but each great event had been engineered to reinforce their enormous wealth and power, and help keep the common man in his place.

So, he wondered as he reflected on his current status and standing, what could the Scroll bring to a man who had everything - a man who had everything yet craved for more?

He answered his own question almost immediately, the Scroll brought infinite opportunity. In a world where true magic was practically non-existent, he would have control over a spell which could create any and all of the great ancient spells. Those spells combined with the enormous global power of the Occultus Populous would bring about the fulfilment of the ultimate dream where the elite would totally control the planet. And he was the elite of the elite.

It would have sounded egomaniacal to most, but he knew it was the truth, he could literally rule the world.

38

The message

Michael was on edge. His software had been shifting money out of IIBE for hours now, but he had yet to detect any response. Surely they must have spotted it by now, he thought, and then he started to worry that he had missed something vital.

He trawled though his hacked email files. There was nothing out of the ordinary; there was definitely nothing which indicated that they had discovered the leak of money. Maybe they were not as efficient as he thought they were. Maybe his little software modules were more difficult to detect that he had reckoned.

To take his mind off his heist plan, he returned his attention to the intercepted, encrypted email to the chairman. The Noviru analyser had been analysing for many hours now and still seemed no nearer to cracking the code. He decided, as a last resort, to switch in the hardware simulator module. He did not have high expectations for this because it only helped with the highest level encryption, the type used by the most secretive and advanced national security agencies. There was no way that the chairman would be involved in that, he thought, no way he would have that level of sophisticated hardware in his possession. He would have been astounded to see that very bit of hardware dangle off the back of the chairman's PC.

He watched the software go though its analysis. Within fifteen minutes he was astonished to be reading the translated message. A particular paragraph grabbed his undivided attention.

'Magic which is outside our control has been used on at least twelve different occasions. Our research has pointed to the strong possibility that the time travellers have arrived with the Scroll.'

His mouth dropped open as he stared at the message. He could not begin to grasp why the chairman of a financial organisation would be involved in this. He could, however, grasp the dangerous threat this posed. He skipped back to the start of the email.

'After solemn and due consideration the European Executive of the Occultus Populous has deemed it appropriate and necessary to convene a meeting of the full Grand Council. This decision has been ratified by the Great Grand Master.'

What was the Occultus Populous, he thought, as he typed it into Google? His query brought back loads of entries for Populous so he tried again with double quotations - "Occultus Populous". It offered him lots of answers for "*Occultist* Populous" but no entries for his specific search.

He shouted for Madrick and was surprised that his voice sounded a couple of octaves higher than usual. He realised he was very worried. Actually he was very scared.

Madrick wandered casually over to the PC corner. He had no inkling of the significance of the discovery he was about to make. He was expecting another funny video because Michael loved showing him funny videos. He was therefore very surprised by the question.

"Have you ever heard of the Occultus Populous?"

"No. It means nothing to me," replied Madrick. "It sounds Salatin and translated to the Anglo-Saxon tongue means something like Special People. For your enlightenment, Salatin was the language which was used for scribing in my time and it was the language of magic scrolls."

"Read this," said Michael as he pointed at the screen.

Madrick read the message and turned white as a flag of truce.

"Someone knows about us? Some secret organisation knows about us? Who are these people? What do they want?"

"I don't know, that's why I was asking you. Listen - don't panic! They may know of you, but they don't know where you are... yet," said Michael. "And they don't know that we know that they are on to you. We have a head start, but we need to move fast. We need a plan."

Michael's flat became a hive of activity over the next few hours.

They collectively panicked as Michael unravelled more detail from the email. He deciphered the recipients of the message - the Council Members. They included the richest and most powerful people on the planet and these people were after them.

They needed to disappear. They needed to become invisible... again. They started with some simple basics - Tung cut Madrick's hair and beard. He looked completely different and the modern clothes from Michael's wardrobe finished off the 'disguise'. Tung was given a similar make-over so at least now the television descriptions would be of little help to anyone trying to spot them in a crowd.

They thought through what could link Michael to the travellers. The biggest worry was the original champagne party in the Ritz. Michael had not booked the lunch table using his own name and Madrick had taken care of their bill so he had not used his credit card. The waiters or the manager or other diners would have spotted them partying together, but no one there knew who he was.

They could probably get descriptions and maybe even a picture of him, but that would be a small pearl of knowledge within a mass of detail. It would be an information pin in a data overloaded haystack, but if someone had enough time and resources they could eventually connect his image to his name. Then they would be knocking on Michael's door. They needed to get away from there and leave no trail whatsoever.

They packed cases with everything they felt would be useful. They gathered money, provisions, clothes and toiletries. Michael parcelled up everything which identified him - credit cards, driving licence, passport - he would destroy it all later, but he wanted anyone who searched the flat to find these things gone. They would think Michael Phillips had bolted. They would not be looking for Michael Baker, the identity he had created eighteen months ago when he started planning his heist at IIBE.

Michael explained what he was going to do next.

"The Council are going to congregate tomorrow. There are forty-eight of them and they're gathering at special locations that are spread across the globe. They will have to use technology to 'meet'. I can hack into the system so we'll be able to watch them. We'll find out what they know and we'll be able to listen in to their plans"

Neither Madrick nor Tung had any idea what this meant, but they could see that Michael was excited so they joined him in a little vocal celebration.

"While I set up the spy software I want you two to create the best possible spell to keep us safe. We are in deep trouble and we don't have any time to lose."

"No time to lose. That's the story of my life," said Tung as he prepared himself.

Michael began to install his spy software. He knew exactly where to start because he had seen the secure teleconferencing facility on the network. He wished now that he had bugged it at the time, but it had not seemed important then. Anyway, it was no big issue, he would be ready to spy in a few hours.

While Michael tackled the bugging, Tung was busy creating and dissipating spells. After a few hours he was totally exhausted and had nothing useful to show for his efforts. He had, among many other things, a chest full of horse leathers, five hundred candles and two extremely ugly bronze statues of goats.

He had also created a beautiful autumn-inspired aroma. It would have been a lot more valuable in his old century and, in particular, in his old street. But it was no good to them right now. It would however have been given a very warm welcome in a fishy hotel room not far away or, even more so, back in Mifal's cell after the great stallion had shown its fear.

The only spell which was potentially useful had given him the power to see in the dark; that would last him a few weeks apparently. Unfortunately that was not going to help them stay safe, but he had a new temporary ability which might come in handy later.

He needed a rest, and some pizza, so he stopped producing spells and started the microwave.

Michael continued work on installing his spy-eye software. It was slightly more complex than he had expected because of the security they had built around the facility. He had just about cracked it though, after all it was impossible to protect yourself against trusted sources and he had made himself a trusted source for every single system within IIBE.

"We are ready to rock!" he shouted out loud, throwing his arms in the air. "We are in."

39

The great and the good

The Members of the Council gathered at the designated locations at the precise pre-arranged hour. This was undoubtedly the most important gathering there had ever been in modern history.

Many of them were often described as 'the great and the good' but they were in fact the greedy and the very bad. Their relentless publicity machines ensured that the world saw them in a completely different light.

Samuel Buckingham took the lead because he was the Chairman of the Council and he was Great Grand Master of the Occultus Populous. He was also in charge of the locale from where the time travellers had disappeared all those centuries ago so he had that extra responsibility. It had always been forecast that the travellers would turn up in his domain if they were going to turn up anywhere.

"We are gathered together on this momentous occasion to fulfil the destiny of our Society; a society which was established over a thousand years ago. Our mission was to track down a pair of renegade time travellers who had stolen the most precious and important of all the spell scrolls. We now believe that those thieves have at last arrived and we are therefore about to complete our mission."

Buckingham had expected that forty-seven pairs of eyes would have watched as he delivered his opening speech. He had expected to be heard by forty-seven pairs of ears. Unbeknownst to him, or the gathering, there were an extra three sets of eyes and ears taking in the spectacle. Michael, Madrick and Tung clustered around the giant TV and watched the world's great men discuss the travellers or, to personalise it, discuss them. It was a little bit frightening, but also quite exciting to think that they were the centre of attention for some of the world's most important people.

"They formed the Society just to catch us?" said Tung feeling rather important.

This did not seem as exciting as being part of a television broadcast, but he felt it was nice to be the centre of attention. He did not fully grasp the significance and danger because he did not understand how much power this group of men controlled.

"They formed the Society just to catch us," he repeated smugly.

"Looks that way," said Michael. "And it sounds as if you guys have been on their most wanted list for a thousand years. They want to catch you, that's for sure."

They did not take their eyes off the screen as they spoke. They did not want to miss anything - although they could, and would, watch it all again because Michael was recording every second of it. That was something which turned out to be extremely fortuitous as events unfolded.

Buckingham went on to describe the actions that had led them to convene the Meeting. A new window opened on the screen showing the sixteen Aethelreds.

"These are what confirmed our suspicions about the thieves. These coins are from the era the travellers left and they are in pristine condition. There were very few fine examples of these coins anywhere and then suddenly sixteen turn up. We initiated an investigation and eventually traced most of them back to an old man - we have his description. We believe it was the same old man who left some very strange items in a hotel room."

He then played a recording of the news broadcast from outside the Ritz. Then he produced the shield commenting that it was from the same time period as the Aethelreds and showing it was in equally perfect condition.

"So that is where that went to," said Madrick.

Buckingham described some of the other mysteries that

had occurred including the great NOISE.

"We concluded that these incidents could only have been caused by magic. So we have initiated a search. We have not got any solid leads yet, but we will continue to interview everyone that came into contact with them. I now throw the meeting open."

"No leads so far. That's good," said Michael. "We mustn't waste any time though; these people have unimaginable resources at their disposal so they will close in on us very quickly."

The Meeting continued for four hours. Many of the Members contributed positively, however many more just asked questions and raised concerns. Towards the end of the marathon session they had developed a detailed three part plan. Part one dealt with the search- it was frightening just how many people would be looking for them. Part two dealt with suppressing current and future stories about the strange events. Part three dealt with what they would do with the travellers when they were caught and subsequently what they would do with the Scroll.

The three listened intently, they felt totally unsettled to think that the most powerful men on earth were talking about how to catch them and the horrible things they would do to them when they did.

"At least we know everything they know," remarked Michael brightly. He knew that they needed to keep their spirits up if they were going to survive this.

His own spirits might have flagged had he known about the secret weapon Buckingham had up his sleeve.

40

Take the money

Michael replayed the Meeting, fast forwarding through the parts he felt would offer him no further insight. He watched certain parts, like Buckingham's initial summary, over and over again because he wanted to understand exactly how these men thought. He wanted to be able to think like them so he could predict their plans and actions. He knew that if he could get right inside their heads he had a chance of evading them regardless of their massive resources. They had a lot going for them, but Michael knew he was extremely clever; clever enough to outwit these old men.

It became very clear to him that Sir Samuel Buckingham was held in awe by the others. It was Sir Samuel who led all the conversations, he called the shots. The others were all extremely powerful men, but they acted subserviently to their leader. There were no egos in the room clouding the issues, there was just a large gathering of men determined to follow their leader and help him gain control over the Scroll.

Michael had no idea what these people would do with the Scroll if they got it, but he did know it would be bad for everyone, except the bad guys, if it fell into their hands. The more he listened to the meeting the more he felt that this was not just a battle for their survival. He knew it sounded a bit grand, but he felt that they were now involved in a battle between good and evil; well at least a battle between goodness and badness. That thought alone made him even more determined to beat these men and fulfil his own dream of changing the world for the little people.

Michael finally stopped watching. He felt he had enough of an insight for the time being and he could always come back to it. He knew it was up to him to devise their escape plan, after all he understood so much more about the twenty-first century and what the hunters could do with the resources they had at their disposal. Tung and Madrick really had no idea. He understood that these people would have connections with the police, the banks, credit card companies and the telecom providers. These people could find anyone, anyone that is, who did not know what they were doing. Tung and Madrick were complacent in their ignorance and he thought it best to leave it that way for the moment. For now, it was solely down to him.

There was something inside Michael which began to make him feel that this was becoming a challenge to his intellect. This was like one of those complex logic puzzles which had always fascinated him. He was genuinely scared of these people, and what they could do to him and his friends, but he was also distinctly excited because he knew deep down that he could win.

He decided, as a defensive measure, to initiate the final phase of his hacking IIBE scheme, but not quite the way he had originally planned. He would hit them with the big steal, but he would send nearly all the money to random individuals because that would leave them chasing shadows and red herrings.

He had already set it up so very large sums would go to various national tax authorities like the Inland Revenue Service in the US and HM Revenue & Customs in the UK. That would cause all sorts of problems when they tried to retrieve that money; they might even write that off rather than open up an intricate can of worms with Government auditors and inspectors.

He had also allocated some huge donations to various well known charities. He felt very good about this. He knew that either the charities would get an enormous influx of cash to help them with their benevolent works or else IIBE would have to suffer crippling bad publicity if they sucked the money back out of these good causes. The good guys win or the bad guys lose.

Right in the middle of this chaos, he would pop a few million into a scattering of accounts he had created for his false identity, but he would not go for the big score he had originally planned. He reckoned that this massive leak of money was bound to drag some of the heat off them. The Council would have no alternative, but to redirect some of the attention into plugging the leak. Every one of the Council Members was bound to be horrified as vast sums of money seeped out of IIBE. They would be terrified of the consequences to the financial systems around the globe. The big corporations would be particularly affected and that would hit these people very hard.

He hit a few keys on his computer and stared at the screen. This was the moment he had been planning for a long time. He savoured it for a full two minutes before he hit the 'enter' key and set the massive theft in motion. He then cleared all traces of the electronic trail that could link him to the fraud.

He had booked eight days holiday from work, more to deal with Tung and Madrick than in preparation to launch his fraud, but that would probably raise some suspicion. He knew that suspicion would be dramatically heightened when he did not show for work once his holiday was over. A little focused investigation at that stage and they would know for sure that it had been him, but then it would be far too late. Right now, all he wanted to do was thoroughly distract them and get a decent head start.

He packed his laptop and all the other paraphernalia that would allow him to access the IIBE systems from wherever he was. He would still be able to watch the teleconference facility. This was vital because being able to watch them meet and discuss their tactics definitely gave them a big advantage that he wanted to hold on to for as long as possible.

Meanwhile, Tung and Madrick were busy creating spells again. They willed up a few more useless ones, but that was always the pattern. There was always lots of nonsense and then bingo, they hit the big one! So they kept going because they were confident that the next great spell was just around the corner. And it was.

Michael heard the cheer and rushed over to the pair.

"Good news?" he asked hopefully. "Have we got a winner?"

"We have the best," shouted Madrick. "We have the absolute best ever."

41

Money is no object

After the Council Meeting, Sir Samuel Buckingham summoned no-title Jim Robinson to his office. He was the Head of Security at IIBE as well as a secret and loyal member of the Occultus Populous. Buckingham had worked with him for many years and he trusted him completely. He had met him through Occultus Populous and had quickly grown to like and respect him.

Robinson had a long and distinguished career in the army. He had combat experience from around the world. He had served with at least one of the Special Forces regiments, however, he never talked about what that had involved, except to Sir Samuel.

Officially, his tours of duty had taken in most of the regions where the British forces had a presence, including Iraq and Afghanistan. Unofficially, his tours had taken him to parts of the world where the British had no military involvement.

He had been wounded twice. Neither injury was particularly severe, but the last one had effectively ended his career. He had been shot in the thigh and there had been some damage to the muscle structure. He was now no longer one hundred per cent fit and that was unacceptable in his Regiment. He could have returned to 'ordinary duty', but after the excitement of his Special adventures he decided against it and accepted an honourable discharge. He missed his army life and often wondered if he had made the right decision. He stopped wondering the day he met Sir Samuel Buckingham.

Within months of meeting, Buckingham had appointed him as the Head of Security at his bank. It was a decision he had never regretted and Robinson had always been particularly grateful for the opportunity. This role, to an outsider, would have seemed a far cry from the excitement of the battlefield, but the outsider could have no inkling of what the bank role actually entailed. It was true that it was a very different sort of excitement, but the challenge of protecting such an important institution from thieves and fraudsters had genuinely inspired Jim. He loved his job. He relished the secret tasks, particularly those that crossed the 'normal' legal and moral boundaries. He felt indebted to Sir Samuel so had a great personal loyalty to him which went above and beyond his loyalty to IIBE.

He had performed his duties professionally and efficiently, and he had shaped the security department into a highly effective shield for the bank. Personally, Robinson had no qualms about doing 'whatever was needed' to protect the bank and Buckingham had used his willingness to carry out a few off-record activities on a number of occasions. There was a strong bond between the two men cemented by some shared dark secrets and Robinson's inherent loyalty.

This loyalty would be sorely tested in the near future when the two men would be at loggerheads because of Buckingham's inability to understand what was in front of his nose. However, that was in the future and neither man knew of the grave consequences of that particular encounter.

Buckingham fully briefed him on the current situation. He knew he could tell him everything. He told him what had been discussed at the Meeting because it was imperative that he fully understood the gravity of the situation. He told him how important the Scroll was to him personally; Robinson already knew what it meant to the Society. He shared every detail of the search for the thieves although that comprised little more than what the original agents had found out by tracking the Aethelreds.

"The search has not been conducted with any real urgency up to this point. That must change. We must track down these thieves and the Scroll. I am placing my trust in you, Jim, to do just that. Bring them to me."

He instructed him to assemble a crack pack to track down the fugitives, he stressed that money was no object. He also stressed the need for secrecy even though he knew that was already clearly understood, but it never did any harm to reinforce the critical messages.

Robinson was to have full authority to call on all the resources of IIBE and the Occultus Populous to catch his prey. As if that was not enough, he was told he could just ask Buckingham for anything else he needed, no matter what, it would be made available.

"Money is no object," he repeated. "And neither are legal considerations. Do what you need to do. I will protect you from any unwelcome consequences."

Robinson knew there were complications within this task because he could not reveal the existence of the Occultus Populous to any outsiders. He knew that he had to maintain secrecy in his team, very few people could be told the full story.

To date, only a small group had been sent out to catch the magic makers, and they had not known exactly what they were looking for. They had not known about the Scroll. They had not known about Sir Samuel's personal interest in their mission.

Everything had now changed. The Council had decreed that this search was top priority, in fact, it was the only priority. More importantly, Sir Samuel had decreed it. Now the gloves were off and Jim Robinson relished the challenge.

He left Buckingham and went back to his office to plan his campaign of attack. He tackled the task with military precision which was what he was trained to do. So first, he needed to work out the best resources to line up against this problem. He started to make a number of lists.

He was, as yet, unaware of the building problem that was

happening right under his nose as an ever increasing trickle of money was being siphoned out of bank accounts that he was ultimately responsible for protecting. When that was discovered, he would be forced to rethink his strategy and redouble his efforts, but in the meantime he concentrated on trapping the time travellers and the Scroll.

42

Believe Me

Madrick knew this was going to be a very tricky spell to use, but he also knew that it had the potential to be their salvation. They would have to plan carefully and a lot of responsibility would ultimately rest with Tung, but he was confident he was up to the task. He had not let them down so far. He had been stupid on more than one occasion, but no task had been beyond him.

He started to explain the spell and its workings to Tung and Michael.

"What we have is the Believe Me Spell. When you invoke the spell you will be seen as totally truthful. Everyone you speak to will believe every single word you say. Whatever story you choose to tell will be believed verbatim, no matter how unbelievable it may be.

"Imagine the power you will have.

"I cannot remember exactly how long your ability will last for. I think it is twenty-four hours, but I am just not sure," Madrick said with a puzzled look on his face.

"I am also not sure how long the 'victims' will continue to believe the story. It is at least the time it takes us to travel once around the sun, but no one knows how long that takes."

"It takes a day," said Tung. "Obviously it takes a day. The sun comes up, the day passes, the sun goes down. So we will have a day. That's not particularly powerful."

"Once around the sun is a year," said Michael.

He did not want to try and explain astronomy and the planet's orbit around the sun to a pair that probably still believed the world was flat.

"Trust me, it's a year. I'll explain it to you both someday."

Madrick looked even more puzzled, but he had learnt to trust Michael. He recognised that Michael knew about an awful lot of things that were still a mystery to him. He was still trying very hard to remember the classes at the Academy. He recalled that they had only scantily covered this particular spell because it was one of the major spells so it was assumed that none of the students would ever be involved with such a powerful enchantment.

"Anyway, we must plan carefully how to use this one. This could be our deliverance if we are clever and careful. We just need to make sure that you get the chance to tell the story to the people that are in control. You need to tell them something which gets us off the hook. We need to have the story ready, practised and perfect.

"You also need to remember that if we," he indicated himself and Michael as he said it, "hear the story then we will believe it too. So you must tell us the truth later. You must undo the lie for us! So, let us work on the story and agree when we should bring the spell into play."

They discussed the options. They knew that they were to be brought before the Council if they were captured so that seemed the perfect opportunity to convince the Members. After all, they were the only ones who could set them free. They also had the power to halt the hunt forever because they called the shots.

"Failing that," said Michael "we probably only need that guy Buckingham to believe us. I'm pretty sure he's the one who runs the show. If we don't get a chance at the whole Council, let's make sure that we get Buckingham to believe us."

"Believe me!" said Tung smugly. "They will buy my story."

"Don't get cocky. This will literally be a matter of life or death if they catch us. You heard what they plan to do to us."

"I'm only kidding. I know how important this is."

"Moving on," said Madrick moving on. "There is one other thing we should plan for."

Madrick explained how it may be possible to stop

someone saying a spell so it was important that the bad guys thought he, Madrick, was the wizard. That should not be hard because Tung would appear to be just too young, as indeed would Michael.

After an hour or so they believed they had made all the preparation they could in the eventuality that they were caught. Michael then started to outline his plan for not getting caught in the first place.

He told them that he had already started robbing IIBE. He did not try to describe how, but he did explain why he thought it would distract at least some of their hunters. He told them about his false identity and how he had created it many months before for the very purpose of making himself disappear.

"Like how we disappeared to escape from Mifal's dungeon?" quipped Tung who knew it was a completely different sort of disappearing that Michael was talking about.

Michael threw him a sarcastic smile and continued to outline their next steps.

"We will head north. I have a house in Liverpool which I bought under my new name. It's quite private and we won't arouse any suspicion with the neighbours when we arrive. We have plenty of cash and I'll have a lot more soon. We won't sell any more gold coins for now because they will be looking out for that. If we keep our heads down for the next few months I don't see how they will ever pick up our trail."

For the next half hour he shared his ideas about how to evade the hunters. Everyone seemed to buy into it and when he had finished, he felt relatively confident that they had a good chance of never being caught. He felt he could do no more so he prepared himself for the Michael Phillips disappearing act. It was the act he had been looking forward to for years.

He went to the bathroom and looked in the mirror.

"This is the face they will be looking for," he said as he

started to shave off his beard and moustache. "No one has any idea what clean-shaven Michael looks like. No one has any idea what Michael Baker looks like!"

He was right. All the photographs that were recorded at IIBE, and indeed Noviru, showed him with his full facial hair. Another bit of great planning, he thought as he washed off the white foam and admired his new look.

43

Shut it down

Deep in the bowels of the IIBE headquarters the bank's top security people were assembled. There was a cacophony of noise as everyone talked and shouted at computer screens and each other. An army of suited men watched the banks of screens which displayed rivers of numbers streaming across them. These digital waterfalls would have meant nothing to the average man in the street, but their trained eyes knew exactly what they were seeing. They watched in horror as tens of thousands of pounds were transferred from their biggest accounts to individual personal accounts all over the planet. The moment they had first spotted these unusual patterns, the account holders were informed. They, in turn, were now frantically checking whether the transfers were valid. As time went by the transfers were getting bigger and increasing numbers of the major accounts holders were being targeted.

Buckingham had convened an emergency meeting of the IIBE Board. Tempers were fraying as the scale of the problem became ever clearer. They quickly realised that their options were very limited and none of the solutions were particularly palatable. They became even more anxious as it dawned on each of them the scale of the damage to their own personal fortunes. That was when the discussion became extremely heated, cantankerous and argumentative. It was a truly despicable sight to see greedy men with immense fortunes squabbling viciously like paupers fighting over a dropped penny.

Buckingham eventually brought the meeting under some semblance of control and brought them back on track, back to working out what to do rather than finding someone to blame.

They all knew it would cause total chaos if they shut down the whole system. They were not even sure if they could. And the shutdown would cost multimillions in itself. They also knew that the bank's reputation would be totally trashed if they went down that line, but they were running out of options as the rate of transfers spiralled.

"We have discussed all the options," said one of the board members. "We know what our choices are so we should table them formally and take a vote. Let the majority decide."

"A vote? The majority? A majority simply means that all the fools are on the same side," bellowed Buckingham. "Shut it down! We have no choice but to shut down the whole system. Find out what has gone wrong and get it fixed. We need to minimise the downtime. Then find out who caused it. We need to make sure it never happens again and they need to be punished. Initiate actions with all the banks that have accepted transfers. We need to get our money back."

With that tirade he stormed out of the boardroom. He was content that he had stamped his authority on the situation; he just hoped that they could follow his instructions. Stop the losses, fix the problem and find the guilty. They knew what they had to do.

He made his way to the secret teleconferencing facility. An emergency meeting of the Council had also been scheduled. In a way it was convenient that the Council Members were all available because of their own crisis. This meant they could use their collective financial might to minimise the effect of this IIBE banking disaster. At least minimise the effect on the Members of the Occultus Populous. As was often the way, it might actually be quite a beneficial outcome if the crisis destroyed legions of ordinary people, as long as the true elite did not bear too much of the burden - preferably none at all. This sort of crisis was good for ensuring that the common man did not climb above his station. It was a bit like a bush fire; it was necessary every so often to keep the bush healthy, but a lot of animals died in the process.

A crisis was needed on a regular basis to weed out the weak and the sick. He knew this only too well because his grandfather had initiated the 'great depression' in 1929 and that had definitely helped his family amass billions albeit at the expense of millions of small investors.

Buckingham had calmed down, at least externally, by the time he reached the teleconferencing facility. He nodded to his fellow Members who were already in the room. He surveyed the large screens and the displays indicated that everyone was present.

He began to outline the latest catastrophe and explained the action he had just ordered. He waited for the initial reaction to subside so he could set out the defensive actions they could all take to protect their personal fortunes. Once everyone realised that Buckingham had thought through the consequences for them personally, things calmed significantly. Many of them were already calculating how much they could make from this situation.

"So we need have no fear as far as our own wealth is concerned. We can engineer restarts and shutdowns that will favour us and knowing exactly when these will happen will allow us all to fully exploit the massive swings that there will inevitably be in the markets.

"But we have other things to which we must turn our attention."

He began to outline his plan to track down and destroy the people who had perpetrated 'these despicable acts of unauthorised magic' as he called them.

"I have put my best man on the job. He is assembling his team as we speak. I have told him that he has our collective resources at his disposal. We will give him whatever he needs to get the job done. He is also tasked with finding whoever has attacked our bank.

"He has been authorised to do whatever he needs to do to

find the travellers and the bank thief. There will be no hiding place. He will find them. Mark my words gentlemen, he will find them.

"These people will suffer. They will all suffer. They have no idea just how much they will suffer."

44

In my Liverpool home

Tung, Madrick and Michael grabbed their packed bags and left the apartment for the last time. Michael knew he could never return. He was noticeably sad because, all in all, it had been a happy place for him.

He had planted a few red herrings before they left because he knew that at some stage the hunters would find the place and examine everything in the minutest of detail. He had also made sure that there were absolutely no useful clues left for them to follow. He had been planning his original escape for months so he felt he was well prepared. He had not had to make any rushed decisions. He knew that rushing things was a recipe for disaster, straight from the cookbook of poor preparation.

They headed to the underground station, paid in cash, and eventually boarded a train headed out of the city. They rode in silence as the carriage hurtled through the dark tunnels. They were all on edge and they watched the other passengers; trying to work out if anyone was taking an unhealthy interest in them.

This was déjà vu for Madrick and Tung. Their lives seemed to be going around in a great big circle. It was not long ago (in their lives it was a few weeks however it was a thousand years for everyone else) that they were being chased by Mifal, and the Black and White Wizards.

"I wonder will we ever be done running," said Madrick. "There is always someone chasing us. Our sad lives are just one damned chase after another."

"Or is it all the same damned chase? Is it actually the same people that are after us but now they are in a different guise?" said Tung.

They consoled themselves with the thought that they had

got away last time, so why not this time? If this was proper déjà vu then that is the way it should pan out.

After a number of train changes, all paid with cash, they arrived in Liverpool. It had not all been plain sailing though, they had two unfortunate incidents on the rail journey.

The first was when Tung managed to get himself locked in the toilet. They needed the conductor to help him out, but they passed it off as him being a bit 'slow' in the brain department. The conductor did not seem fazed at all. He had already dealt with fare dodgers, a punch up in the buffet car and a couple of drunken party girls. Someone locked in the lavatory was light relief, he thought, pleased with his mental toilet pun.

The second incident was a bit more serious. They had decided they needed some food. Madrick stayed to keep the seats while Michael and Tung headed to the buffet car to buy some sandwiches. There was no problem with that because Michael did the talking - three bacon butties and a couple of ham sandwiches would certainly fill the gap nicely.

Tung led the way along the corridor back to their seats. The man in the wheelchair seemed to come out of nowhere and bumped gently into him. He reacted instantaneously to the 'danger' because he had developed lightening quick reflexes after years of living on the dangerous streets of Mifal's Thamesius. He had never seen a wheelchair before and he was taking no chances. Before the man could apologise for nudging him, Tung knocked him backwards, tipping man and chair onto the ground. Michael could only gawp in amazement as Tung stood aggressively over the man shouting.

"Get up. Get up and fight. Is there something wrong with you?"

It took all Michael's diplomatic skill to stop the incident escalating into something that would draw in the growing band of on-lookers. He calmed Tung and sent him back to

Madrick. He righted the chair and helped the man back into it.

"I am so sorry. My friend had a nasty accident once when he was knocked down by a bike. He's scared of anything with wheels now."

The words were out before he realised just how ridiculous an explanation that was.

"Actually he's on a day out from a mental hospital."

He made the universal 'he's nuts' sign with his finger. The man was shaken, but he seemed to accept the apology. Before he could change his mind, Michael dropped the bacon and ham sandwiches in his lap.

"Here. Please take these. It's our way of saying sorry."

He was so embarrassed that he did not even wait for a reaction. He turned on his heels and hurried after Tung. The man in the wheelchair could only watch him in disbelief.

"Surely he must have seen my skull cap?" he said to the nearest bystander. "Is this some kind of sick joke? Why else would he drop a load of pork on a Jewish man's lap?"

"I think they're probably both on a day out from a mental hospital," said the bystander. "But you would think there would be someone sane to accompany them."

"You're probably right. No real harm done, I guess. And here, would you like some sandwiches?"

"Are you having a laugh, mate? Look at the beard. I'm a Muslim."

Michael knew nothing of the ethnic chaos he had left behind him. He thought he had dealt with the problem quite well, but he was nevertheless glad to get back to find Tung sitting quietly beside Madrick.

"You are a troublemaker," he said totally unaware of how much worse he had made the situation.

"Where are the sandwiches?" asked Madrick.

"You don't want to know. Trust me, you do not want to know," he replied as he gave Tung the dirtiest of dirty looks.

Apart from that it was an uneventful journey. They had not noticed anyone following them and there were no strangers paying any special attention to them. As time went on they felt that they had put some distance between them and their pursuers. The first part of their escape had been a success.

They gathered their bags and got off the train. They walked along the platform and saw the man in the wheelchair being helped off. Michael waved but the man ignored him.

"How rude! I wish I hadn't given him our sandwiches now."

Michael decided they would walk from the station to his Liverpool home rather than take a taxi. It was a couple of miles, but he felt that this was a sensible precaution because then there was no trail for anyone to follow. They also walked separately. Madrick was fifty yards behind Michael and Tung a further fifty yards back. This meant no one would have seen three men walking together. Maybe he was being overly cautious, thought Michael, but they might as well leave as little as possible for their hunters to pick up on.

As Michael passed a narrow entry, about ten minutes from the station, a small man leapt out and knocked him to the ground with a rather dramatic karate style kick. Michael was stunned, but he was not going to let go of the backpack which the man was trying to tear from his grip.

The man, who looked of Japanese origin, pulled a small gun from his pocket and pushed it into Michael's chest.

"Let the bag go, man," he growled. "I'll shoot you in the face if you don't let go of the bag - NOW."

Suddenly the man released his hold and dropped heavily to the ground. Above him stood Tung who had just landed a fearsome, double-handed blow to the back of his head. Michael looked up at him gratefully. He was shaken but not badly hurt.

"This is what I do," said Tung looking rather pleased with his work.

"That was really brave," said Michael as he got up unsteadily and brushed himself down.

"Weren't you afraid of the gun? Weren't you worried that the gun might have gone off when you hit him?"

"What's a gun?" asked Tung.

"I'll explain later."

This was another occasion when Tung's ignorance of the modern world left Michael wondering how he had survived so long.

"That was random; I've never been mugged before. Let's hope he was just an opportunist thief and not something to do with the men who are after us.

"Let's move on before we attract any attention to ourselves. At least we can be pretty sure that this guy won't be reporting anything to the police!"

They moved on, again fifty yards apart. Tung felt slightly sorry for the mugger, because a man has got to make a living, he thought to himself.

Michael had quickened his pace; he wanted to get to his house as quickly as possible. They needed to get behind closed doors and away from curious eyes as soon as they could. He hoped above hope that the attack had been the work of an opportunist and not something more sinister; only time would tell.

They arrived at the house without any further incidents. Michael opened the door and waited for the other two to squeeze in past him. He closed the door with some relief and pushed home the big bolt. He immediately felt safer now the world was shut outside.

It was an imposing Victorian brick house which lay about two miles south east of the city centre. He had bought it eighteen months earlier using money he had been left when his mother and father had died.

He began to think back to that dreadful night when he had been given the news. His eyes literally filled with tears as he thought about the moment his uncle George and a policewoman had broken the news to him. Madrick broke into his bleak reminiscences.

"This is a beautiful house. Why did you live in the other place when you have this wonderful home?"

"This was always my secret getaway place. I bought this as my safe house where I could hide after I robbed IIBE. No one can link this house to my old identity. This is where I planned to lay low for a while and then start my new life, clear and free. And now it is working for all of us. As far as our pursuers are concerned, we will have disappeared off the face of the earth."

"Yes," said Tung. "Been there and done that."

They all felt a great sense of relief. Things were surely on the right track for them now.

"That's quite a bump you have on your head," Tung said poking Michael's skull. It was nice to see someone else getting head bashes, he thought.

"Yep. I've taken one for the team."

Michael was still a bit concerned that the Japanese martial arts mugger might have connections to IIBE, but he kept that to himself.

"It's a bump, but it's not a major ninjury," said Michael smiling.

Tung looked at him with a blank expression.

"You don't know what a Ninja is, do you?" said Michael disappointedly.

"No more lessons for a while, Michael," chipped in Madrick. "Let's have some relax time. I think we all deserve it."

"That's fair. We do deserve some down time."

"I think we have found the plot," said Tung feeling pleased with how his language was adapting to the twenty-first century.

"How do you mean 'found the plot'?" queried Michael

wondering when Tung would get a better grip on twenty-first century language.

"Well, things are pretty good now. When things were going bad you told us we had 'lost the plot'. Well, I think we've found it now."

Michael nodded, it actually made sense and things were 'pretty good now'.

Clearly they were not aware of exactly what their pursuers were up to.

45

An information haystack

The resources that had been dedicated to the manhunt were frightening. Agents had been assigned to every sighting of the old man and his accomplice; every sighting was fully investigated. They had already tracked the trail of most of the coins back to 'Buy your Gold' stores or small antique shops. They returned to each of these places and tried to establish where the old man had gone to and where he had come from. They used CCTV images, witnesses and intuition. Gradually they began to fill in the route that Tung and Madrick had followed to the Ritz. Eventually they also pieced together everything the pair had done since they arrived at the Ritz.

They had a couple of lucky breaks which helped them complete the trail back to their starting point at the beach houses on the coast. They found plenty of evidence around the huts where they had holed up for a few days. They checked out each of the break-ins and gathered the random magic debris and the Aethelreds which had been left. Frustratingly, the trail went completely dead at that point so Robinson concluded that it must have been where the time travellers had landed. That made sense because it was relatively near the point where they had disappeared nearly a thousand years earlier.

It was imperative to gather every shred of information, but this was the least important part of the tracking. It was all very well to find out where they had been; what they really needed to know was where they had gone.

The back tracking was merely the tip of the manhunt iceberg because there were even more agents (and agencies) trying to follow their route from the Ritz.

They had names from the hotel register, Tung and

Madrick Tide, father and son they were told. They did not know whether these were false names, or whether these people were indeed related, but at least it gave them labels for their prey.

The names were run through every database they could access, but to no avail. There were no entries which matched. Early on in the name tracing exercise someone had noticed something which made them sure that the names were made up.

"Tung Tide. Say it out loud."

"Right, 'tongue tied', that has got to be a joke."

Tung could have told them about the origin of his name. It was a joke, but it was also, sadly for him, his real name.

Their agents had interviewed everyone who had been in contact with them at the Ritz; this was very time consuming, but it helped them build a picture of two men who were clearly out of place in this environment. In fact, as it turned out, out of place in this millennium.

There was only one worthwhile lead that had come from these enquiries. It related to one night when they had partied with another man and woman. They had all retired to their suite and the unknown couple had stayed with them overnight. The thing that was particularly interesting was that the man had returned on a number of occasions after that and he had been with them when they checked out of the hotel.

It appeared that this man was in league with them. They had a full description of him - young, modern with a trendy beard and moustache; but better than that they had pictures of him, and of Tung and Madrick.

They had gathered a wealth of CCTV coverage from the hotel and from various camera systems in the area. They had employed leading experts to sift and analyse the footage so they now had top quality images of their targets, along with accurate heights and weights.

Some of the CCTV images had shown the modern man using a mobile phone. They had cross referenced the exact time and location against databases from all the mobile phone companies. It had been extremely time consuming, but it had given them a list of potential names which they could filter using the other information which was accumulating.

They knew exactly what they were looking for. They had not yet worked out exactly who they were looking for.

Their teams continued gathering information and their analysts kept analysing it. Their perseverance eventually identified Michael Phillips as the third man.

They immediately dispatched a team to his last known address where they found a whole series of clues and leads amongst the debris of the, obviously recently abandoned, apartment. Small teams were allocated to follow up each of the new leads.

In addition to feet on the ground, they were continuing to use facial recognition technology, mobile phone records, credit card transaction analysis, CCTV fractional identification and a host of other hi-tech techniques to help them close in on their targets.

Eventually they got footage of them boarding a southbound train, but the trail went cold when they could not find where they disembarked. They had some pointers that suggested Dover, but this was based on credit card payments which, unbeknownst to them, were part of the elaborate red herring trail which Michael had laid.

They scoured the Dover area for clues and also dispatched a team to France in case they had jumped a ferry. There was plenty to check out, but Jim Robinson was not convinced they were on the right track. It was possible that the trail had gone cold. He sensed that something was wrong. He sensed that they might be half way through a wild goose chase. He had, however, no choice other than to follow the leads they had, particularly those which related to Michael Phillips.

Once Phillips had been identified it did not take long for them to know every detail about him. The most important being the fact that he worked in the computer department of IIBE.

Robinson did not believe in coincidences. The magic and the fraud were linked; he could not explain it yet but they were definitely linked. Phillips had perpetrated the fraud and he was in cahoots with the travellers. He had been very clever because they had not yet worked out how to stop the money leak and repair the damage. Here was a cunning opponent who could not be underestimated, and he had magic on his side.

While a large contingent of the field agents followed through on the Dover and France angles, other smaller teams continued to gather evidence at the Ritz and at Michael's apartment. Collectively they were amassing huge quantities of information which all needed to be analysed. They had so much now that they were beginning to suffer from information overload. They were now in danger of losing the vital piece of knowledge because it was buried in a mountain of dross. Even though this was a risk, they continued to gather CCTV footage and scour each of the hot areas for witnesses or evidence of strange occurrences.

A further, very technical, group had been assembled and deployed to tackle the IIBE problem. This group included computer specialists, IIBE security personnel and, secretly, Occultus Populous agents. They were supplemented by teams, from other Council Member organisations, who were working backwards from where the money had ended up. They were checking out the receiving accounts to see how they were all connected. The perpetrator must be linked in some way to these accounts, they deduced, otherwise what was the point?

In parallel, the IIBE teams were trying to work out how and why the money had been dispatched. Was there a common thread that determined which accounts had been targeted?

Finally, a crack team from Noviru was in place. After all, their software was meant to offer total protection so they were under immense pressure to find an answer.

The IIBE financial systems had now been shut down for nearly four hours and the world was taking notice. Statements and press releases had been issued about computer malfunctions, but they would only hold up for a short period and then the panic would start with a potentially crippling effect on the world financial markets.

In total, there were over three thousand people dedicated to fixing the problem and finding Michael, Tung and Madrick. That did not include all the other eyes that were hunting them. The police, border control and all the security agencies had their photographs so they were on the look-out too.

Buckingham surveyed the mountain of information that had been gathered. He knew that they had made fantastic progress in a very short time. They had identified the three men - the two travellers from the past and their collaborator, Michael Phillips. They had plugged the IIBE system. The Noviru team had quickly spotted where Michael had disabled parts of their software and once they had been reinstated the intelligent software quickly cleansed the system. IIBE systems were up and running again, but the fraud had allowed nearly three hundred billion pounds to leak out to accounts all over the globe. They had already recovered about fifty billion, but Buckingham knew the recovery would be slow and he accepted that they would never claw back all their funds.

There was also the untold damage that had been done to their reputation and this would get even worse as soon as the story of the fraud got out, as it inevitably would. He would deal with that particular difficulty when it arose. There was no point in fretting about it now, he told himself.

He was satisfied that they had minimised the problem at IIBE, but it had been a serious distraction. They needed to find the three men quickly, but he was concerned that the trail seemed to have gone cold. They had mountains of information, although in reality they had no rock solid leads to follow. He decided he would allocate even more resources to the hunt. He had to find these men, the Scroll and the reason why the time travellers were working with Phillips to defraud IIBE.

Buckingham reported everything to the Council. He was totally unaware that prying eyes were watching.

46

Home free

Michael, Madrick and Tung watched the Council meeting on the big split screen. Michael was horrified to hear himself referred to by name. It made the whole 'they are after you' thing seem so much more real and personal. He had expected them to identify him eventually, but he did not think they would have been so quick. These people were not to be underestimated.

The three of them listened to Buckingham describe the chase so far and they high fived when he talked about the search leading to France. Hopefully, the majority of the search would be diverted to that continental wild goose chase.

"They've followed a shoal of the red herrings that we left in my flat," said Michael. "They think we're in Dover and heading for France. Or, even better, they think we're in France already. I am a smart boy! Hopefully they'll soon pick up some of the bogus credit card purchases which we planted. Keep your fingers crossed, we may have fooled these people. We just may have thrown them off our scent."

Michael had laid the false trail with his real credit cards. He had supplemented that evidence with a few cleverly constructed electronic paths left on his 'dummy' computer. All the cards had now been destroyed along with all the other Phillips' identification. As far as he could tell there was nothing to link the old Michael Phillips with the new Michael Baker.

They listened intently to the rest of the meeting. Michael was disappointed they had plugged the IIBE system so quickly, but was delighted to hear that they had no further leads on him and his friends. He was also very pleasantly shocked to hear that he had extracted over three hundred billion pounds from their coffers.

The Council was just about to start describing the next phase of the hunt when Michael's screen went blank.

"Damn it!" he said. "What the hell has happened?"

He checked all his connections and ran a few software routines.

"Damn it!" he repeated. "It looks like they've found my spy software. That's the end of us knowing what they are doing. At least we know that we haven't left any loose ends or made any silly mistakes.

"So let's not get too worried. They know a lot about us, but they don't know what to do with all that knowledge. It's like knowing that a tomato is a fruit, but not understanding that it doesn't go in your fruit salad. Too much information can just blur the objective."

Madrick and Tung looked puzzled. They reckoned it must be one of those modern expressions that went straight over their heads. Michael saw the puzzled looks and realised that what he had said did not make much sense to him either. He decided it was easier to leave it and move on.

For the next couple of hours they discussed how they would keep a very low profile and keep themselves well below the radar. Michael told them that they needed to avoid high surveillance areas such as seaports and airports. He also pointed out that, for their longer term survival, they would need to create modern day identities for Tung and Madrick. He stressed how important it was, but explained that it was not particularly urgent. There really was no rush, they could take their time creating these new personas.

Michael thought hard about what had led up to this point. He could not see any way that their trail could be followed. As far as he could work out, they were home free. By way of celebration, he ordered a Chinese carry-out to be delivered and the three of them settled down to enjoy the meal when it arrived.

"We need to be extra careful how we go on from here. We all want to have fun and enjoy our lives, but these are powerful people and they will not stop looking for us. I mean, they've been looking for you guys for a thousand years!"

They all pondered that statement. It was true and a bit frightening. These people would never stop. They were like an ancient Terminator, thought Michael, but he had no intention of trying to explain that particular thought to the others.

"It's all quiet now. We seem to have shaken them off and it's clear they don't have a clue where we are or what they should do next. Let's make the most of this space."

"Maybe it is just the calm before the storm in a teacup," said Tung.

Michael tried to analyse what Tung had just said, but gave up quickly. It would be great if all they faced was a 'storm in a teacup' but he suspected that they had a lot more than that to worry about.

They did not want to spoil the meal with serious conversations. Madrick steered them away from the heavy subjects.

"There are lots of things that I've accepted about the twenty-first century - electricity, cars, planes, television - but there are so many other things I just don't understand."

Michael was happy to go down this road. He reckoned that Madrick was right to move the talk to something more trivial. They all needed a break from the stressful situation they had been dealing with over the last few days. He expected to spend the next while trying to explain complex issues like the Internet, nuclear power and maybe even space travel. He was surprised by the list that Madrick sprung on him.

"What's the deal with credit cards, gymnasiums, drugs, charity shops, dentists, parliament, poodles, social workers and lipstick? I've got plenty more questions, but that lot will do for starters," he said as he popped a spring roll in his mouth. That'll do as a starter as well, he thought.

It was as if he had been compiling his list for an occasion just like this and, in a way, that was exactly what he had done. He had come across references to these modern phenomena, but had not had a chance to find out about them.

"Yeah," piped in Tung. "And what about broccoli, chewing gum, cricket and pantomimes? Oh yes, and zebras?"

"Hold on guys, hold on. One thing at a time. Which one do you want to start with? Not broccoli or pantomime though, because I don't get them either."

Madrick picked gymnasiums as the first topic and Michael spent the rest of the meal trying to explain the purpose of tiring yourself out on pointless machines. He found it hard to satisfy Madrick's constant queries.

"Why have machines to run on when you can just run outside? I don't get it, what's the point? Actually, why would you want to run anywhere, if you don't need to be there in a hurry?"

It was a fun conversation and they laughed a lot at the anomalies of modern life.

When they finished the meal they chatted about what they should do in the short-term. They made some plans, but Michael was agitated. He was missing something. He felt an overwhelming need to talk to Faith, but he recognised that IIBE must know about his relationship with her. He knew he needed to be extremely careful.

"It is a long time since I have seen Faith face to face," Michael tried to say. It came out more like 'Faith faith to faith'.

He tried again, but it came out exactly the same way.

"I haven't seen Faith in person for ages," he said, giving up on his tongue twister. "I really want to call her and make sure that she is OK. I'd love to get together with her again... no, I need to get together with her again. But I know it's just too risky for now. I need to find a way to see her that is safe enough for everyone."

He thought hard about how he could talk to her without compromising either his secret identity or his location. There had to be a way, he thought, and I need to see her very soon before it is too late for our relationship.

Madrick and Tung were horrified at the prospect.

"You need to think inside the box about this," said Tung.

"What? What are you talking about? What do you mean, 'think inside the box'?"

"You told us we had to 'think outside the box' when the answer wasn't obvious."

"So what's your point?" asked Michael, although he was pretty sure he knew what the point was.

"The answer here is so obvious. Remember you told us that zebra thinking was ignoring the obvious answer? Making things too complicated. You said 'when you hear hooves coming up behind you, you should think horse, not zebra.' Remember that?"

"Yes, I remember," said Michael, not quite sure where this was going.

"Well, this requires 'horse inside the box' thinking. The answer is blindingly obvious.

"The answer is 'don't be an idiot, don't contact her'," concluded Tung, folding his arms across his chest for emphasis.

Michael knew he was right. It would be stupid to contact Faith. It was such an idiotic idea that even Tung thought it was mad. So, he decided, he needed to find a way to make it seem sensible. He would find a way to make it seem sensible.

47

Bad news gentlemen

Buckingham finished outlining progress to date to the Council, oblivious to the fact that they were being watched by the very people they were trying to catch. The Members were feeling increasingly anxious because progress had become a little tenuous since the three fugitives had left Michael's flat. However, Buckingham had one piece of information which he knew would completely settle their nerves. He had been holding back the most important and positive news until the end. He was just about to share it with the meeting when his phone rang.

He looked at the display, apologised to the meeting and pressed the 'answer' button. He did not even say 'hello'. He had left strict instructions that he was not to be disturbed. Everyone knew he would not be taking any calls. This was different, he knew who was calling and he knew that they would not disturb him unless there was something critical to report. He held the phone to his ear and waited to hear what was so important.

He listened carefully to the voice on the other end of the line. He knew that every word was carefully thought out, and true. His face drained of colour just before it reddened with anger. He hung up. He had not uttered a single word.

"I have some very bad news gentlemen," he said addressing the meeting. "It appears that our secure teleconferencing system was not as secure as we were led to believe. The system was compromised, by Michael Phillips, so the fugitives have probably heard everything that we have said up to this point. The only positive news I was given is that the system is now totally guaranteed to be secure so we can talk candidly."

There was immediate bedlam as the implications of the revelation sunk in. Everyone realised that the fugitives now knew every detail of how they had planned to catch them so they could clearly take evasive action. Worse still, these people now knew about the Occultus Populous and could identify the inner Council. Not only could they identify them, it was possible they had recordings of the meetings which meant that they had absolute proof of their existence. Would they leak it to the world? That was the question that each Member was now contemplating. Individually they were horrified by the potential consequences, collectively they were totally incensed.

This was by far the most serious threat to the organisation since it was founded nearly a thousand years before. Their secret, which had been treasured and protected for a millennium, was now in jeopardy. To make matters even more galling, it was not a major government or a popular global movement which threatened their very being. The threat came from a small band, three to be precise, of rogue thieves.

For at least ten minutes there was complete mayhem and there was no way that anyone could intervene and bring order to the proceedings. However, when the commotion died down a little, Buckingham took his chance to restore some semblance of control. He knew he had one small, but very significant, glimmer of hope to offer to the Council.

"Gentlemen, gentlemen, please let me speak. I have some very important news for you. I was about to tell you something extremely positive before we were so rudely interrupted. Please listen carefully because things may not be as bad as you think."

There was a distinct calming of the tension as they turned their attention to Buckingham. Things were still very edgy, but they seemed willing to listen to what Buckingham had to offer. Each Member was praying for something to lift the gloom.

"Before we were given this dreadful disclosure, I was

about to give you some good news," he announced. "We have something which we are convinced will help us capture our enemies very soon indeed. And once we have them we will ensure that they talk to nobody... ever."

48

It's lovely to hear your voice

Michael was absolutely determined to talk to Faith. He was really worried that she could be feeling that he had abandoned her, which effectively he had. He had not seen her for what seemed like absolutely ages, indeed, he had not even spoken to her for more than forty-eight hours. He felt he needed to make immediate contact; he could not shake the feeling that if he did not speak to her very soon, then the trust would be broken and their fledgling relationship would be over.

He spent the next hour carefully setting up an anonymous connection so he could make an untraceable call to her over the internet. He knew that would give him a completely safe and secure way to call her, indeed to call anyone.

He rang the mobile number that he had in his secret little book and waited for an answer. He felt extremely nervous. It was the same kind of feeling he had when he was asking someone for a first date, but much more intense. He had only had a few experiences of that first date question, but he hated the gut-wrenching feeling it created. This was a thousand times worse!

"Hello?"

"Hi Suzie, it's Michael," he said. "I really can't explain why I'm calling you, but I need to talk to Faith on this phone. Is she there?"

Suzie was Faith's flatmate and he knew they had been best friends for many years. Apparently, they had met in primary school and had hit it off straight away. He knew they shared everything from hairdryers to make-up and from secrets to boyfriends. He did not know just how deep the friendship was.

"Michael? Where on earth have you been? Faith's been worried sick about you."

"I really can't explain. Is she there? Please, can I speak to her?"

"I'm not sure I want to allow you. You've really let her down."

"Please Suzie. This is really important. I need to talk to her. I will explain everything to her."

"OK, but you'd better not mess her around or I'll have to kill you. I'm serious, do not hurt her or I really will kill you."

There was an interminably long pause.

"Hold on, I'll get her."

There were a few clinking sounds and a background conversation that he could not make out. Then he heard Faith say his name. He felt a strange surge in his chest immediately he heard her voice and all she had said so far was 'Michael'.

"Hi Faith, yeah it's me. It's lovely to hear your voice," he said nervously.

"Michael! I've been trying to get in touch for ages, but your mobile's dead. Where have you been? What's happened? Are you all right? Where are you?" she asked frantically. "I want to see you, I need to see you. I've missed you terribly. I've been so worried."

"I know, I know. I'm so sorry. Things have been really hectic. I'll tell you all about it when I see you."

"OK, can we meet now? Can you come round here or can I come to you? Where the hell are you?"

"Listen Faith, we need to be extremely careful. I think I am in big trouble. In fact, I know I am in big, big trouble. I can't explain much over the phone and I know this will all seem weird, but I need you to trust me."

"You've got to give me something Michael. You can't just disappear off the face of the earth and not tell me anything. Give me something."

"OK. But like I said, this will all seem weird."

He warned her that some very scary people had probably tapped her phone; that was why he had called her on Suzie's mobile. He told her there was no way they could talk freely on Suzie's phone either because they may already have made that connection.

"It's unlikely, but they may have hacked her phone as well. I need to talk to you properly; away from prying ears," he said.

He implored her to go to the phone box outside the pub where they had had their first drink. Only they knew where that was so, hopefully, that would give them some privacy.

"Don't say the name," he warned her. "Just tell me that you know where I mean."

"Of course I know," she said slightly peevishly. "Why all the mystery? You're not James Bond you know. Are you sure you're not imagining all this?"

"I'm not imagining it. I will explain when we have some privacy."

"Michael, you are beginning to frighten me. What have you done?"

"Trust me," he said. "Be beside the phone at 10.30 today. I will ring you. I'll explain more then. Please, please be there. I miss you."

He hung up and prayed that she would not be too spooked to go to the phone box and wait for his call. He reckoned that even with their immense resources it would be impossible for the hunters to listen in to a call on a, to-date unknown, public phone box. He had noted the number some time ago in preparation for just such an eventuality. He had collected over fifty numbers in the past eighteen months; he had prepared well. He appreciated that they could follow Faith to the box, but he would have had his private conversation with her by the time they got a line tap organised. So far, so good, he thought as he planned his next move.

An hour later he called the phone box, but it rang out without being answered. He waited a couple of minutes and called again; it rang out again. He decided to give it one more go. He rang again and it was picked up on the second ring.

He heard a voice say 'hello', it was Faith.

"I am so glad you came. I've called a few times. I thought I had maybe scared you off."

"I know I'm a few minutes late, but I got held up. And I think I'm being followed. I tried to shake them off, but I don't think I did. There's a man across the road who I'm sure is watching me. I'm scared Michael. What on earth is going on?"

"I know this seems crazy, but please trust me. I wouldn't be surprised if there was someone on your tail. I know this is easy for me to say, but don't worry about it. They are only interested in you as a way to get to me. Turn your back on him, let's give him as little to work with as possible."

She turned away from the man she suspected and held the phone tighter to her face. She cupped her hand over the mouthpiece to add to the secrecy.

"Now please listen really closely, I'm going to tell you some things which will sound unbelievable, but if you stick with me, this could be the start of our dreams coming true. So please, please bear with me."

"Grrrrr Aarrgh," she said impersonating a bear. It was an old joke, but it eased the tension a little. She heard him chuckle at the other end of the line.

Michael spoke for the next fifteen minutes or so; Faith merely added 'uh-huh' sounds at appropriate points. He did not tell her very much about Tung and Madrick, in particular he said nothing about time travel and magic - that would have been just too unbelievable for now. He did tell her about hacking the IIBE system and stealing the money. He told her he was doing it to destroy a monster, not to become rich himself. He did however mention that he had seeded away a couple of million, but he reminded her that that was small beer compared to the billions that he had sucked out of the bank.

"It's mainly gone to random accounts," he explained "but I popped twenty grand in one of yours. Go to your bank straight after this call and withdraw as much cash as they'll let you have. It'll help you to cover any expense over the next few days.

"We need to meet up. I really need to see you."

He had not realised just how much he missed her until that very moment.

"Go and get as much money as you can. Then go to the public phone at the Ritz, the one just outside the restaurant. Be there at 3.30, I'll call you then.

"Stay strong," he added and then, for the very first time, he told her that he loved her.

49

I'm scared

When Faith came off the phone to Michael she was literally shaking, she had never been so nervous in her life. She walked around in little circles for five minutes to try and calm herself. As she did, she casually checked out all the people in her immediate vicinity. The man that she thought was watching her had moved on, but there were a couple of others who looked a bit suspicious; she memorised their faces. She knew it was going to be vital that she kept her wits about her. She needed to be aware of everything that was going on around her. This could all become very dangerous so caution was the watchword.

She wanted to be completely at ease before she made her next move. It took a while, but once she felt a bit calmer, she went back to the public phone and made a few calls. Then she headed for the bank. She was going to try and withdraw the money.

Her bank was about half an hour away. She thought about taking a taxi, but she reckoned the walk would do her good. The walk would help to keep her calm. When she arrived at the bank she studied the interior. She saw an area where people were filling in forms. That was perfect, she thought, she could position herself there for a while and watch the door to see who came in after her. She grabbed a pen and a couple of forms and, as casually as possible, pretended to fill them in. After about thirty seconds, a man she recognised entered the bank. He stopped just inside the door and did a sweep of the foyer with his eyes. As soon as he saw her he looked away, backed out of the door and was gone.

She doodled on a couple more forms for a few minutes and kept watch. No one else came in, so she joined the short queue for the cashier windows. While she waited she mentally practiced the words she would say when she reached the counter. She was really nervous, after all, she had never asked for twenty thousand pounds in cash before. She had never even seen twenty thousand pounds in cash before.

Her turn arrived so she took a deep breath and made her way to the cashier desk.

"Hi there. I'd like to close this account please," she said, sounding a lot more confident than she was feeling. She handed over her card and the girl tapped the details into the computer.

"Ahmm. There's a lot of money here. It's way over the limit for withdrawals. I'll have to check with the manager. Can you hold on please?"

The cashier disappeared through a door and left Faith standing at the counter. She shuffled her feet nervously and fiddled with the contents of her bag by way of distraction. She felt as if everyone in the bank was staring at her. Then she noticed one pair of eyes which she definitely recognised, a pair of eyes that were definitely staring at her. They belonged to the man who had been watching her at the phone box; he had come back into the bank. She was now one hundred per cent certain that she was being followed. Michael had told her it was a possibility and he seemed to know what he was talking about. Before she had time to worry about it, the cashier returned and pointed to a door at the end of the cash windows.

"Please come on through, the manager would like to have a word with you."

Faith walked quickly over and went through the door. She was ushered into the manager's office. She had never felt so nervous in her life. She reckoned it was guilt that was affecting her, but it could also have been the stress.

"Hello Miss Tamworth, please take a seat."

Faith sat and held her breath, but maybe not in that order. Was this all some sort of extravagant ploy? Was he going to keep her there until a bunch of security guys arrived, she wondered? She said nothing and waited to see how this was all going to pan out. She had no choice now.

"I'm sorry to hear that you want to close your account, you have been with us for a long time. Is there anything we can do for you that would make you change your mind?" he asked in a tone that started to put Faith more at ease.

"No, really, thank you. I just want to get my money out please. I'm moving and I want to have all my cash in my hand. I've got some debts that I want to sort out before I go. I need the cash to sort them."

This was her practiced speech, the one she had been going over and over in her head. She thought it was plausible enough and it did not leave much scope for questioning or argument. She said it very firmly so she left no room for doubt that she had made up her mind.

"Fair enough, I respect you wishes, we would never think of trying to pressurise customers to stay with us. I'm sure you appreciate that I have to ask. You'll have to give us about half an hour to organise that amount of cash. Do you want to wait or come back? We'll happily supply you with a briefcase for your cash. It's a small gesture, but we want you to leave with a good impression of us. Maybe we'll get you back as a customer sometime in the future!" he smiled as he rose from his chair and extended his hand.

After a brief handshake she was shown to a waiting area where she would spend the longest half hour of her life. It seemed to take an eternity. She listened nervously to the sounds of footsteps in the corridor and she froze every time anyone came into the room.

Eventually two uniformed men entered. Security had arrived. Her heart stopped.

"Miss Tamworth?" asked the larger man.

"Yes, that's me."

"We have your money, all you need to do is sign a couple

of forms and then you can be on your way."

She took a cursory look at the documents which he held out in front of her. She did not even try to read them, but she played the game and went through the pretence. She took her time because she did not want to be seen as over hasty. She took the offered pen and signed the forms on the line where the second man pointed.

"We will leave you here to count it," said the first guard as he handed her a black leather briefcase. "Just call someone if there is a problem. Otherwise, thank you very much for your custom."

The two men left the waiting room and Faith just stared at the case. She flicked the catches and literally gasped when she lifted the lid and saw the bundles of twenty and fifty pound notes. There was a printed A4 sheet on the top. It had her name, account details and a line that said 'Total withdrawal £21,674.77'. There was also a white envelope which contained £4.77. She realised that was the odds and sods; the shrapnel.

She closed the briefcase and headed for the door. As she walked out of the bank she sensed the man who had been following her was somewhere nearby. She deliberately did not look round, but she 'felt' him leaving the bank behind her.

✿ ✿ ✿

Michael was totally stressed by his last conversation with Faith. He had felt like a schoolboy in love - heart pounding, gut turning and his words drying up. He was only now realising how much he adored this girl.

There was however something that was severely troubling him. He could not put his finger on it, but there was something about the way Faith had talked to him that made him feel very uneasy. Was she scared, he wondered? Had being followed made her over anxious? Or was he more frightened than he liked to think? Had he missed something that would allow these people to pick up his trail again?

He thought through all the precautions he had taken. He was sure they could not trace the phone call he made. He knew they could keep a tail on Faith, but he had a solution to that particular problem which he would bring into play later.

At exactly three thirty, he rang the phone outside the Ritz restaurant. He was expecting the usual tense wait, but she answered on the first ring. She did not even give him time to speak, she was so excited.

"I got the money! They gave me all the money! I have over twenty thousand pounds in a case at my feet."

"Calm down! Calm down! I knew it would work. I told you I had planned all this meticulously and I am good."

He said this with tongue-in-cheek and hoped she understood. He was actually very surprised that they had given her all the cash at such short notice, but that was great. It meant that they would have no money issues to deal with for a while. Cash was always good to have because it was untraceable.

"Listen Faith, now that you have had a little time to think about things, how do you feel about the prospect of starting a completely new life with me? We had talked about it as something way in the future. How do you fancy making it happen now?"

"I don't know if I'm coming or going right now. I have no idea what to think. You have just robbed a bank and I'm standing here with twenty grand at my feet. I'm sure this will come as no surprise to you, but I'm scared and confused."

"Look, I know this is bound to be a massive shock, but we always talked about taking the big chance when it came along. Well, it has come along. Trust me, I can make this work for us. It sounds trite, but I really can make our dreams come true."

They talked for the next forty minutes. Michael tried to paint a picture of how things could be for them in six months time when they had created new lives and put IIBE far behind them. He talked of travel, money, luxury and assured her that, if they were extremely careful, they could disappear off everyone's radar forever.

Faith talked about her fears and concerns. She was worried about getting caught and also questioned what would happen if their relationship did not work out; after all, they had only been seeing each other for a matter of weeks.

They talked it out, but Faith kept expressing her doubts. Then suddenly, nearly out of the blue, like a switch being thrown, Faith said she was ready to do it.

"OK Michael, you're on. But don't you let me down. I am putting my faith in you. I can't believe I'm doing this. I love you. I can't believe I'm saying that!"

She took a long, deep breath and then asked him in a very serious tone.

"What happens now?"

He explained his plan. He said he still could not tell her where he was because, at this stage, the less she knew the better. The less she knew the less chance of an accidental slip of the tongue. He told her he would phone her soon on her mobile and she needed to react as if that was the first contact. They would plant a false trail when they talked. She had to play along and follow whatever instructions he gave her, as if she believed them to be the real thing. They would talk again soon. It was to be yet another public phone and he gave her the place and time.

She clutched the phone to her chest after he hung up. This was what she had been waiting for. This was the pinnacle of her life so far. She knew she had to be super careful, but she knew she could do it.

"Don't be scared," she told herself. "Don't be scared".

50

Are you crazy?

Tung, Madrick and Michael were all very happily settled into the Liverpool house. It was quite a grand old mansion with comfortable, period furnishings. The main reception room was particularly comforting and welcoming with its stylish furniture and open fireplace. There were plenty of sizable bedrooms so everyone had space to spend some time on their own when they wanted to. It also had a well equipped kitchen which had, at its centre, a large farmhouse style table that was often the social meeting point, particularly when there was food around.

It was day two in the house - lunchtime. They were all sitting round the table enjoying a steaming bowl of tomato soup and discussing the excitement of the last week. Madrick said he thought life was pretty near perfect and Tung too was in his element. He could happily watch television all day long or just sleep, and there was no shortage of food. Tung raved about modern food; he had fallen in love with the tasty soups, fabulous crusty bread and the overall quality of anything that contained meat, in particular, he loved pizza. In his mind, it was worth waiting a thousand years for that innovation.

Tung talked about food constantly. He was like most teenage boys; he could not be filled no matter how much food you tried to shove into him. Michael had already introduced him to lots of the modern staples, but pizza was, far and away, his favourite. Stuffed chicken breasts were a close second on his list and he was talking about them again.

"I love stuffed chicken breasts nearly as much as pizza," he said between slurps of soup. "I mean I love chicken, I love breasts and I love stuff. So what could be better?"

Michael sensed the calmness in the air so decided now was

the time to break the news.

"I've been in touch with Faith. I'm going to get her to come and join us."

"What? Are you crazy?"

"I miss her. I miss being with her. I need to see her because I just can't be happy without her," he said and waited for the bad reaction he knew was going to come.

"You can't do that," said Tung. "You told us we had to stay low. You told us that we had to take no chances. Low profile, you said. This would be a massive risk, you said so yourself."

"I know. But listen guys, I really do miss her. And you know how careful I am and how well I plan things. I've already been able to get her a heap of money which she's now carrying around with her; that will help us big time and keep us comfortable for months. Once she's here, then we'll be able to keep a really low profile. We will become invisible."

"No, no, NO," shouted Tung as he jumped to his feet. "You are putting us all at risk for the sake of a stupid woman. You wouldn't let me do something like this. You'd call me an idiot if I suggested it."

This was obviously risky and he was worried about this disrupting his new lifestyle. He knew he was being a bit selfish, but he really did not care. Madrick put a hand on his arm and helped guide him back into his seat.

"I'm not happy either, but to be fair, I think we should trust him, Tung. After all, he has got us this far and he has looked after us well. He has put himself out and taken risks for us. We would have been in big trouble without him."

He turned to Michael and just looked at him quizzically as if to say 'I can trust you, can't I?'

"Honestly guys, I will be super careful. Remember, I'm in as much danger as you. I'm as scared of these people as you are so I wouldn't take any chances. I won't take any chances."

After a bit more discussion Tung agreed reluctantly. He

knew they owed a lot to Michael, but he also knew this was going to be risky no matter how well he planned this rendezvous.

"We trust you, Michael. We're not happy but we do trust you."

"Thanks guys, I promise I won't let you down."

He was genuinely moved that they had accepted his idea so quickly. He had expected a battle. He knew that he would have fought much harder if the boot had been on the other foot. He thanked them again as he went upstairs to make the calls he had been planning in his head for ages.

The first call was to Faith's mobile. As agreed they both played the 'we-haven't-spoken-for-ages' game and it seemed convincing. In fact, Faith was so convincing that Michael almost believed her. Michael was sure their call was being monitored and he was right; a team of IIBE security agents was listening in.

After the initial small talk Michael felt it was the right time to start introducing the deception into the call. This was the start of the plan and would hopefully throw the listeners off the trail.

"I'm in Newcastle," said Michael. "I really want to see you. I have missed you so much. Will you pack some things and come up here? You could get a train and be here by tomorrow."

"Newcastle? What on earth are you doing in Newcastle?"

"I'll tell you all about it when you get here. It will all make sense, please trust me."

"I don't know. It's a big step for me and..."

"Please. You won't regret it."

"I can't just pack in my normal life on a whim. You can't ask me to do that."

"Just take a few days holiday. Think of it as a short break. We'll play it by ear and see how it goes."

The pleading went on for five minutes and Faith played the

part of the reluctant party brilliantly. Michael was beginning to think she had forgotten the point of the conversation and was never going to agree to meet him. Finally she gave in.

"OK Michael, you're on. But please don't you let me down. I am putting my total faith in you. I can't believe I'm doing this. I love you. I can't believe I'm saying that!"

It was nearly a verbatim repeat of their last 'real' conversation; she thought that was a nice touch. He told her what to bring and what to do when she arrived. He explained where the restaurant was and finally he gave her a time to meet. It was all set and the plan was all systems go.

"I love you so much, Faith. I didn't realise just how much you meant to me until we were apart. I can't wait until I see you, it'll be a long couple of days. Be careful. Be very, very careful."

He hung up, but held the phone against his face for a good five minutes. It was like he was trying to cuddle her voice. He reluctantly dropped the phone onto his desk and went downstairs to join the others. They both looked at him quizzically when he entered the room.

"It's done. She's coming."

"I hope you've done the right thing," said Tung.

So do I, thought Michael, so do I.

51

Derby Day

It was far and away the biggest fixture of the football season in the North-East. The Toon Army, as the Newcastle United fans were called, would tell you it was the biggest fixture anywhere in the land. Newcastle were playing local rivals Sunderland and the city was buzzing.

Faith stepped off the train and, even though she was immediately consumed by the crowds on the platform, she was still aware of the three 'casual' strangers who had been tailing her since she left London.

She had a holdall with her. It contained a few days worth of clothes and some misleading 'clues' which were designed to confuse anyone stealing the bag; false clues that would confuse all but the cleverest of people. During Michael's secret phone call to her, he had listed exactly what she was to pack. It seemed a bit over the top to be so definite about each item in the bag, after all, she was meant to leave it in the left luggage office and never pick it up again. Anyway, because she wanted to follow his instructions to the letter, she deposited the bag and left the station. It was chilly outside so she stuck her hands in her coat pockets, hunched her shoulders and headed up the hill towards St James' Park, Newcastle's home ground. All she had with her now was her handbag, into which she had crammed the twenty thousand pounds worth of notes. She kept that very close to her chest.

The town was heaving with football supporters and there was a very strong police presence. Now she understood why Michael had chosen here, and today, for her to lose her trackers once and for all. As instructed, she stopped off at The Emerald Palace, a Chinese restaurant near the stadium. She picked a table as far away from the door as possible and positioned herself with her back to the wall. That way, she could see who else was dining there and, more importantly, she wanted to see who came in after her. She had to wait a few minutes before the waiter came to her table and, after a short discussion, she ordered the match day, three-course special. She also told the waiter that her name was Faith.

✿ ✿ ✿

Michael had been in Newcastle the day before and had paid way over the odds for a match ticket. He also bought a black and white striped Newcastle football top, black tracksuit bottoms and white trainers; all Faith sized. A blonde wig and a pair of glasses would complete the disguise. He had a quick lunch at the Emerald Palace and afterwards paid the manager five hundred pounds to pass the parcel with the clothes and match ticket to Faith.

He kept a close eye on his time and, at the appointed hour, he made his way to the public phone in the restaurant. At the end of his last conversation with Faith he had given her a phone box location, and they had agreed exactly when he would call it. Now was the time, so he dialled the number of the public phone box. He prayed that Faith would be there and, after only three rings, he breathed a deep sigh of relief when he heard her voice. They exchanged a few pleasantries and then he explained the plan to Faith. She checked every little point as they went along so she was clear on every part of the plan. Her attention to detail meant Michael knew she was taking the whole thing extremely seriously. This is going to work, he thought to himself, this is actually going to work.

Once they had finished the private call, Michael phoned her mobile and they laid a false trail for the eavesdroppers that he knew would be listening in. She played her part well. She had clearly understood both the plan and the precautions. He just prayed that they were both clever enough to fool the snooping wiretappers.

He ended the call by telling her how much he loved her and then he hung up, left the Palace and headed to the station to start his journey back to Liverpool.

✿ ✿ ✿

Faith finished her lunch and ordered a coffee. The waiter smiled and pointed out that she was in danger of missing the start of the match. He knew that practically everyone in the place was destined for the game, so this bit of friendly advice could boost his tip.

"Thanks for the warning," she said. "I'm not going to the match."

She said it louder than was really necessary. The excess volume was for the benefit of the two groups of men who had arrived in the Palace shortly after her. She was determined to play her role to the letter, after all she thought, you never know who is watching.

After a second coffee, she paid the bill and asked where the toilet was. She made her way past the few remaining occupied tables, the place had virtually emptied half an hour before kick-off. Just as she was passing the last occupied table, a man stood up and blocked her way. Her heart stopped.

"Not going to the match then, pet?" he said with a thick Geordie accent. His voice was slightly slurred from at least one glass of wine too many.

Faith's heart restarted when she realised this was just a clumsy pick-up attempt.

"Sorry. Excuse me. I really need to get passed," she said as she slipped round the man.

She rushed the last few yards, keeping her eyes straight ahead, and dived into the ladies room. A few minutes later, a waitress followed her in and handed her the package which Michael had left. It contained the change of clothes, the match ticket and the disguise. She tucked the package under her arm and left the restaurant without looking back to see what was going on behind her. She did not run, but she did walk her fastest walk the short distance up the hill to St James' Park. There were very few people about because the match was already half over so everyone was inside the stadium.

It took her a good fifteen minutes, and a couple of enquiries, before she found the right entrance, handed in her ticket and made her way into the buzzing, crowded ground. The men who were following her were stuck outside. There was no way to get into this match without a ticket, and there was no easy way to get a ticket.

Faith immediately made her way to the ladies' toilet where she changed into the striped top, the black bottoms and the trainers. She got the twenty thousand pounds out of her bag and slotted it into a money belt which she carefully strapped round her waist. She then ditched all her own clothes, her handbag, her mobile phone, her credit cards - everything. She donned the wig and glasses. She looked in the mirror and did not recognise herself. That was a good omen. She took a deep breath and made her way to her seat among the fifty thousand plus crowd; half of them dressed in tops exactly like hers.

When the match was over, she was invisible in the horde of people that streamed out of the ground. The crowd was in buoyant mood because the home team had beaten their local rivals 6-1; 'Howay the Lads' was the deafening chant which surrounded her.

She stayed with the biggest group of fans until she was over half a mile away from the stadium, then she hopped into a taxi and asked the driver to take her to Darlington. He was a bit taken aback by the distance, but she waved some of her cash in his direction and he happily settled in to a nice-earner of a journey. After about an hour's driving, he dropped her off at Darlington railway station, by which time she had swapped the striped top for a plain black jacket. She blended in again, but she was sure that she had lost her tail. She was confident there was no one around to notice her blending.

She bought a one-way ticket for cash and waited on the platform for the train to arrive. Even though she was sure she was in the clear, she kept a keen eye out for anyone who might be watching her. About ten minutes before her train was due she spotted a couple of men who looked out of place among the other travellers. They seemed to be anxious and every so often she felt their eyes fall on her. Were they watching her, she wondered, or were they worried that she was watching them? Her question was answered when the pair both hopped on a train going in the opposite direction. She watched them go and that seemed to bother them. They obviously had something to hide.

Within minutes, her own train pulled into the station. She had one final look around the platform before she boarded the carriage that would take her to Manchester. She found a window seat and settled in for the journey, but she could not relax. She had, more or less, stopped worrying about being followed, now she was worrying about how she would really feel when she saw Michael.

The journey passed quickly and it seemed like no time until she was stepping off the train in Manchester. She made her way to the taxi rank where she grabbed a cab to take her to Liverpool.

There was no turning back now, but that did not stop her wondering if she was doing the right thing. She knew that all her bridges would be burnt the moment she met up with Michael. Her life was going to change forever, so she prayed she had made the right decision.

52

We lost her

There was complete pandemonium at IIBE where the security team was gathered. Before the report came in, there had been a muted excitement as the expectation built of capturing the fugitives. The planning had been extensive and they had deployed some of their top men to track Faith.

They were proud of their efforts and confident that the inside line they had got from tapping Faith's phone gave them all they needed to set the perfect trap.

The message that came through changed all that. The message was from the agents who had been following Faith and it brought the worst possible news. They had lost her. The lead agent of the HQ team had taken the call.

He listened impassively when the report began, but he became increasingly agitated as the story unfolded. The room went silent as everyone watched his mood change. It was clear that he was getting some very bad news.

The caller explained that, as instructed, the pursuit team had positioned themselves in and around the restaurant where the girl was supposed to be meeting Michael. As a safeguard, they had assigned three men to follow her all the way from London to make sure she went to Newcastle and the restaurant. No one was taking any chances.

They had people inside, posing as diners, and people outside covering the front and back. They had all been extremely careful to look casual so they did not alert their target. They were ready to pounce as soon as Michael showed up.

She had eaten a meal, as expected, but there was no sign of anyone else. She had dined alone and then she had unexpectedly left the Palace alone. At the time they could only surmise that something had spooked them and they had aborted the meeting. There had been one unusual development though, a development which made them think that they may have been tricked. Had they been played all along? Had Phillips known that they were listening in on his plans?

"What was the development?" he asked as casually as possible. These were the first words he had said since he had taken the call. He listened again and was told that she had picked up a parcel in the toilet. They had no idea what was in the parcel.

They followed her to St James' Park, but she had been able to get into the ground. She had somehow got herself a ticket. It had presumably been in the parcel. They had tried everything from bribery to threats to get in after her, but they failed to get past security. Eventually they paid crazy money for a couple of tickets in another section of the ground, but as soon as they went inside it was clear they were not going to find her.

They explained how they deployed all their available manpower at key locations around the ground, but they knew that was going to be futile. Also, more in hope than expectation, they had also stationed a few men at the train station left luggage in case she showed up there to retrieve her bag, but of course, she never showed up.

The manager who was coordinating the mission from the headquarters building was absolutely livid. He listened carefully to the report, but even the fact that they had not really made any mistakes did not quell his anger. He screamed a barrage of abuse at the phone and then slammed the receiver down in a rage. Deep down he knew his men had done a good job, they had just been outplayed by clever planning. That was the only mistake they had made - underestimating Phillips and the girl. Now he was going to have to take the fall for the situation so he was dreading having to report this to his boss, Jim Robinson. He was dreading having to take the abuse that he had just dished out. He knew that Faith was the last solid lead they had and she had slipped through the net, at the football match, on his watch.

He passed on the guts of the message to his team which caused pandemonium as everyone started pointing fingers. No one wanted to take the fall for this.

He had no idea what they would do next. That was the worst part of this problem. That was why his failure was so catastrophic.

He braced himself and made the call to his boss. Robinson listened to his report and seemed to take the news relatively calmly. That was nearly worse, he thought, he had prepared himself for a screaming match and now he was left not really knowing how his boss felt about him. He was very troubled as he hung up the phone.

Robinson considered what he had heard very carefully. He smiled to himself before he made his own call on a secure line to Buckingham.

53

Together at last

Faith stepped out of the cab near the world famous Royal Liver Building. She had never been to Liverpool before, but she knew immediately that she was exactly where she was meant to be. The Royal Liver Building was a great place to meet because it was so recognisable, even for a stranger to the city. She now stood in front of the great concrete structure and knew the next few days were going to be the most dramatic of her life.

She looked up at the iconic birds which were perched high above her and remembered hearing the rumour from a Liverpudlian friend that every time a local virgin walks past, the Liver Birds flap their wings, but no one had ever seen them flap! She knew that the more official legend was that if either of the birds was to fly away then the city of Liverpool would cease to exist and that is why both of the great bronze birds were chained to the building.

She looked around the crowded street. Her heart was pounding. She was especially nervous and anxious about how this meeting was going to go. Would she be able to hold herself together, she wondered, would she be able to see this through to its desired conclusion?

She saw Michael before he saw her. She recognised him immediately even though the beard and moustache were gone. Had he shaved especially for her, she wondered? She ran over, threw her arms around him and hugged him tightly. He seemed momentarily startled, as if he was not expecting her at all.

"I didn't recognise you," he said. "That wig works really well! Take it off please, I want to see the girl I love!"

She took off the disguise and he could do nothing for a few seconds as he stared at her. He had been waiting for this moment for so long. He broke the stare and they hugged some more. Michael had never felt as happy as he felt that very moment. A wave of relief spread through him; they were back together and everything was right with the world.

"It's fabulous to see you; there is so much I need to tell you. Are you all right? I've missed you so much. Have you missed me?"

He realised he was babbling so he stopped talking and gave her another big hug.

"Let's get going. We're going to take a walk to my house. It's not too far and it'll give us a chance to talk. We'll be there in about twenty minutes and then we're going to meet up with a couple of old friends."

He hugged her tight and felt a sense of total calmness engulf his body. He always had a little anecdote for every occasion and one suddenly popped into his head.

"I remember reading that 'faith isn't faith until it's all you're holding on to' and, right now, I know exactly what that means."

She laughed and he held her. Then they set off on their way.

They chatted and hugged and kissed as they walked slowly to Michael's house. She told him how smart she thought he was. She always made him feel good with her words. She talked of how the plan had worked perfectly, just like he said it would. She showed him the money belt around her waist and did a little happy skip as she started to describe her encounter with the bank manager.

He told her about his journey to Liverpool. He apologised again for 'running out on her' but he had had to leave in a hurry once he had started to steal the money. He could not hang around and allow IIBE to snare him.

"I really couldn't say too much to you for your own safety and mine. But I knew I'd be able to make it right. I knew I could make it all alright."

He had decided to keep the serious and crazy bits for later when they were relaxing at the house so he said nothing about the Occultus Populous, magic spells or the Scroll. That was not going to be an easy conversation so it was best left until they could concentrate on it properly. Best left until he had some things around him which would help him convince her that he was not absolutely bonkers.

When they arrived at the house Tung and Madrick seemed genuinely pleased to see her. There was a bit of embarrassed should-we-hug-or-not dancing and eventually they settled on not, after all Faith had only met them once and it had taken her days to get over the resulting hangover.

For the next half hour they sat round the fire and talked. It was largely small talk and more about how Faith had been and what she had been doing.

Michael was waiting for the right moment to get on to the important stuff. Eventually he started to tell her about Tung and Madrick, but she seemed a little distant, as if she was not really listening. He assumed that she was exhausted by her travels from London to Newcastle to Liverpool, as well as the tension of having to lose her tail. Logic told him that that was the case, but his gut told him different. There was definitely something that was bothering her and Michael was worried about it.

"Are you all right?" he asked. "I know it's been crazy over the last few days, but you seem to be a bit, ahmm, vacant."

She snapped out of her own little world and smiled sweetly at him. He loved her smile and immediately felt more at ease.

"I'm really sorry," she said. "I just feel so incredibly tired. This has all been a bit too exciting for me. I'm not used to having any sort of adventure, never mind one like this."

"No worries," said Michael and he slipped his arm around her shoulder.

He knew a hug would do him good and he hoped it would help Faith calm down and relax. He was disappointed, and a little bit hurt, when she shrugged him off.

"I'm sorry, I'm just not feeling myself."

She excused herself and went to the bathroom. She locked the door behind her and sat on the edge of the bath. She stared at the floor for a good five minutes. She closed her eyes and rubbed her face with her hands as if she was unsure what she should do. But she knew exactly what she had to do.

She took out a small mobile phone which was hidden in her sock. It was the phone which Jim Robinson had given her.

54

Faith

The 'modern' IIBE bank had been established in the early sixteenth century, but its roots stretched back to the early Saxon attacks on Britain. The Danegeld tax had been introduced to finance forces to oppose Viking invaders. The taxes needed to be collected and a formal bank was established to manage the money. But the system was quickly infiltrated and subsumed by the Occultus Populous. They recognised the power that money and debt would hold over people. From the day they gained control, the bank helped create massive wealth for the owners so it soon became one of the Society's most prized assets.

Everything went smoothly for centuries. Then there was a major theft from the bank in 1820 perpetrated by one of the senior managers. That sent shock waves through the highest echelons so, to protect their interests, the owners set up intricate networks of spies within the organisation. Those spies were the forerunners of the present day security department.

Today, the IIBE security department was extremely well organised, completely ruthless and highly secretive. It had at its disposal a whole arsenal of weapons, spying devices and covert techniques which were there to protect the bank from every conceivable kind of attack.

As time went on, the department became more and more powerful within the bank and its methods evolved over the years to ensure it was prepared for the ever-changing threats which it faced. The most significant change happened when they recruited a senior Stasi operative in the 1980s. She had been one of the most ruthless commanders in the East German Secret Police and she had completely remodelled the organisation.

One of its most successful strategies was to use spies to form close, short-term relationships with all new employees who could potentially compromise the bank. Michael was one such employee and Faith was one such spy.

Faith Tamworth had been recruited by IIBE when she was only sixteen and just about to leave school. The IIBE training centre was located nearby and they employed quite a lot of local people to work in the centre although very few were ever chosen to work in the bank itself.

They had offered her an extremely generous salary and the opportunity to travel all over the world working in a number of the IIBE international branches. She was to spend six months or so in each branch, ostensibly carrying out receptionist duties, but her real job was to befriend designated employees and report anything that might be of interest to internal security. They portrayed the role as essential to protect IIBE from cheats, fraudsters, scammers, thieves and liars and, they were keen to point out, they needed help because they were always a target for these criminals. They also convinced her that anyone who was part of that protective inner circle would be extremely well looked after and handsomely rewarded. This would be a long-term commitment by both parties, they told her, and she would never regret it.

As soon as she signed up, she underwent an intense four month training and induction programme. Half of the programme was about the tricks and techniques of forming relationships. There was some very devious stuff and it prised open the eyes of an impressionable young lady.

The other half of the training was effectively brainwashing; all of it aimed at convincing her to believe that IIBE was a totally benevolent organisation that deserved her complete loyalty. At the end of the course she felt very grateful to IIBE for the opportunity and she felt very special and privileged.

There was one particular incident which cemented her

loyalty to the bank very early on.

✿ ✿ ✿

Faith was nearly half way through the IIBE training course when Brian Clarke came back into her life. He was the bully from her childhood that she had humiliated in the school playground. He had sworn vengeance on Faith and her friend Suzie, but he had never had the opportunity until they met again, by chance, nearly ten years after the original incident.

Brian Clarke was still a bully - some things never change. He had been expelled from school soon after his encounter with Faith and had subsequently failed at everything he had done. He had had a succession of home tutors who had all given up on him as lazy and stupid and nasty. Eventually he got a minimum wage job as a junior porter with a small catering company. He carried boxes and washed dishes - badly.

The company he worked for provided catering services for the IIBE training centre so he was often there carrying out a variety of menial tasks. His life was a meaningless humdrum until the day he spotted Faith. He could not believe it, he had all but forgotten about her.

He watched her at every opportunity. Then, one day, they bumped into each other. She recognised him immediately and she was horrified. Clarke, on the other hand, was delighted because he could see the distress in her eyes. They exchanged pleasantries, with no sincerity, and then Faith quickly went on her way. She hoped that would be the end of the matter because, even after all these years, she still hated and feared Brian Clarke.

As is often the way with bullies, Clarke held petty grudges - not for days but forever. He decided he was going to hurt, really hurt, this person who had shattered his reputation all those years ago.

He planned a very crude revenge as that was all he was capable of doing. He watched Faith's movement each night when she left the centre. She always left just after five and made her way across the waste ground that sat behind the IIBE training building. She crossed a couple of back streets until she arrived at the stop where she got the bus that took her home.

The waste ground, he decided, was where he would do it. That was the perfect place. It was very secluded, so that would give him plenty of time with her; plenty of time to get rid of those years of frustration and resentment.

Faith had been unsettled by her encounter with Clarke. She had casually mentioned it to her course supervisor. It was a casual comment, but he had taken it seriously and he told her not to worry. He reminded her that she was one of the bank's key employees and they would look after her. He reported the conversation to the internal security department where Faith would eventually work.

Clarke watched her for weeks and noticed that Wednesdays were the quietest days, often no one crossed the waste ground for hours. He had gathered together his 'kit' which comprised some duct tape, a small cosh and a razor sharp folding knife. He crouched in a dark corner and waited.

Faith had enjoyed her day, but she was looking forward to getting home. She walked quickly because she did not like this place, but the shortcut saved her at least ten minutes. Clarke jumped out of the darkness and her heart stopped.

"The time has come Faith. Just like you knew it would."

Clarke did not know what hit him, literally! He felt something hard smash into the back of his head and he crumpled onto the ground. The darkness was the perfect cover for an assault, but this was not how he had envisaged it. Two men now stood over his prone body.

"Everything is fine, Miss Tamworth. You go on home and we'll deal with this," said one of the men. She vaguely recognised him from the training centre, but she was not going to hang around long enough to find out exactly who he was. Her instincts took over and she walked away, moving even faster than before. She did not look back, but she heard Clarke being dragged along the ground.

The two men pulled him into the corner where he had been hiding and beat him mercilessly. They left him with multiple cuts, heavy bruising, two broken legs and a message. While he lay, bleeding on the ground, one man whispered menacingly in his ear.

"This is a gentle warning. Never talk to Faith again."

He never did. He knew that this was the time to drop his grudge; even stupid bullies know when to stop. As soon as he recovered, he left his job and moved to Liverpool which, he hoped, would be far enough away.

The day after the assault, Faith received a couple of photos on her phone. They showed Clarke beaten and bloodied. She realised at that point that she was working for dangerous people. But these dangerous people were looking after her and she liked that.

✿ ✿ ✿

Faith absolutely loved her job and she was very good at it. Her great looks and delightful personality, coupled with the tricks she had been taught, made her an instant hit with the young men who became her targets. There was something special about her physical appearance which drew people in and that, of course, was one of the reasons why she had been selected in the first place.

To date she had managed extremely well with every task the bank had set for her. As directed, she had formed a close bond with each target from very early on. She had never been rumbled and had even managed to stay friends with the marks after she had been instructed to move on.

She had already worked assignments in New York, Chicago, Sydney, Toronto, Birmingham and Edinburgh. Up to this point however, none of her relationships had identified any threats to the bank. That was good news for the bank, but Faith was a little disappointed because she had hoped that her hard work would have produced some real results. Sometimes she had wondered if there really was a threat to the bank or was she employed to protect it from phantom shadows?

Faith's latest mission was in London targeting Michael Phillips, a computer support specialist. She had quickly formed a friendship, but even she was surprised how it had developed. She knew he was already very fond of her. However, things were not quite as they should be because, for the first time, she was becoming quite attached to her mark. There was something about him that was very appealing and endearing; and she was falling for him.

Even in the very early days of the relationship she had felt that Michael was a little bit different, particularly in the way he treated his job. He was not the normal nine to five employee and there was something about the way he acted that had set off alarm bells in her head.

The fact that she liked him was not going to change how she went about the task, but she was worried that this was going to turn out to be the first assignment where the target did actually mean harm to her employer. She was hoping with all her heart that this was not the case.

Michael had said a few things to her which had made her feel that his work aspirations were unusual, but there was nothing specific. She had not pushed him too hard on the matter because she did not want to raise his suspicions. She did, however, take every opportunity to give him the space to talk about his work. She had reported all the conversations to Jim Robinson, her boss, but he had just said to keep monitoring and to keep probing gently.

It all changed when Michael was identified as the perpetrator of the big fraud.

She was briefed about his activities and shown the evidence which proved his guilt in the fraud. She was not told anything about Madrick and Tung except that they were now, apparently, working with Michael. She decided that there was no good reason to pass on the few details that she remembered about meeting them. She did not feel that what little she knew was relevant and she was still very embarrassed about her behaviour that night.

Michael was now the focus of a lot of attention, so Robinson was interested in everything she knew about him, every little detail. He also stressed that she must notify him if Michael made contact so, immediately after they had talked on Suzie's mobile, she reported the whole conversation to Robinson. He had come back to her less than ten minutes later and told her to go ahead to the phone box. He also said he would assign a team to follow her and watch her back. He assured her she would never be alone and that they would protect her. She did not feel in danger, but this assurance comforted her. She really did not feel that Michael posed any threat to her, but then again, she had not realised that he was a thief.

Robinson did not tell her that no one below his level knew about her. That meant the men who would follow her believed she was part of the fraud. They would see her as a rogue employee who would eventually lead them to Michael Phillips. If she had known that, she might have been less comforted by the men who tailed her; the men she wrongly thought of as her 'guardians'.

As instructed, she reported back immediately after her conversation in the phone box. Again her boss called her back after less than ten minutes. He told her to go to the bank and said he would clear the way for her to withdraw all the funds.

After she picked up the money she headed for her three-thirty appointment at the Ritz. She was sure she was being followed, Robinson had not let her down; there was someone watching her back.

She had her long conversation with Michael and she was sure she had acted her part well enough so as not to raise his suspicions. She then summarised the whole conversation for her boss making sure she did not leave out any important details. He, in turn, reported it all to Buckingham.

Faith was instructed to go along with Michael's plan to the letter. She had to play her part well so as not to raise any suspicion. Robinson also gave her a mobile phone which she was to keep with her at all times. It would allow her to get in touch with him immediately, at any time of the day or night, and its GPS would allow him to know exactly where she was.

"When you are in the location where he is holed up with the other two thieves then, and only then, call me."

He stressed the importance of waiting until they were with the 'other two thieves' but he did not explain why. She would never be told that they were the real target of this manhunt because they had the Scroll.

"As soon as I get your call, we'll come and get you."

55

Déjà vu all over again

It was dark when the thirty man team arrived at the house in Liverpool. It was a larger team than would be normal for this type of operation, but this was crucial. They were not going to fail because they were under-resourced for this final step. Unusually, Jim Robinson had left the nerve centre of the headquarters building to co-ordinate the assault. This was way too important to leave in anyone else's hands.

The men had all been thoroughly briefed and every individual knew his role inside out. They silently took up their positions around the secluded mansion. A team of six armed men assembled at the front while another team of seven positioned themselves at the back. Simultaneously both teams burst through the doors shouting at the top of their voices so as to create the maximum amount of confusion and fear. They charged through the ground floor of the house fanning out to check each room they came to. They quickly found their four targets in the front room. They were paralysed by surprise, like the proverbial rabbits caught in the headlights.

Tung was the first to react, in fact, he was the only one to react. He had plenty of experience of being on the wrong end of an ambush. Without any warning, he darted for the window and, without any thought, he threw himself headfirst at it. He expected it to smash and for him to perform a graceful roll outside before he rose to his feet and ran free. He expected it to be exactly the same as his escape from the three bearded men back in his day, his famous spring roll. Unfortunately, he was unaware of double glazing and its inherent strength. Welcome to the twenty-first century! His head might as well have smashed into a brick wall and that was certainly the way it felt. Here comes another mammoth headache he thought as he crashed to the floor, inside the room.

Robinson walked into the room and surveyed the scene. There were two men sitting stark still and another one groaning on the floor. Faith sat, trembling a little, near the fire. Everyone was accounted for and everything seemed to be under control.

"Subdue the prisoners. Get them ready for their trip," he ordered.

His team moved forward and very professionally secured the three men with plastic ties. They were led out of the house and away to the waiting vans. Once inside they were hooded and their feet were bound with more plastic ties. The whole operation had taken less than five minutes.

Jim walked over to where Faith was sitting, she was still startled even though she had been expecting something like this. It had just been a lot more sudden than she had prepared herself for.

"Fantastic job!" he said. "You have done us proud and you'll be well rewarded for this. We just need to find all Phillips' computer gear. Oh yes, and have you seen an old bit of parchment that the old man had?"

He had added the last bit as casually as he could. He was the only one on the team who understood exactly what this operation was about. Everyone else believed the priority was to capture Michael. They believed the other two were just accomplices and the girl was a relatively innocent bystander. No one else knew about the Scroll and that it was, in fact, the most important part of the mission. No one else there knew about Faith and exactly what her role had been.

"Thanks. That was the most nerve-wracking thing I have ever done. Look at me, I'm trembling," she said holding out her hands to demonstrate how shaky she was.

She had not really heard what he had said or at least she was far too disoriented to take any notice of it in. She had certainly not heard the vital question.

"The Scroll? Have you seen a scroll?" he asked with more urgency.

"No sorry. I know all the computer stuff is in a room at the top of the stairs, but I haven't seen a scroll."

"No problem, we'll find it," said Robinson as he started to direct the search teams.

Within fifteen minutes they had collected all the computer equipment, but there was still no sign of the scroll. They rummaged for a further half hour but with no success. That was when Robinson decided it was time for him to get the prisoners back to London; back to his boss. That was what he had been ordered to do; secure the prisoners and bring them back to base.

He left four men to stay in the house. They would retrieve the scroll once the prisoners told them where it was hidden, and they would tell because they were about to face the most extreme interrogation, an interrogation which would break any man.

He took Faith by the arm and led her out to the black Mercedes which was now parked at the front of the house. He opened the car door and helped her settle into the back seat before running round and jumping in the other side.

On his instruction, the Mercedes took off followed by the vans which held the bulk of the team and the three prisoners. The convoy headed for the motorway which would take them to London. This would be a very uncomfortable journey for the prisoners, but it would seem immensely preferable to what awaited them.

✿ ✿ ✿

The three captives were carried through the back entrance of the IIBE headquarters building and deposited roughly in the corridor that led to the secure teleconferencing facility. It was in a part of the building that only the most privileged employees were authorised to go. In fact, only members of

Occultus Populous were allowed in that special and secret labyrinth that lay under the grand old building. It had been built hundreds of years earlier and was the most secret of secret places.

Robinson waited with the prisoners until he was joined by six member agents. They carried the prisoners through the heavy door which Robinson unlocked with a very old iron key which never left his person. They carted them down steps, along corridors and down further steps. They took them deep underground and, when they could go no deeper, they were finally dumped into an authentic dungeon.

Tung, Madrick and Michael were still bound and hooded, but they could sense they were in a cold, damp place. They heard a heavy door slam followed by a solid metallic bolt engaging. Then, all was silent.

Dark, dank, and putrid were the words an estate agent might have used to glamorise this miserable dungeon. There were no words horrible or nauseating enough to describe what it was really like.

It was déjà vu all over again for Tung and Madrick. They felt they had been in exactly this predicament before. The only real difference was that they did not know what was planned for them, but they knew for sure it was not going to be pleasant.

"We are in big trouble, aren't we?" said Tung.

"Yeah, big trouble."

"That was a rhetorical question," snapped Tung.

"That's not a rhetorical question. What are you talking about?"

"I think it was. You told me that a rhetorical question was a question that didn't want an answer. I didn't want that answer."

There was a silence because there was just no answer to that. This was an inappropriate discussion that was going nowhere and they had a lot more to worry about than semantics.

"We shouldn't talk," said Michael. "They are bound to be listening. Just remember what we agreed."

"I remember," said Tung. "Don't worry, I remember."

56

Mission accomplished

They had no idea how long they were in the cell for, but it seemed like an eternity. They were all extremely uncomfortable and scared. The ties were digging deep into their limbs and the hooded darkness just intensified the pain and fear. They did, however, derive some comfort from the fact that they had a plan and they believed that their plan would get them out of this hole.

Suddenly, the door crashed open and they were dragged to their feet. The ties around their legs were cut and they were led out of the cell, up steps, along corridors and eventually into a warm room. The hoods were removed and the three immediately shut their eyes and turned their heads to the floor, blinded by the lights.

When he was able to focus, Michael looked up and realised they were in the teleconferencing facility. The members of the Grand Council appeared on giant screens and a further two Members were with them in the room. They recognised one of them as Sir Samuel Buckingham. This was exactly what they had hoped for; this is what they had heard the Council plan for them when they had eavesdropped on one of their planning meetings.

"I know you know who we are and why you are here," began Buckingham. "We are going to give you a chance to answer our questions here and now. That would be the civilised way for all concerned. Otherwise you will suffer unbearable and unimaginable pain until you give us what we want, and that will not be civilised.

"Just to be very clear, we want the Scroll and we want any records you have of our meetings. We know you were watching us.

"Do not try and deceive us. We will get to the truth.

And I warn you, our patience is nearly exhausted. We have expended a lot of time and money to find you and we do not plan to waste any more of either."

As agreed, Michael kept quiet while Madrick caused a distraction. They wanted nothing to get in the way of Tung saying the spell.

"If you know about us then you know my name is Madrick and I am an accomplished and respected wizard. I have cast spells that few wizards in the history of time could even have dreamed of. I was once the Royal Wizard, by appointment to King Mifal…".

"Enough. We have no interest in your history. What we want is the Scroll. Where is it?"

While this exchange went on, Tung was trying, as inconspicuously as possible, to say the Believe Me Spell that was in his head. He was now well practiced and no longer fainted or fell over. There was very little external indication that anything strange was happening, in fact, no one who was watching noticed anything unusual about Tung. They did not know that they were about to be comprehensibly and magically deceived.

"Believe me," said Tung as he started his well practiced speech. "You have the wrong people. We are not time travellers or thieves. We did not rob you and we do not have a scroll. We have nothing that you want. The people you are looking for are dead and the Scroll has been destroyed.

"We will not remember anything about your organisation or being here. You must send us home and never bother us again."

There was a silence in the room. The Members were stunned. Buckingham broke the silence.

"There has been a terrible mistake. I am so sorry gentlemen. People will be punished for putting you through this ordeal."

He summoned the guards who were outside in the

corridor.

"Untie these men," he ordered. "Immediately!"

One of the guards stepped forward and cut the ties on all three men.

"Show these men out. Take them to our best car and instruct the driver to take them to wherever they want to go.

"Gentlemen, again all I can say is how extremely sorry I am about our dreadful mistake. I cannot apologise enough."

"Believe me," said Tung. "We will hold no grudges - if you give us money before we leave."

Michael and Madrick would have both been astounded by his stupidity had they not totally accepted what Tung had just said. If they had not been enchanted, like everyone else who heard him speak, they would have been horrified that he would risk such an idiotic deviation from the plan, just as they were about to be gifted their freedom. But it was different this time, Tung had pointlessly jeopardised their escape, but this time, everyone was happy. Everyone that is, except Jim Robinson who could not believe his eyes when he saw the three men being led out towards the exit.

"Sir Samuel, what is going on? Why are you letting these people go?"

"They have nothing to do with our problem. We have made a dreadful mistake."

Robinson could only stand open-mouthed as he watched everyone leave. He would demand a private session with Buckingham as soon as he was available. He would have to get to the bottom of this. He did not know that this was the beginning of the end of his special relationship with his boss.

Tung, Madrick and Michael were escorted out of the building and led to a chauffeur driven limousine. The door was opened for them and they slid into the white leather lined compartment. Just before the door closed, Buckingham handed Tung a thick white envelope.

"Again I cannot apologise enough. I hope this small token of our appreciation of your understanding will help you forgive us. Goodbye, gentlemen."

With that, he turned and walked back into the building. Tung smiled his 'see I told you' smile and tucked the envelope into his pocket without even looking to see what was in it. He thought that his casualness would further rub Michael and Madrick's noses in his little victory. He had forgotten that they were oblivious to what he had done, because they believed the story as much as Buckingham had.

After a brief conversation, the chauffer started the long drive to Liverpool while the three passengers enthusiastically explored the drinks cabinet.

"That was a bit scary and weird," said Michael. "What on earth made them think we had robbed them and what is the scroll that is so important to them?"

"I am very confused," added Madrick. "I have very strange memories which do not fit in with the picture I have of my life."

It was then that Tung remembered that they too had been affected by his spell.

"Believe me," said Tung. "I can help you."

And that is exactly what he did. He reminded them of who they were and what they had done. He undid the lie for them.

"Right. That makes a bit more sense now."

"Yes. It makes sense to me too. I can see now why I felt so strange."

Back in the teleconferencing suite, Buckingham was bringing the meeting to a close. They had agreed that everything was back to the way it should be and their secret organisation was safe. They further agreed that they would change the stated mission of the Occultus Populous because the hunt for the time travellers and the Scroll was over. The time travellers were dead and the Scroll had been destroyed.

They would instead concentrate on further building their power base and wealth. They would continue to strive for a one world government which they would control.

There was still work to be done to retrieve the money that had been stolen, but that was well underway. There was also a major exercise required to restore IIBE's reputation and to stabilise the global financial system. They agreed a plan to achieve this and they collectively promised massive resources to ensure it happened quickly.

Buckingham was pleased with the outcome. They had not retrieved the Scroll, but crucially, it had not been left in the control of commoners. The time travellers were dead so that also closed off that part of their ancient mission.

He thanked the Members for their dedication and, with tongue in cheek, wrapped up the meeting.

"Thank you again gentlemen. I will see you all in about two hundred and fifty years."

57

The A+ Team

The car drew into the driveway at Michael's Liverpool home and three, very happy, passengers disembarked. They thanked the driver and Tung gave him a departing 'Believe Me' to make sure he had not picked up any incriminating evidence from their conversations. He drove away feeling sorry about the ordeal that these poor, innocent folk had been put though.

They crunched across the gravel driveway and made their way into the house. Tung retrieved the Scroll from its hiding place in the garden. That had been clever. It would have been virtually impossible to find it without digging up the whole of these substantial grounds.

They made their way into the house. It seemed even more welcoming than usual. They were home and they were home free.

As he closed the door, Michael sang 'In my Liverpool home' - just those four words over and over because that was all he knew of the song. He set a fire in the large grate in the front room and the three of them settled down in front of the fledgling flames. They were relaxed and feeling very satisfied with their work.

"It is wonderful when a plan comes together," said Michael. "Full marks for the A team. In fact, we are the A+ team!"

Neither Tung nor Madrick had any idea what he was talking about, but they were happy. Tung tried his own rendition of 'Liverpool home' but he did not even know four words so it was pretty poor.

"Now our destiny is in our own hands. We definitely came up with a great plan to go with a great spell! Now we don't have to simply react to what others are doing, we decide what happens next," said Michael in an attempt to halt Tung's warble.

"We have a year to sort out our plans. They won't be after us for at least that length of time. With any luck, they may never come after us again."

Everyone was calm. There was no need for urgency, but there were still things to be done.

"The first thing I am going to do is post all the footage we have of the Occultus Populous meetings on the internet. We are going to totally obliterate that organisation. We are going to make sure that they never again have the power to destroy people's lives. And they won't have a clue that it is us doing it. I love it. Even if they remember us in a year, there'll be nothing of the organisation left to chase us."

"The first thing I am going to do," said Tung, "is order three of the world's biggest pizzas. We need to celebrate and we need to celebrate big!"

"The first thing I am going to do," said Madrick, "is get some sleep. I am wiped out. I am shattered. A man of my age cannot endure this kind of turmoil without it taking a toll on the body. I need to rest. I need to sleep."

So Madrick slept, Tung ordered pizza and Michael went to work on his computer.

He retrieved all the video files he had of the Occultus Populous meetings. He watched segments of them and quickly realised just how damning this footage was. He edited together a compilation of the juiciest bits and posted them on a number of popular forums on the internet. He knew that the world's media would very quickly pick these up and they would shine a very bright spotlight on this shadowy organisation. He was confident that this exposure would destroy these people and their secret society and they would have no idea who had done it to them. The Council members believed he was an innocent bystander; they would continue to believe that, no matter what evidence to the contrary was presented to them.

Well pleased with his work, Michael joined Tung and, shortly afterwards, the pizza arrived. They ate, they talked and they enjoyed the warmth of a fire that was now roaring like a ferocious lion.

Eventually Madrick appeared. He had slept for an hour or so and was totally refreshed. There was no pizza left, but he was not particularly hungry.

"Are we good?" he asked. "Are we ready to do something for ourselves? It will make a pleasant change for all of us if we could make a dream or two come true."

"I'm all for that," said Tung. "I can't remember the last dream I had that came true. I remember plenty of nightmares that happened though and a lot of them were very recent."

"I know," said Michael. "We deserve some joy after what we've all been through. And I'm nearly ready.

"But there is one last thing I need to do before we start thinking about our own futures. I need to talk to Faith."

58

The jagged rocks of world attention

Much of the Occultus Populous Members' wealth was inextricably linked to the fate of IIBE, but because they had the inside track, they were shielded from any significant losses. In fact, most of them had made money from the financial disaster. Just as Buckingham had promised, by knowing when the IIBE systems would be offline, they all had numerous opportunities to 'bet' on market movements which they knew, for sure, would happen. The uninformed investors were losing millions in the chaos, but these, already immensely wealthy, individuals were sucking up profits like there was no tomorrow.

However something very bad had happened in the midst of the financial free-for-all. Secret footage of their recent meetings had been leaked into the public domain. This was a disaster.

The pressures on the Occultus Populous were immense. The Council Members had no idea who had exposed them, but they were determined to minimise the damage by stifling as many information outlets as possible. They had all committed massive resources to the task which, so far, had been relatively successful. They collectively owned many of the national and international newspapers so they made sure that no part of the story was printed in the press. They also managed to shut down most of the on-line news feeds which meant that only a comparatively small number of small-traffic blog sites and forums continued to carry the article.

These successes were nowhere near enough to change the way Sir Samuel Buckingham felt about what had happened. His world had basically disintegrated. He had been forced to make the transition from being the man who had fulfilled the destiny of the Occultus Populous, to being the man who was at the helm when the organisation's thousand year old secret was exposed. If they did not kill the exposé completely, then he would be known as the man who had destroyed this incredible Society and steered it onto the jagged rocks of world attention.

He had not slept for days because he had spent every hour marshalling all the organisation's resources to kill the story. Most of the effort was concentrated on plugging the leak, but a small contingent was tasked with finding the source of the story. This small group presented reams of evidence which clearly identified Michael as the guilty party, but because of the 'Believe Me' legacy, Buckingham dismissed the evidence. In fact, he became extremely angry when the same evidence was re-presented to him as being indisputable.

"Stop wasting my time and yours," he bellowed. "This man has nothing to do with it. He is completely innocent. Do not trouble me again with these stupid and false accusations."

His men were left in the very unenviable position of knowing exactly who had caused the problem, but they were totally unable to convince the powers that be that they were right. They could do nothing because they understood the dire consequences of acting against the instructions of their bosses. They were left with nowhere to go because every other investigative line was totally pointless. Jim Robinson was particularly frustrated by Buckingham's ridiculous refusal to recognise the undeniable.

Buckingham also, was totally frustrated. He could not understand how his, usually reliable, lieutenants were making such little headway in their investigations. They were generally infallible in their endeavours, so this latest incompetence was adding dramatically to the pressure he was feeling.

The pain in his chest came on very suddenly. He was in his office when it hit him. It was as if a ton of bricks had been dropped on his chest. His life did not flash before him, nor did he think lovingly about of his family. His over-riding thought was to wonder how he would look lying on the floor; he wondered if he would be able to get himself into a dignified position before he became totally immobilised.

He mustered all his strength and pulled his phone from his inside pocket. A sense of duty drove him to call Jim Robinson, rather than summon medical help. The phone was answered quickly, as it always was.

"What can I do for you, Sir?"

He always answered the phone the same way; he never wasted time with frivolous small talk. He did not know that 'not wasting time' had never been so important.

"I want you to promise me that you will not allow my son to destroy the organisation we have both served so loyally."

"I'm sorry, Sir. I don't understand."

Sir Samuel spoke two more words. They were the last words he ever said.

By the time his secretary found him he was dead. He looked surprisingly serene as he laid stock still on the plush carpet. The immense anxiety of the last few weeks had combined with a genetic weakness to bring on a massive heart attack.

The news spread like a wildfire through both the organisations that he led. It compounded the panic that had been growing within the Occultus Populous, but it had tried and tested procedures to cope with this very eventuality. The Great Grand Master is dead, long live the Great Grand Master. Marcus Buckingham, or Sir Marcus as he now was, the eldest son of the deceased Sir Samuel, would lead the organisation. It would take a few days for him to be briefed and to give him time to read and absorb the family history which would now be revealed to him for the first time.

IIBE had procedures too and an emergency board meeting was convened by the deputy chairman. It was an unsightly meeting because the directors were more concerned about the opportunity they each had to elevate themselves, rather than any compassion for Sir Samuel. Personal greed and self-aggrandisement definitely ruled in the IIBE board room. They agreed that they would vote for a new chairman at their next scheduled meeting.

An uninformed observer would probably have felt that the death of Sir Samuel Buckingham was a serious set-back for two very evil institutions. That observer would have been quite wrong because this event would, in fact, result in a much nastier presence coming into the ascendancy.

59

Does this make my bum look big?

"I need to talk to Faith. I know you'll think I'm crazy, but I really need to do this."

Michael knew from their faces that they were deeply concerned by this bolt out of the blue. He understood why they were so shocked, but he felt this was a necessary evil. This was the sort of idiotic thing Tung would do, thought Madrick, as he tried to muster his arguments against what he considered to be madness.

"But she betrayed us. You can't want to talk to her. She will just mess you around and maybe even put us all in danger again. You need to forget you ever met her. She is bad news. You must know that talking to her doesn't make any sense at all."

"I know why you think that. But I can't forgive her for what she did to me, what she did to us. I want a little bit of revenge before I forget about her. I've lost my Faith and I want her to suffer for what she's done. She needs to learn a lesson; a hard lesson."

Michael did not generally approve of petty vengeance, but this particular situation was different. This woman had broken his heart and she had happily given them up to a ruthless enemy who would almost certainly have killed them had they not been so well prepared. He knew they would have suffered horribly had it not been for the Believe Me Spell.

On top of that, she had made Michael feel incredibly stupid in front of his friends. He had been humiliated to the point where he almost felt as if it was he personally, and not her, who had betrayed them. He was not planning to hurt her physically, the way she had planned to hurt them, but he did want to hurt her mentally. He also knew he needed to do something, for closure. He wanted revenge, but nothing too cruel because, inexplicably, he knew he still loved her.

He talked through his plan with Tung and Madrick. They listened, and the more they heard, the more relaxed they became. They began to understand why he wanted this, why he needed this. They also saw that it was virtually risk free. When he had finished outlining his thoughts, they all laughed and agreed it was a good and just retribution. She deserved it.

"When do you want to do this?" asked Tung.

He was the main man in the plan.

"Now is as good a time as any. Are you up for it?"

Michael phoned Suzie's mobile, it was the only point of contact he had for Faith - he certainly did not have the number for her secret phone. Suzie was reluctant to let him speak to her friend, but after a brief discussion she called Faith and Michael's heart jumped when he heard her say his name.

"Michael, I am so, so sorry. I never meant it to end the way it did. I thought they just wanted their money back. I didn't know that they would haul you away like terrorists. And now I find out that you weren't even involved in the fraud and that they had the wrong people. How can I ever make it up to you? Will you ever be able to forgive me?"

He had not had the chance to say a single word. She had launched straight into her apology the second she had come onto the phone. She sounded so sincere and remorseful. He started to have second thoughts about hurting her, so he handed the phone to Tung before he changed his mind.

"Believe me, you want to listen to everything I am about to tell you. You do not want to hang up. You are madly and deeply in love with Michael. There will never be anyone else who you will be able to love. Michael used to love you, but your deception has hurt him so much that now he hates you. There is nothing you can do that will ever make him change his mind. Everything that is wrong in your life is your own stupid fault. You are going to be very unhappy and you will hate yourself for what you have done."

Faith listened carefully and the more she heard, the sadder she felt. He eyes filled up and she was biting her bottom lip. Suzie could only watch, although at one point she tried unsuccessfully to take the phone from Faith. She hated seeing her best friend become so upset. Faith shrugged her off and continued to hang onto every word that was being said to her.

"Oh yes… and everything you wear makes your bum look big."

Tung hung up.

"I hate myself," said Faith as she handed the phone back to Suzie.

She burst into tears. She had never felt so sad and pathetic in her life. Suzie tried desperately to console her friend, but she failed miserably. Faith tried to thank her for her kindness, but got choked by sobs. She told Suzie she needed some time in her room; she needed to be alone. As she walked away, she caught sight of her reflection in the full-length mirror. Her eyes were drawn to her bottom and her wailing suddenly became uncontrollable as she broke into a headlong dash for her bedroom.

In Liverpool the mood was completely different. Everyone was feeling buoyant. The three men high fived and gave each other arm's-length man hugs.

"Thank you for that, Tung," said Michael. "You have helped me put a sad and unfortunate chapter of my life behind me. I thought she was going to be the happiest and best thing that ever happened to me, but it turns out that she was the complete opposite. But because of what you've done I reckon I'm now ready to move on. No more looking back for me, I'm ready to plan for our futures. The sky's the limit!"

"Don't tell me the sky's the limit," said Tung, "because I know... it is not."

He had not quite remembered the end to the expression, but everyone knew exactly what he meant. Everyone agreed wholeheartedly.

Tung and Madrick were both pleased that Michael had suggested this last interaction with Faith. They had both been a bit nervous about it, but it was clear that it had been the right thing to do. They all knew it was a bit mean to curse the rest of her life the way they had, but she deserved it and it had definitely given Michael the closure he needed. Anyway, in reality, it was not for the rest of her life; it was only for a year if Madrick's memory of the spell was anything to go by. They all knew that it was now time to move on; it was time to leave the past behind and concentrate solely on the future.

Tung thought that now would be the perfect time to cement his friendship with the others. He had never really had friends in his life, before Madrick, and now Michael. He did not want to lose them. So why not make sure, he thought to himself, why not make sure that they stayed friends forever?

"Believe me," said Tung. "I am the best friend you guys will ever have. I am honest, kind and reliable. You will love me forever and cherish my friendship."

Madrick and Michael looked at each other and smiled widely. They both knew that that particular spell had now run its course.

"Good effort," said Michael wondering if Tung had planted any other lies in their heads. He realised he would never know the answer to that particular question.

"And by the way, I really do cherish your friendship. No need for a spell."

They all spontaneously, albeit a little uncomfortably, embraced in a proper group hug. It was not at arm's-length this time and it felt surprisingly good.

"Right," said Madrick breaking the moment and moving away. "It is time to see what spell the Scroll throws up next. The sky's not the limit."

60

Tributes

Marcus Buckingham was enjoying his third holiday of the year in the south of France when he was given the news of his father's death. He said nothing for over a minute while he assessed the information. He tried to show proper grief, like he felt he should, but inside he was joyous. He had been looking forward to this moment since he was a young teenager. He hated his father nearly as much as he hated the rest of his family.

"That is dreadful news. What happened?"

"I'll explain everything when you get here. I must ask you to come home immediately," the voice on the phone told him. "I will make all the arrangements. Please get yourself ready to travel."

Sir Marcus hung up and smiled widely to himself. He quickly packed and got himself prepared for what lay ahead. He was looking forward to everything.

The journey home took less than four hours which was a credit to the man sorting out the logistics - a private jet and two helicopter rides helped.

He stepped out of the jet black, twin engine Sikorsky which now sat on the manicured lawn which fronted the fabulous Buckingham stately home. The sleek aerodynamic lines of the helicopter contrasted starkly with the architecture of the house. It was a beautiful Elizabethan limestone building which had been the family 'pile' since it was built in the late fifteen hundreds. It was a massive mansion with over ninety 'proper' rooms supplemented by numerous halls, corridors, bathrooms and service areas.

He strode purposefully towards the entrance where he was met by two of the house menservants.

"Welcome home, Sir Marcus. We are so sorry it is in these

awful circumstances."

He rudely, yet typically, ignored their greetings and marched through the grand hall into a reception room where two women were seated. It was used as the family room even though it was massive and would have seemed a very formal place to most 'ordinary' folk. Grand oil paintings of ancestors adorned the walls and, in one corner, there was even a suit of armour which a medieval relative had worn in some ancient battle. Everything in the room had a history. Everything in the room was authentic Buckingham family, even the two ladies. They were drinking tea and both deliberately and pointedly ignored his arrival.

"Mother. Aunt Lily," he said, more to the room than the women. "This is the most dreadful news. It seems so very sudden, after all, he showed no sign of illness. I will miss the old man dreadfully. He was always the mainstay of our family, but I am ready to take on his responsibilities. I am ready to step up and do my duty."

Neither woman so much as acknowledged him. His opening lines fell on deaf ears - two of the four ears were literally deaf. He was not in the least bit bothered. He crossed the floor to his mother and kissed her formally on the cheek. He placed a hand on his aunt's shoulder and squeezed it gently.

"This is a very sad day, but there is much for us to do to make sure father's legacy does him justice. I will get started straight away."

That was enough, he thought. They all hated each other so there was little point in prolonging this embarrassing masquerade. He felt he had made the appropriate gesture towards his mother and her sister so it was now time to get down to the important business.

"We can talk again later," he said sarcastically as he left the room.

He made his way to his father's study, his study as it now

was, where four sombre, suited gentlemen awaited him.

"Sir Marcus. May we convey our deepest condolences? Your father was a great and honourable man. This is indeed a very sad day."

Marcus waved away the comments dismissively with his left hand. He took his place behind the early Georgian walnut desk that had been his father's pride and joy. He remembered well, as a child, trying to attract his father's attention away from the sheaves of papers that always littered this highly polished desk. He never succeeded. The most humiliating times were when his father summoned one of the servants to take him away. When he thought back to those days, he knew that this indifference had sown the seeds of the contempt he now felt for his father and everything associated with this family.

"Thank you, but enough with the platitudes, gentlemen. There is serious work to be done, so let us get on with the real business of the day."

The men were disappointed that there was to be no time set aside to reflect on the life of Sir Samuel, but they accepted that there was now a new boss in town and they were duty bound to serve him. They knew that Sir Marcus was renowned for his abruptness, so they knew that he was not going to be a pleasant man to serve.

One of the men moved forward with a great, leather-bound volume which he placed on the desk in front of Marcus. It was beautifully embossed and showed all the signs of age, without any signs of aging.

"This book is nearly a thousand years old and it charts the history of the Buckingham family; your family. It will reveal to you secrets which will change your life forever. Once you have read this, you will understand your destiny and..."

"Hold on," interrupted Marcus. "Let's get some of the basics out of the way first. Do I inherit all the money? And the house? And the title?"

"Of course, Sir Marcus. As the eldest son you are entitled to everything, however, as you know, you have responsibilities for the other family members. In the same way that your father had."

"We'll see. They never treated me with much respect, maybe now they will wish they had been a bit more generous with their…" he paused while he struggled to find the right word, "tributes."

The four men were somewhat taken aback by this statement, 'tributes' was a very strange word to use. They knew they needed to be very wary of someone who was looking for tributes. They had always known that this man who stood before them was not going to be as easy to serve as his predecessor, but it looked as though things were going to be a lot tougher than they had ever imagined. Here was a totally self-centred man who, given any level of power, was one to be greatly feared.

"OK, that's good. I inherit everything. Now, tell me about this book."

"Sir Marcus, what you have before you is the great tome which charts the long and prestigious history of the Buckingham family. The book is nearly a thousand years old and can be read by no one except the head of your family and the executive of the Occultus Populous."

"Occultus Populous? What is that?"

"You must read the book. The book will reveal all. You must read it carefully because it sets out both your history and your destiny. We are here to answer any questions you may have and to guide you through the process as you take your rightful place as leader of our great Society."

"This makes no sense to me. All I want is my title, this house and all the money. The rest is irrelevant. Why would any of this 'history' be of any interest to me?"

"Sir, I beseech you. Please, take the time to read the book, learn your history and understand your destiny. The world as we know it depends on you."

"That's a bit dramatic. Look, why don't you just explain it to me and then I can get on with my life and enjoy the privileges that I have just inherited?"

"Sir, there are parts of the book that even we have never seen. You must read it so you can truly inherit all that is rightfully yours."

He drew a long breath just to indicate his frustration, then he opened the great leather volume and began to read. He had expected to lose interest very quickly, but within a few minutes he was completely engrossed. His ancestors were incredible and it was almost unbelievable that the line stretched back so far. The history itself was mind-boggling, but surely all this magic stuff in the early days was merely ancient myth.

He began to question the four men who had watched in silence as he read the ancient pages. They answered all his questions about magic, spells, Gravalar, the Scroll and the Occultus Populous - past and present.

The session went on late into the night as Marcus worked his way through the historic book, guided by the four Under Masters. He became more and more excited as he learned the secrets of his family and the true source of their unimaginable wealth and power. He had always known that they were a very special family, but he could not have imagined just how special they really were.

From early childhood, his parents had told him that he was in line for great privilege, but he had never imagined anything as spectacular as this. If this was true, if even half of it was true, then there seemed no limit to what he could do.

This was a stunningly good day for Marcus, but it was a disastrously bad day for the ordinary people of the world because Marcus was an evil and selfish man who would have no reservations about abusing his new found power.

Marcus worked his way through the great Buckingham tome and asked for guidance when he came across entries which were unclear. He had many queries because the story was so incredible. There was so much history, so many great men, so many great deeds. The Under Masters dealt matter-of-factly with all his questions and used their collective experience to explain the mysteries which surrounded the family. It was a gruelling, yet very exhilarating session. He now understood where the family had gained its unequalled power. He was a part of an incredible dynasty which had spanned a millennium.

He was flabbergasted that he had had no inkling of the truth up to this point; it had all been a closely guarded secret and he understood why. He also understood why he needed to keep it that way. He knew that some of the information was known only within the Society and he was to share it with no one outside the organisation. Most importantly he realised that there were some parts of the story that only he and the book knew. Parts that his instincts told him to share with no one.

He had no problem with keeping all the secrets as long as he could exploit this new found power for his own personal ends.

His father had been hard-nosed and greedy, but he had felt some compassion for those less fortunate than himself. He did not seem to exploit his power ruthlessly which, as far as Marcus was concerned, was a sign of weakness. Marcus had no such scruples, no such weakness. He was determined to maximise the opportunity he now had and he saw no reason to respect anyone else in the pursuit of his own individual goals. He did not even care about what happened to other members of his family never mind other members of the Occultus Populous. This was an opportunity for him, Sir Marcus Buckingham, so why should he give any consideration to anyone else? This was his birthright and it was not to be squandered.

Marcus was unmarried and had no children. He realised that if something happened to him then the story and the power would pass to his younger brother. What a waste that would be, he thought, my brother is a wimp. He had spent his adult years being a 'home-maker' and had three sons already. He had followed the family tradition of starting young and having lots of boys. His brother was a do-gooder if ever there was one. He would not know what to do with this immense power and he would undoubtedly waste it. Marcus was determined that he would not be given the chance. He would find a wife as soon as possible and produce some heirs. This is all for me, he thought, and then my sons in due course.

The men advising him were gravely concerned. As time went on they could see that Marcus was not respecting the culture of the organisation. They could see his blatant selfishness and they worried for the future.

"Remember gentlemen, I do not care what anybody thinks. Since my father died I am in charge. I will do what I want. It's all about me now."

This was the first time in history that the great traditions of the Society were not being honoured by its own Great Grand Master. Never before had such a greedy and evil man been at the helm. The world was in for a very rocky ride and there was nothing these men could do about it because they were duty bound by sacred oath to serve the man who stood before them.

Marcus realised that his first task, his priority task, was to cement his own position and to protect the organisation he now led. He would ensure it continued to prosper because that was what gave him his power. He would therefore address the Council and set out his short term plan. He would show them what a dynamic leader he was by identifying and punishing the people who were causing his organisation so many problems.

From the briefing he had been given, he knew exactly who the culprits were. The evidence was stark and clear so he could not understand why his father had not seen it too. He had no idea that his father had been hexed by Tung's 'believe me' story - his father and the Council. He simply did not understand that it would be impossible to convince anyone who had heard that story, that the story was a lie. He instructed the four Under Masters to open communication channels with the Council.

In parallel, he wanted to be appointed as the chairman of IIBE because it was the perfect cover for his activities and he also liked the public prestige that the position would bring. This appointment would not be a problem given the size of the shareholding he had in the bank, coupled with the influence his family had over each of the other directors. Again the Under Masters were instructed to make it happen.

He was restless and wanted to get everything underway immediately, but he accepted there would be a necessary delay before he could be firmly established in both of the positions that his father had held. There was also the inconvenience associated with his father's funeral and all the ceremony which went with it. Then, there was the rest of the family to deal with.

He quickly accepted that there was nothing much that could be done until he had put his father's legacy to rest. Then he could fully assert himself.

He would allow the existing efforts to protect the Occultus Populous to continue. They were actually being relatively effective in stifling the exposé, however, they were totally useless with respect to finding the culprits. He accepted that he needed to be patient. He was not going to jeopardise his own position by rushing in and trying to change too many things too soon. After all, he had a lifetime to mould everything to his will.

He dismissed the men from the room and sat in silence for a long while. He thought about some of the terrible atrocities which his family had engineered - the wars, the famines, slavery, mass poverty and devastating global financial crises. His ancestors had shaped the world with their greed and their contempt for the poor. He was genuinely proud of their efforts, but he was determined to outdo all of them.

61

The future past

It had been five days since Michael had leaked the footage of the Occultus Populous meetings. He had spent a lot of time relaxing, but along with Tung and Madrick, he had kept an eye on the various news channels to see how his internet exposé would play out. He was very surprised that there was so little mention of what had to be the biggest global saga for many years. This was the ultimate conspiracy, yet there was hardly a mention of it anywhere.

Michael had checked the forums where he had posted the videos and had found that most of his entries had been removed. He re-posted them and also started populating the less well used channels and blog sites. He was determined to get the information out there. He was now on a mission to destroy the Occultus Populous. He hated it more than he had hated IIBE and anyway, this was two birds with one stone, given the many ties between the two organisations.

What he did not fully appreciate was the stranglehold that these people had on the world's media organisations. They were working frantically in the background to stop the story leaking out although, even with their great influence, the story was gradually seeping into the public domain. There were just too many routes to block, although it seemed as though the initial rush he had hoped for had been stemmed. The global television networks had been completely stifled and they had taken down the entries from most of the main internet sites which had been hosting the story. Some sites had actually been shut down so they could not be 're-infected'.

Michael was disappointed, but not despondent. After all, he thought, even a few negative messages should hurt the Occultus Populous and anyway, his original target had been

IIBE and he had certainly damaged it. He felt very good about what he had achieved so far, and he knew he could do more.

They all agreed that Michael should get back on the internet to see what further mischief he could concoct while Tung and Madrick worked on the next spell. This time they were not looking for something to protect them from their enemies; this time they were looking for something that could inject some magic into their futures.

When he sat down at the computer, Michael reckoned that he had three specific tasks to tackle. The first was to further damage IIBE and the Occultus Populous. The second was to keep moving the money he had stolen for himself to make it impossible for the bank to track it down. The third was to create modern identities for both Madrick and Tung. They were not being hunted, as far as he could tell, but they would need all the relevant paperwork and reference documents if they were going to survive comfortably in the contemporary world.

This last task, creating identities, was reasonably straightforward, although it would require a bit of time and patience. He knew the process well and had successfully created a completely new identity for himself already. His alter-Michael had every conceivable form of documentation from a passport to a driving license; from a bank account to utility contracts.

The first thing you needed was a birth certificate. You always started this process with finding someone who would have been of a similar age and who had died as a child. He smiled when he remembered that both Tung and Madrick were about a thousand years old.

While Michael dealt with his challenges, Tung was busily creating new spells. He really was very adept at it now so it was a quick and virtually painless process. Madrick marvelled at how the young man had come on, he was genuinely proud of him although he often worried about just how much he was needed now. The more adept Tung became, the less crucial Madrick was; he just hoped their developing friendship would keep them together. He did not want to be abandoned in this crazy new world.

As was always the pattern, the first few spells were totally valueless, however one did produce a very unusual tree which now grew in the corner of the large lounge. It had numerous interwoven blue branches and perfectly round, red leaves. They hoped Michael would like the new addition to his décor, he would have little choice really because it was very big and looked firmly rooted.

Tung kept on creating and dissipating spells. He had become very blasé about the process and no longer marvelled at the smaller feats of magic. After another string of innocuous creations he gave birth to a giant crystal ball which seemed to excite Madrick greatly.

"This will show us pictures of the future. It will not, however, show our personal futures and that, I think, is a good thing. Personally I would rather not know what life holds in store for me, particularly if the last few weeks are anything to go by.

"What it will show are great events and significant happenings that are destined to take place sometime in the future. We can choose how far ahead we want to see. The longer we hold our hands on the orb, the further into the future it will portray. From my memory of this rather obscure spell, you can see as far ahead as two hundred years."

They called Michael. They wanted to share this rather beautiful and wondrous contrivance. Michael, rather reluctantly, paused in his work and joined the others in the lounge. It was probably time for a break anyway, he thought, as he entered his favourite room in the house.

"What the…" he yelled. "What have you done to my beautiful room?"

He was surveying the debris that the spells had deposited in his lounge. It was like the flotsam and jetsam you might find on a beach after a particularly violent and surreal storm. It could be tidied, he knew that, but what on earth was the bizarre and enormous tree growing out of his floor?

"I know," said Madrick. "It is an interesting feature. I think it will grow on you - it will certainly grow on. I think it is very well rooted."

After he had calmed himself down a little, he realised there was no point in getting upset. They were all learning to deal with their new situation; this was just another part of the adventure that they were on. Anyway, the tree might be nice to sit under in the summer and it might even start a new trend. He had definitely seen weirder things in some of the televised makeover shows.

"That is not what we wanted to show you although it's good to get it out of the way. We were worried you might be cross. Look, this is what we really wanted you to see. It is the future!"

Both Madrick and Tung dah-dahed as they ostentatiously presented the great orb, much like a cheesy conjurer would show the results of his grand finale trick.

"This marvellous crystal will show us great events from the future. Let me demonstrate and show you what will befall us as we progress through time."

It was a bit of a silly introduction, but Madrick was enjoying the showmanship that he believed the new creation deserved. He laid his hands on the crystal ball as they all peered into its centre. Misty images began to form although they were constantly shifting and changing. Madrick took his hands away and the images started to come into focus. They all moved in closer and eventually recognised what looked like ancient soldiers racing into battle. The scene then focused on the king of one of the armies who had been speared in the eye with an arrow. Michael knew exactly what was happening in the scene.

"That is not the future," he said. "That happened in 1066, nearly a thousand years ago."

Madrick tried again holding his hands on the great crystal globe for much longer. Again it was obvious that the new image was also ancient. After some thought, Madrick reckoned he had worked out what the problem was. He realised that the globe was seeing the future as it was before they had time travelled. It was a bit confusing. There were so many anomalies that time travel could throw up.

"The future ball is trapped in the past. It is stuck in the age we travelled from. It will never be able to show us the future from where we are now."

They all looked disappointed, but there was an air of 'it doesn't really matter' as they were not under any real pressure right now. No one was hard on their heels. As far as they knew, no one was chasing them so they could create spell after spell at their leisure.

"What a shame, we can't see the future," said Tung. "But it will make a fascinating centre piece for your room Michael. And it'll distract attention from the tree!"

"Let's take a rest," said Michael. "I think we're all tired. We have plenty of time. We don't need to kill ourselves by over-working."

"Let me try just one more," said Tung. "I'm feeling lucky. I think this is going to be the one."

He was right, he was about to create the spell that would change the world forever.

62

The Good Will Spell

Michael and Madrick watched as Tung went through the routine. It had all become very easy and seemed surprisingly normal. He read the words on the Scroll and then concentrated hard on the picture in his head. His mind's eye scanned the picture and he described it in great detail. His description was precise and measured.

Madrick pondered for a long while, but he was unable to come up with any interpretation of the new spell. His search of the libraries of his memory came up empty. He asked Tung for more detail of the picture, but the few extra details he extracted did nothing to help solve the mystery.

"I really do not know this one. I can usually give some alternatives when I am unsure. This one is a complete mystery to me. I know I have always advised against this, but I can think of no other way. This time, it may be a case of just say it and see."

"I don't want to do that. This one feels different in my head. I have a really strong gut feel that this is an important one and one not to be wasted. I don't want to risk wasting it. We need to find a way to work out what it is. After all, for once we are not in a life or death rush."

There was something deep inside him which told him that this was a very significant spell; one of the principal ones which Madrick always harped on about. No matter how hard he concentrated on the picture, he could find nothing that he had not already described to Madrick. He stared at the words without concentrating on the individual letters, but unfortunately they offered him no help whatsoever. Madrick stared into space in the hope that something would come to him; like the revelation about the Invisibility Spell. It was not quite a 'eureka' moment but Madrick eventually came up with the solution.

"Then there is only one choice. You must tell me what the words are, without of course 'saying' them. I am going to teach you to read. I had thought about this before, but there was never time, there was always someone about to pounce on us. We have the luxury of time now, so it is time for you to go back to school with me as the teacher."

Tung thought about it. His mind drifted back to his last day at school. He had been seven years old and the teacher had beaten him remorselessly because he had been unable to say how many coins were left if you took two coins away from four. He could not see why the answer was not none - everybody knew that you would always take all four coins. Why on earth would anyone leave any? He lost focus as his mind replayed some of the painful incidents from his schooldays. It was a horrible series of memories, however, he realised things were very different now.

"Did you hear what I said? It is time for you to go back to school."

"Fair enough. It is time for me to learn to read. Mind you, you will need to be patient with me, I don't learn fast."

Madrick set about the rather daunting task of teaching Tung to read. They realised early on that they did not actually need to teach him reading as such, all he had to do was be able to recognise the letters and relay them to Madrick. This turned out to be much more difficult than either man expected.

Michael gave Madrick the modern tools he needed, namely sheets of paper and a thick marker pen. Madrick used these to draw each of the letters of the Salatin language. It was the language that had preceded, and was in fact the root of, Latin. It was also the language of all magic and spell scrolls.

He carefully drew each of the forty-eight primary letters and spread the sheets out across the table. He had already decided not to worry about the sixty-six secondary letters; he would only introduce them if it became absolutely necessary.

They started trying to get the letters out of Tung's head.

"Look at the first letter in the spell and tell me which one of these it matches."

Madrick was amazed by Tung's sustained level of concentration; it was not long ago that he had the attention span of a distracted gnat. The problem was that, no matter how hard he tried, he could not seem to match the images that Madrick had drawn with the images that were in his head. No matter how hard he concentrated, the images seemed to change shape each time he looked at them. A modern teacher would have realised that Tung was, in fact, dyslexic. They struggled for hours and managed to get some letters matched.

Madrick scribed what Tung extracted from his head. There were some letters that he just could not pin down so Madrick used a '?' and there were others he felt were not right, but he had little choice other than to accept Tung's best guess. Eventually they ended up with 'devenoienti? e?t bov?tus'.

That made no sense to Madrick so he decided to take it away and work through the possibilities. Tung went away for a lie-down after his exertions. This learning is harder than creating spells, he thought. I remember now why I hated school.

It was two hours later when Madrick shouted excitedly.

"I've got it! I think I've got it."

By this stage Tung and Michael were eating a pizza and chatting about nothing in particular. Madrick burst into the room still shouting.

"I've got it. I'm sure I've got it."

"Benevolentia est donates!"

They looked at him hoping for an explanation. Michael now knew what it was like for Tung when a modern expression went right over his head. Madrick's words meant nothing to either of them.

"Is this good?"

"Good? Is this good? That's an interesting question. You'll understand why I say that when I explain what we have got.

"This is indeed a principal spell. You were right Tung. You were right about its specialness and you were right not to waste it. I can see why it felt different to you. Anyway, I know what it is now, but I have no idea what we can do with it. Let me explain."

"Not before time," they whispered in unison.

"This spell will create a set of words which will cause any reader of the words to become kind, caring and benevolent. He will not know that he has been hexed and he will be compelled to perform good and selfless deeds. How long it lasts depends on the individual - the crueller and more unpleasant the individual, the longer the spell will force him to do kindnesses.

"This spell is one of the most ancient of all spells. It was solely intended to transform the behaviour of the rich and powerful. After all, they were the only ones who could read."

He threw Tung a funny look when he mentioned reading.

"The rich folk were the only ones who could make a worthwhile improvement to other people's lives. And most rich folk were cruel and horrible people who could do with a change of attitude. Not much has changed if our experience in this century is anything to go by!

"Of course, the Words themselves could not be reproduced easily because only a select few could write."

He threw Tung that funny look again when he mentioned writing.

"So, back in my day, the spell could only bring its magnificent benefits to small, isolated pockets of humankind. I guess it might be a different story today."

Michael listened with great interest. He had always wanted to make a difference and his attack on IIBE had been his attempt to benefit many ordinary people who had been cheated and suppressed by that global monster. Maybe, he thought, he could make an even bigger contribution to the planet. Maybe this was his chance to change things for the better; forever.

"Exactly what will the spell create? Will Tung see the words in his head? Or does it create a bit of paper with these special words?"

"Right second time. We will have a small parchment with the Words inscribed on it. We can create other parchments or indeed any reproduction of the Words; they will all work. We can make as many copies as we like - I guess it will be much easier nowadays to produce lots of them."

"Too right," said Michael, his brain was racing with the possibilities.

"Tung will be immune from the Words. They will have no effect on him. We can be immune too if we are touching him when he says the spell. The wise one who created the original spell knew that his own actions could become unpredictable if he was affected so he built in that protection."

They all pondered the possibilities although Tung's thoughts quickly turned to pizza. His lazy gnat attention span had kicked in again, but to be fair, it had been some time since he had last eaten (10 minutes).

"I have an idea," said Michael. "I know exactly what we should do.

"I think we should try and spread the words as widely as possible. Affect as many people as possible. Make the world a better place for everyone. With my skills we can exploit the internet and global communications to get the Words out there. I always wanted to make a difference and to bring some happiness to the masses of ordinary people who seem to be constantly slapped down by the Big Man. This is the opportunity to change everything. We should do this!"

Madrick and Tung still had no idea what 'the internet and

global communications' were; all they knew was that Michael could definitely exploit them. He was excited about the possibilities, so they were too.

"We will be legends," crowed Tung. "We will go down in history."

He was right, but not in the way he thought. What none of them realised was that they were mere players in a great dictacy cast a thousand years earlier. They were bringing together two good things, Michael's aspiration and the great spell, and they were going to destroy the influence of evil.

Madrick was as excited as anyone, although he had some reservations. He could not put his finger on them, however, he knew there was something about the idea that made him uneasy. He had no way to articulate this feeling so he decided to go with Michael's plan. After all, he thought, what harm can be done by thousands of people doing good deeds? He did, however, make one suggestion which turned out to be the most important thing he had ever done.

"I don't know why I feel this way, but I think we should make ourselves immune."

"No problem," said Michael. "We're good enough people already. We don't need any help to get us to do the right thing. After all, look at the gift we are about to give the world."

The three men held hands and Tung spoke the spell in his head. There was no blinding flash, no thunderclap or anything else that might indicate the power of the small piece of parchment that appeared in mid-air and now floated gently to the ground. Michael picked it up and saw eight beautifully inscribed words. He held the parchment tenderly and nodded sagely to the others as he took the parchment to his computer room.

"Spam email and internet forums," he whispered to no one in particular. "Plus a sprinkling of WikiLeaks, YouTube, Google Buzz, FaceBook and Twitter."

Anyone watching would have realised that here was a very

knowledgeable man who was extremely happy in his work. He wanted people to see the Words, to read the Words, and he knew exactly how to achieve that. The Words were going to get out there and they were going to get out there even faster than Michael could have imagined.

As Madrick had said, when the spell was created it was virtually impossible to reproduce the magic words, but that was then. This was now, and now was very different. It was clear that even the ancient, wisest-of-the-wise wizard who had created this Good Will spell, even he could not have foreseen the impact of the internet in the twenty-first century.

63

Marcus phone home

Sir Marcus Buckingham had been appointed chairman of IIBE by way of a unanimous vote at the specially and rapidly convened board meeting. It had been a formality once he had put his name forward and exerted the pressure that his family name allowed. Not everyone was happy about the outcome, however, no one had any option other than to allow Sir Marcus to step into the role of Chairman.

He now sat in the office formerly occupied by his father and pondered his position. He was very happy. Everything was going exactly according to his plan, and his plan was the only plan that mattered.

He had the power he craved, derived from his great wealth, his inherited leadership of the Occultus Populous and his recent appointment as chairman of IIBE.

He had dealt quickly with his family issues. They had laid his father to rest with a very dignified ceremony. Many highly influential people from around the world had attended to show their respect. Many of them also wanted to try and ingratiate themselves with Marcus.

Once the formalities of the funeral were complete, Marcus tackled the other family issues. He had actually enjoyed informing them all that they would no longer be receiving generous allowances and that they were on their own. Basically he had cut them off from the family fortune. He knew this was not the tradition, but he did not care.

In particular, telling his mother she was no longer allowed to live on the estate had been very satisfying. He hated that woman. She had never paid him much attention and, in later years, had actively ignored him. He had nothing to thank her for except his independent spirit and his coldness towards other human beings. She had once described him as having all the qualities of a poker, but without the occasional warmth. It was very satisfying to return her indifference in spades.

He felt he had firmly established himself as 'the man in charge'. He was in charge of the family, the Occultus Populous and IIBE. Everyone knew who the boss was, so it was now time to pursue the perpetrators of the vindictive exposé of his secret organisation. The first step was to convince the Council that this was the right course of action. They had already been presented with blindingly clear evidence, but like his father, they seemed adamant that the evidence was wrong. He was however, determined to find a way to impose his will.

It would be a very bad day for Michael, Tung and Madrick if they fell into this man's hands. He was the epitome of evil and he would make sure they suffered horribly. This revelation would be nothing new for Madrick and Tung, but it would have shaken Michael to his very core.

Marcus perused his emails and noticed a strange news story which referenced the spread of an unusual chain letter. The thing that was particularly bizarre about it was that the text of the letter was apparently in Latin so most people would have no idea what it meant - so why would they send it on to their contacts? Normal chain letters either promised good luck if they were passed on or dreadful consequences if they were not.

He decided to investigate in case the 'letter' was in some way linked to the odd occurrences which had become so prevalent in recent times. Although a link seemed unlikely, it was definitely worth a few minutes of research to find out a little bit more.

A quick Google search brought him face to face with the Words. They meant nothing to him. He read them out loud to see if they made any sense, but still he could find no meaning in the eight foreign words. He popped them into the Google Translator and it came back with '*I hope your day is good. You are welcome.*'. That made no sense at all.

He was about to sign off from his email account when he realised that a strange sense of calm had engulfed him. Ever since he first read those strange words he felt… different.

Before he signed off, he emailed a copy of the article to all the Council members and all the IIBE Board members. He did not know why he had done that; there was just something that made him feel it was the right thing. As a final action, he emailed the article to everyone in his address book. Why not, he thought, as over eight hundred emails hit the ether.

He clicked off his computer and leaned back in his chair. He decided to phone his mother, just to see how she was keeping. Halfway through the conversation he began to tell her of the great things he had planned. He wanted to use half the family fortune to help some of the unfortunate people in disease ridden countries, just as Bill Gates had done, but on a much grander scale. She never found out what he had planned with the other half of the fortune.

Sir Marcus noticed a red spot on his tie. He tried to flick it off. He realised, too late, that it was the dot from a laser sight. The high velocity bullet smashed through the window and slammed into his chest. He was dead before he hit the floor.

In a room in an office block across the street Jim Robinson began to pack away the sniper rifle that had served him so well during his time in the Special Forces. He had one last look across the street and could see panic in the office of his former boss. He had carried out the dying wish of Sir Samuel Buckingham. He had carried out his final order from Sir Samuel. 'Kill Marcus' had been the last words spoken by his great friend.

Jim Robinson had no idea what would happen next. He had no idea what would become of his life. He did not care because he had done what he needed to do.

"The Great Grand Master is dead, long live the Great Grand Master," he said as he closed the door behind him.

Somewhere, at the centre of the universe, an invisible record was being ticked as the first events in the last ever dictacy came to pass.

64

Good Will to All Men

The Good Will Spell spread virally across the internet like a wildfire. It was truly unbelievable how the count of views racked up… hundreds of thousands in the first few hours, millions within a day. There had never been anything like it. Not even the fat kid and the Numa-Numa song, the Intel bum-bum-bumbum ads or the Kung Fu cats had spread with anything like the speed of the Good Will words.

Michael knew it would colonise the internet faster than the speed of light. These extraordinary words compelled readers to do good deeds and the best deed of all was to pass the Words on to everyone they knew.

Tung, Madrick and Michael were surely the unlikeliest of heroes and now it seemed that they were genuinely going to change the world by spreading this supernatural set of magically fashioned words; mystical words which forced people to become wonderful human beings. It was not going to be a super-power government or a global religion or vegetarianism that was destined to change mankind forever - it was this unique, paranormal combination of the ancient and modern.

Over the next few days, they watched the twenty-four-hour news channels to see how their phenomenon was being reported and to admire the impact of their gift to humanity. They were settled in front of the giant plasma TV expecting to be constantly patting each other on the back as their gift spread across the earth and made the planet an infinitely better place. They were the ultimate Miss World - 'I want to help all the poor people in Africa and I want every human being to be as happy as me. Oh yes, and world peace'.

Things felt good, but Michael realised that their contribution to humanity, as they saw it, might not be all plain sailing.

"Remember, being good doesn't mean being smart," he reminded Madrick. "Some folk will do some really stupid stuff, albeit with the best of intentions."

He was thinking of Miss World when he said this.

At first, the gift was harshly portrayed as the most virulent, malicious and pathetic chain-letter ever. The sheer volume of messages had slowed down many of the main email services, indeed some had even ground to a halt. Many people were receiving hundreds of copies of the good-word emails because all their friends and acquaintances were sending them. Interestingly, no one seemed to be getting annoyed by it.

Soon isolated random-acts-of-kindness stories started to filter through... like the Boston billionaire who donated all of his fortune to a well-known, third world charity. There was the London 5-Star hotel owner who threw open every one of his four hundred rooms, free of charge, to the homeless. There was the South American crime boss who gave himself up to the authorities, along with hundreds of his subordinates, associates and partners. And so it went on.

There was the chief executive of a Fortune 500 company who gave every single employee a massive bonus... although the sudden cash drain caused an immediate drop in the share price and the company effectively fell out of the top 500. There was definitely more trouble brewing on the global stock markets.

Airports in every first world country were chock-a-block as thousands rushed to travel to underdeveloped countries where they thought they could make a difference. People doing this had always been known as SUVs - spontaneous uninvited volunteers. Now there was SUV overload. These poor, unfortunate countries were being overwhelmed by a tidal wave of do-gooders. The surge quickly slowed, however, because so many pilots refused to take their polluting flying machines into the air.

As time went on, every kind-act story seemed to have a 'but' at the end of it. Each good deed seemed to have some negative consequences. Newton had more or less summed it up with his third law - 'For every [good] action there is an equal and opposite [bad] reaction.'

Things were deteriorating extremely quickly and then, disastrously, the whole phenomenon was dramatically accelerated when one of the TV channels actually broadcast the Words. Unbelievable, there they were on the screen, seen by millions... *'Spero vestri dies est bonus. Vos es exspectata.'* Soon every channel, every newspaper was showing the Words. Soon there was hardly a human being on the planet who had not read them. The effect was devastating.

People lost their competitiveness and drive. More and more people became totally selfless and thoughtful which resulted in less and less of anything constructive getting done anywhere. The stock markets crashed (and no one cared), workers stopped working, businesses closed, shops gave away their produce (and were not restocked), farmers released their animals into the wild; and so it went on.

The first total traffic grid-lock came shortly afterwards; it happened in Paris. The city ground to a halt as drivers became over courteous; who would have thought that an over preponderance of non-aggressive drivers would bring everything to a total stand-still? The problem was, of course, compounded by cars running out of fuel and being abandoned. Very few people got angry about it and nobody had any way to sort it out. It was spreading fast and soon Mumbai, Seoul, Tokyo, New York and London all followed the pattern. The world's great cities were grinding to a halt. The world was grinding to a halt.

The ancient dictacy was coming to pass, however, the Universe had once again played a terrible trick on mankind. The two goods had indeed come together and replaced the influence of evil with an overwhelming influence for good. That, it seemed, was worse.

As the three watched the unfolding disaster they knew that they were totally responsible for this epic catastrophe.

"Oh, this is not good," said Michael. "This is not good at all. We need to fix this."

Lightning Source UK Ltd.
Milton Keynes UK
UKOW051416091211

183486UK00001B/11/P